THE GAMES WE PLAY

BALANCE OF POWER
BOOK 3

BERLIN WICK

A note to the reader:

The book explores themes around sexual exploration and is intended for mature audiences 18+.

Trigger Warnings: Please visit my website at www.berlinwick.com

❀ Formatted with Vellum

CONTENTS

DEDICATION

To all the bookish girls:
Who suddenly become red and green colorblind when a 6'2 ex-
NavySEAL moves in next door.

A NOTE TO READERS

As much as this is a Second Chance - Neighbors to Lovers (kick your feet and giggle) romance story with a very broody but wicked funny MC, **there are some serious triggers**. If you don't have any triggers, read on my friend! If you do, please take a moment to visit my website at www.berlinwick.com to review prior to reading.

Side note: If this book somehow landed in your hands (or on your Kindle) and you are reading these words, it means you probably ignored the other 17,234 books on your TBR for this one and I can't tell you how grateful I am!

PLAYLIST

- NICE TO MEET YOU - MYLES SMITH
- WHERE ARE YOU NOW - LOST FREQUENCIES & CALLUM SCOTT
- CRASH INTO ME - DAVE MATTHEWS BAND
- NO GAMES - SICKICK
- POWER OVER ME - DERMOT KENNEDY
- THONG SONG - SISQÓ
- SOMETHING TO SOMEONE - DERMOT KENNEDY
- GETTIN' JIGGY WIT IT - WILL SMITH
- IS THIS LOVE - WHITESNAKE
- STARS WILL ALIGN (ZERB REMIX) - KYGO & IMAGINE DRAGONS
- NIGHTS LIKE THESE - BENSON BOONE
- DANGEROUS HANDS - AUSTIN GIORGIO
- STARGAZING - MYLES SMITH
- PUT YOUR LIGHTS ON - SANTANA FEATURING EVERLAST
- DAMAGED - PLUMB
- FEELIN' LOVE - PAULA COLE

Playlist

- Fighting For - The Score
- Empty Clip - Matt Schuster
- Perfect - Ed Sheeran
- My Girl - The Temptations

Playlist available on Spotify

PROLOGUE
SEAMUS

17 Years Old

"Sea-ma…Sea-mass Matthews." I roll my eyes hearing the overly dramatic pronunciation of my completely butchered name, just like it has been my entire life.

I don't mind my name, until someone new tries to say it.

"It's pronounced 'Shay-muss'," I reply slowly to the camp counselor with the least amount of disdain in my voice as possible. I'm not trying to get on their shit list the first day.

"Hmm, okay, Seamus." Saying it correctly but snarky as hell. She hands me a red name tag that says, Hello My Name is, printed out with my first name written in black Sharpie underneath.

"Put this on and head over in that line for a lice check. You'll get your cabin assignment after the health check is complete."

My eyes shift in the direction she pointed, seeing another line of campers waiting. One person stands in front of a counselor who is filling out a form on a clipboard, while another gets their hair sorted by what looks like a popsicle stick.

A lice check?

I understand why my mom wanted me to come here this summer, but I hate it.

Most kids go to summer camp to enjoy the experience, make friends, and break up their summer routine—not to hide away from life at home.

In her eyes, putting me in here for two weeks out of the summer is better than spending it at home with a father who spends half his day drinking, and the other half telling you how worthless you are.

He's gotten worse this past year.

She's right by saying that. Except the truth is, he's gotten worse with me as I've gotten older.

But, the way I see it, at least he takes less out on her.

And that's worth it for me.

I've never been to a summer camp before, but it's clear as I look around the room at the lines of people that everyone else here has.

There are others around my age and some younger, I think around twelve or thirteen, all lingering around with their over-sized backpacks, sleeping bags, and suitcases, caught up in conversations with each other. Some of them are running to each other, jumping up and down while screaming and hugging.

I suppose they only get to see each other this one time in the year, and it's a very happy event for them. Not awkward like mine.

I make my way through to the front of the line. The clipboard counselor asks me a few questions, checking off a few items on her form, then directs me over to the lady wearing plastic latex gloves as she grabs another popsicle stick out of a plastic bin.

I sit down, removing my baseball cap as my dark hair flops down over my forehead.

I didn't have a chance to get it cut before I left, but I've also been intentionally growing it out this year.

It doesn't go past my ears, but it's long enough that the strands fall over my face, making it feel like a barrier from me and, well, everyone else that I have no desire talking to.

"You're clear," Latex Glove Lady says gruffly, as she tosses the wooden stick in the metal bin at her feet, making a ping sound echo through the room.

Standing, I slide my hat back on over my head and grab my backpack, placing the strap over my shoulder.

There are two guys standing at the front of the line talking to each other. One stops as he looks at my name tag, back up at my face, then down again. He taps the arm of his friend and pats his own name tag while popping his chin up at me.

I look down to inspect myself, when he says, "Semun, your name is actually *Semun?"*

There's a mix of a snicker and a snort before they both burst out in exaggerated laughter.

My backpack strap is covering a portion of the last letter, and the front of the tag is bunched together, removing the "A" from the middle, completely messing up the print.

Fucking great.

My fist clenches tightly around the strap of my bag as I step toward him. I don't have friends here, so getting into a fight with an idiot whose maturity level rivals a five-year-old doesn't sound like the smartest idea, but I won't be the new guy that everyone uses as a punching bag.

My dad already does that.

Neither of the guys are too big. One is roughly my same height, sitting at about 5 '11, the other just slightly shorter. Although, the shorter one is heavier than both of us by at least forty pounds.

I open my mouth to reply when I feel a hand wrap around my bicep, giving me a slight tug in the other direction.

"I see the year hasn't done anything for your maturity

levels." Her voice is soft like velvet, but the sharp tone of irritation is obvious.

My neck swivels down to her hand, then trails up slowly. My gaze moves from her dainty wrist and olive skin—that looks freshly sunkissed—up to her collarbone and smooth neckline, and over the contours of the most beautiful face I've ever seen.

Her dark chocolate eyes meet mine, and they're the kind you get lost in, the kind that pulls you in and traps you unknowingly, but willingly. Her midnight hair compliments her gorgeous, almond-shaped eyes, and I'm officially speechless.

A confident smile spreads over her lips, and I can't help but mirror it.

"Come on, Seamus, I need help finding my cabin." She says my name perfectly, and it sounds like my new favorite song that I'd like to play on repeat forever.

"Hey!" the guys call out. "We were just messing around. He's totally one of us, tell her, dude." He points at me, begging with his eyes, like I'm actually going to save him right now.

Lifting a shoulder, I shrug with a matching one sided smirk, then turn to follow the goddess currently residing on my arm toward the bungalows.

"Every year those guys find someone to pick on," she says as she leads us away from the check-in chaos. "They're so annoying," she adds.

"You were behind me and couldn't see my name tag. How did you know my name?" I'm instantly irritated with myself realizing that is the first thing I've said to her.

"I heard you when you checked in—sounding out your name. Plus, my grandfather's name was Seamus. He was my grandfather on my mom's side. He died before I was born, but we have a big Irish family, so I'm familiar with the name." She smiles as she turns to look at me.

"You're Irish?" I ask with skepticism, because I'm full-blooded Irish, and she doesn't look just Irish.

"My dad is Japanese, so I'm half, officially." She smiles again, and I'm already half in love with her. "I'm Mimi."

1

SEAMUS

Present Day

"**M**iller, check in?" I ask into my two-way radio.

"South exit is clear—" His words are mumbled, and there is a pause as he smacks his lips. Rocco side-eyes me from his position at the front entrance.

"Are you eating a lollipop?" Rocco asks through his headset.

"Shit," Miller whispers. "I was hungry… and bored. There is no action back here."

Both Rocco and Miller are guys from my squad. When we served together, it became a tradition to celebrate a successful op or mission anyway we could.

You could never predict what could happen, and since we didn't have much, a candy nightcap was what we did. It was something we all looked forward to, because it meant we were all still breathing.

Old habits die hard I suppose, because we still celebrate the end of each night when we work together. Even now, retired from service, working for my security company that I built specifically for events like the one we're overseeing tonight.

"Put the lollipop down," Rocco threatens, "those have a purpose."

"Fine," Miller whines out as he grunts, clearing his throat as he repeats himself. "South exit is clear, sir."

I glance around at the crowd, congregating at the front entrance of Afterburn. We expected a lot of people, but the amount of people who have shown up to attempt to get into the newly established lifestyle club tonight far exceeded anyone's expectation.

The waitlist line has at least a hundred people in it. It's trailing the side of the building and wrapping all the way around to the back. If anyone exits through that side, there's a possibility that someone might attempt to sneak their way in.

"Good, keep it that way. I don't want anyone who doesn't go through a full security and member check to enter this building."

"Yes, sir," Miller replies.

I watch as Rocco pats down a member before granting him access. He'll be one of the few standby members that will be getting into Afterburn tonight. We will have to turn away a majority of these members, and I hope it doesn't turn into a full blown riot.

We already have the protestors for that.

My eyes bounce over to the fence line the police officers put up on the sidewalk. It provides a barrier around the parking lot, blocking them out. For now, at least.

Fortunately, I know enough people who knew someone at the Seattle Police department, so we were able to get more than enough to help on that side of things.

"I'm going to make a round inside and check in with Ember," I share with the team as I walk up to the front entrance. Rocco opens the heavy oak door with a curt nod, and closes it as swiftly as I walk through it.

The ambient change is immediate.

The chaotic sounds of the crowd diminish immediately, replaced by a more synchronized sound of chatter.

A large oval shaped welcome desk sits in front of a floor to ceiling waterfall backdrop, with the words *X-Connect Live* embedded underneath it. The cascading water allows for a three dimensional look in front of the lettering, giving it depth and meaning.

The deep red lettering of AFTERBURN glows over the top, bringing the word, and foyer, to life.

X-Connect is the website that started this whole venture with a live club. Christian Ford, the CEO of Ford Enterprises, created the X-Connect app, a matchmaking platform but for specific needs. Sexual needs, to be exact.

When he hired Ember, she had an idea which ultimately led to the creation of Afterburn, a club where members can meet safely to explore kinks and sexual desires in a judgment free space.

It was a risk to do something like this.

But, here we are on opening night, packed to the brim, with people begging to get in.

I pass through and enter the main area of the club, which is now booming and lively. There are people at the bar and high tables, talking excitedly amongst each other, all wearing masquerade masks or veils—which I hate.

None of my security guys are wearing them. Ember didn't like the idea. She wanted us to blend in with everyone to appear less intimidating, but that would defeat the purpose of why and what we are here for.

This is not a standard dance club, this is a lifestyle club. A high-end one, albeit, still a lifestyle club. And people can be…unpredictable.

Although, I do have a couple of guys in masks, playing the role of patrons, because I never take anything to chance.

Scanning the room as I pass through it, I catch sight of my

best friend, Hudson, talking with Ember's assistant, Cruz. It's natural they've become close since Ember is technically his wife.

I use the word *wife* loosely, since they got drunk married during our last trip to Vegas and ended up staying married for reasons that benefited them both. Regardless, there's something way deeper there than either one of them is leading anyone to believe.

My instincts are never wrong. Ever.

Too many years in the Navy and being trained to read people and places is an occupational hazard, and an annoying personality trait according to the few friends I do have.

I spot Ember and wait for her to peek over my way. When she does, I nod my chin toward the back of the club, and she immediately excuses herself from the small crowd of people she is talking to.

As she walks up to me, her rose gold dress sparkles over the dim lighting. She looks elegant and sexy at the same time, and I'm certain Hudson is doing everything in his power to refrain from taking her home and ripping it off of her.

"Hey, Seamus, everything okay?" she asks with a bit of concern.

"Absolutely, everything is great. I just wanted to give you a quick update," my reply is monotone and even. Though she has a quick sigh of relief, her head tilts at me with raised eyebrows.

"You know, you need to notify your face that everything is okay. This permanent scowl you wear does nothing to make anyone feel at ease." She gives me a playful punch in the arm, but my face doesn't change. I just look at her dumbfounded, that she would purposely ask me to do such a thing.

I don't know if I know how to *notify my face* of any other emotion other than dead serious with a hefty side of death stare. I've had too many years of military service with multiple tours and a government job that prevented me from getting close to anyone. Using my facial features to be unapproachable is my favorite tool.

Taking this job to do security for Ember was purely a favor to Hudson. Most of my old squad are all recently retired and just do contract work like me; it's a good reason to get us all together. Plus, it keeps us fresh. This is natural for us, and easy compared to what we've done in the past.

Ember shakes her head with a defeated smile. "Okay fine, I give up. What's the update?"

"The protestors are getting a bit more rowdy, but the police department has sent some additional officers to help manage the crowd. There are about a hundred people lined up to come in, and we're going to monitor the occupancy levels, letting members in as others vacate. But… well, no one is leaving. So there are a lot of people still waiting."

Her eyes widen as she turns to look at the front entrance, like she'd be able to see the extent of the line outside.

"I'd really like it if everyone had a chance to make it in. Are we really at max?" I understand she's concerned about the members and wants everyone here to experience opening night, but it's just not possible.

"Everyone who reserved in advance is in. All of those people waiting in line are waitlist members who didn't plan accordingly or couldn't get a reserved space tonight. We can't accommodate everyone. So, you have to get that need to make everyone happy out of your head now," I reply, probably too crass, but it's a fact. "It's just not going to happen."

She chews on the inside of her cheek, but nods.

"Okay, but let's get as many in as possible. When someone leaves, someone else comes in. And I want all the member names for those that don't make it in tonight, so I can reach out to them myself," she replies, and I can't help but internally smirk at who the serious one is now.

Ember is so unassuming and surprising. Her petite frame

surrounded by a mountain of red hair appears so innocent until she talks about the club. Afterburn is Ember's baby, and it's clear in the way she talks about it.

"You got it," I reply, because there's no fighting back with her on that.

"Thanks, Seamus. Now, lighten up, grumpy pants." She takes a few steps back, using her fingers to make a fake smile with her lips before turning around back to the bar. Remaining stone faced, I head the other direction to make my rounds through the voyeur rooms and private sections.

The voyeur room is packed. People are crowded close to each other as they peer through the floor to ceiling glass window, observing a couple inside the room.

I hear the distinct sound of a wretched, moaning man before I can see anything.

Curious, I crane my head through the crowd of people. Fortunately, I'm taller than most of the people here.

The bed is empty with only ruffled silk sheets splayed over the side. Following the line of sight of the other spectators, I see a woman with her back fully splayed up against the corner of the glass. She's kneeling in front of a man whose palms are planted against the viewing window, caging her in with his body. His anguished face is up close and personal to everyone watching. He's looking down at her as his cock pushes in and out of her mouth, driving himself deep down her throat, groaning with immense pleasure after every thrust.

It's clear by the short breaths and blushed faces of those surrounding me that everyone in this room is thoroughly enjoying this show.

There are two other women kneeling on this side of the glass, mirroring the woman's position on the other side. It's like they want to join, and are egging him on even more. They are both touching themselves, each other, and the glass barrier. The mix of moans fill the room, not only between all of them, but with all the other people watching, too. It's a symphony of sounds that's broadcasting through the open space like its very own theme song.

I step toward the back of the room, and now, I can only hear the couple on the other side of the window. The rooms are equipped with microphones connected to speakers into each viewing room. Anyone performing has an option to turn them on or off, and right now, all three rooms have them on.

When standing in one room, you really get the surround sound of just that room, but I have impeccable hearing, so I catch on to the light murmuring and echoes from the others.

As I step over to the next room, this one has just as many spectators. This time, there are two couples behind the window. This foursome is using the over-sized bed placed in the middle of the room, and I can see the faces of the two women. The blonde one sits on the edge of the bed with a man's face between her legs. Her entire body is bouncing, synchronized with the pounding the woman next to her is getting.

The blonde cups her hands around her man's cheeks, pulling him to her face. She kisses him deeply before bringing her lips to his ear, whispering so the microphones don't catch her words.

So I hone in on what she is saying by reading her lips.

One of my most useful traits.

Are you ready to fuck him now, baby?

The man's eyes trail over to the man next to him. His eyes are hooded, jaw slacked, as the woman wraps her hand in between his legs and strokes his cock.

His forehead dips to her shoulder and he nods, almost ashamed of his silent confession.

Releasing his cock she interlaces his hand in hers, then reaches over, caressing the back of the other man still pumping in and out of the woman who is laying on the bed. Slowly, she trails their locked hands down to the globes of his ass as the muscles flex with each thrust.

In between thrusts, the man glances over at the couple and smiles, then grabs the man's forearm, pulling his body behind him.

The crowd is silent as they watch, everyone engrossed in them.

I spot one of my undercover guys in the crowd. He's blending in well—maybe too well. He's also entranced with the couple in the room, shifting back and forth on his feet, like he's feeling a bit antsy.

I only agreed to help Ember with the opening. We're just extra security due to the nature of the club and all the protestors. I know she intends to hire a permanent team for their special events, and I'm going to suggest to her that she thoroughly vets each individual team member. They should be tested in a live environment, as well.

I know there will be nights with rowdy couples or jealous rages, and you need guys who can not only ignore their baser instincts, but proactively spot the start of that kind of behavior before it's too late.

As I turn to head toward the next section, a delicate hand caresses my forearm. I peer down at the bright, neon pink nail polish that is connected to the fingers that is now wrapped around my suit jacket. I trail my eyes up, taking in the features of the woman next to me. Her face is flushed behind her crooked mask as another woman explores her neckline with her tongue, gropes her breasts through her thin, skin tight dress.

"Want to join us?" she asks, all breathy and desperate.

"No."

I step out of her grasp and make my way over to the third room. It is most definitely for the more experienced couples—a full blown red room with bondage galore. It has a smaller crowd.

Not because there aren't as many people with this kink, but it's hard to make your way through when you have two other rooms to get preoccupied with.

It's like the crowd in all three rooms have been frozen in time, with the exception of a few couples groping each other or some solo individuals secretly touching themselves. It's easy to spot movement out of the corner of my eye with how still everything is. A body slinks off behind the thick, black curtain that separates the voyeur rooms from the private rooms. There is supposed to be an employee or security standing guard there, but there is no one to be seen.

Scanning the area, I catch the side of the mask marked with the red X, indicating an employee. They've made their way to the corner of the glass window, peering in to see the show.

Shaking my head, mentally noting to deal with that later, I make my way through the thick, black-out curtain and peer down the long hallway, following the figure. There are six doors that lead into separate private rooms.

A woman walks carefully down the hall. A pale glow casts over her body as she passes by the light that hangs over each door, creating a shadow on the ground. Her perfect, hourglass outline paints the floor as she tiptoes through the hallway.

My eyes trail over her white dress. It's brighter than everything that surrounds her due to the contrast of the dark room and I'm easily drawn to the curves of her hips and the strong lines of her legs.

Members can reserve and pay to use the rooms, however, you need a keycard to enter. She might have one, but the way she snuck past the curtain and her current body language leads me to doubt that.

I hold my position and observe her for a moment. She appears to just be curious, but she shouldn't be back here.

Steadily and silently, I make my way toward her as she

reaches the last door—room six. It's at the end of the hall, and there is nowhere to go except past me to get out.

This is the only room not operational tonight, but for some reason, the door is cracked open.

She slows, as do I, placing her palm gently on the door, tilting her head to peek through the crack. Her high cheekbones are apparent in her profile, and I can see that the contours of her jawline and nose are absolutely stunning, even though the mask covers half her face. It's silky and white to match her dress, but has feathers over the top that move as freely as she does.

She's so absorbed in the moment, she doesn't hear me creep up behind her. Her long, black hair falls forward over one of her shoulders as she leans toward the crack of the door, the other half lay loosely over her back.

The thin straps of her dress cross over her upper back and connect to the fabric of her silky, white dress. It's loose and lays low on her back, fitting snugly around her perfectly, peach-shaped ass.

I don't normally find myself interested in women sneaking around sex clubs, but there is definitely something about this one.

Pulling myself out of the distraction that is her gorgeous ass, I voice my presence—my tone deep and commanding. "What are you doing?"

She jumps with a squeal, turning around urgently and backing up against the wall.

"Oh my God, you scared me." Her hand is splayed out over her chest. The silky material on this side of her dress is tight around her waist, but hangs loosely over her breasts, exposing the channel between them.

My eyes naturally follow the fabric of the upside down triangle that ends just above her belly button, then back up to her eyes.

My breath catches in my throat and my heartbeat stutters.

Perfect, almond-shaped eyes, the color of the richest dark chocolate, stare back at me through the holes in her mask. I'd recognize those eyes any place, any time, in the darkest of rooms.

"Mimi?" I whisper.

2

SEAMUS

"*Mimi?*"

Her name bounces off the walls between us.

For a brief moment, I'm confused. I think I'm dreaming, being that I've previously questioned whether or not she was real. She disappeared, and when I tried to find her, it was like she was never there. I drove myself crazy for so long, wondering if I actually conjured up everything between us.

And now, she's here. Right in fucking front of me.

Her head tilts as her eyes squint through the mask. I step forward, bringing myself closer to her and into the small stream of light peering out from the open doorway.

As the light hits my face, her mouth falls open and her eyes widen.

"Seamus," she whispers with shaky breath.

It was real.

She *is* real.

The feathers on the top of her mask flutter with the movement of her neck as her eyes bounce around the crowded space between us, taking in her surroundings.

"What are you doing here?" I ask as I step toward her.

Aligning my body with hers, I trap her between me and the end of the hallway.

"I was just curious, that's all." She pushes herself further into the wall as her eyes glance over to the door, still slightly ajar, then back to me.

"No. What are you doing *here*?" I ask with more urgency, stepping closer.

Her eyebrows twitch with confusion.

If she is here, she's a member of X-Connect. She is a member of a website that you share your sexual desires and kinks with, so that you can find partners to explore with.

She's a fucking member.

Rage explodes from every corner of my body, and my fists clench so tightly my knuckles burn.

The glossy material of her dress shimmers in the light with the rise and fall of her chest. Her breathing is heavy and deep, and I can see the panic radiating from every inch of her lavish body. Her eyes look between mine, but she can't hold the stare. She glances behind me, I'm guessing to look for an exit, but she's not going anywhere.

"Where have you been?" I reach up, placing my palm on the wall behind her, caging her in. "Where did you go?"

It's been *years* since I've seen her—other than in my dreams —despite multiple attempts to find her. She's the only one I could never find. It was like she wasn't ever real. A figment of my fucking imagination.

The confused look she's displaying morphs into anger.

"*Me*?" she accuses. "Where did I go? Where did you go?" She presses her palms into my chest, and tries to push me back, but I don't budge. "*You* left!" The anguish behind her voice as it cracks is powerful and real.

The accusation makes me flinch.

It was more than ten years ago, since that two weeks at camp. Ten years of wondering what happened to her. Ten years beating myself up for not being able to find her. Ten years of wondering if I was insane.

And she thinks I would fucking leave her intentionally?

"You left…you just left me there." Her voice is a harsh whisper that slashes through me worse than any wound I've ever had.

"Mimi—" Before I can finish, she slaps me. Hard. Her palm feels like tiny razor blades that pierce my skin, and the sensation rips through my entire body.

I step back, confused. I'm so fucking confused. My gaze is trained on the ground, attempting to recap every goddamn memory as I question the last night I saw her. But I don't need to. It's been branded to my memory and comes to me easily in daily flashbacks.

I know what happened between us.

My eyes trail her body slowly, from the ground, up her silky, muscular legs, between each side of her hips, onto the olive skin that peeks through the middle of the opening of her dress.

Jesus, she's so beautiful.

She's everything I remember, and still better than I ever imagined her to be.

I step forward, reaching to cup her face. She steps forward, and for a moment I think she's doing the same—until her hands land on top of each side of my shoulders and she kicks her knee up directly between my legs, nailing me in the balls.

"Fuck," I grunt out as my teeth grind together. I fall to my knees as I buckle to the ground. I was not fucking ready for that. My eyes squeeze shut for a moment as I curse through the pain bursting through every cell in my body.

Slowly, I open my eyes, but my vision is distorted, blurred beyond any recognition. I push myself up off the floor, just to stumble down again. Jesus, she couldn't have centered that more perfectly.

I finally get to my feet and peer down the hallway. She's

already through the black curtain barrier, and as I run toward it, I hear the distant moans of the people inside the voyeur rooms. They are much louder than they were earlier, but they're easy to ignore this time with my new objective. I crane my neck over the crowd to see a row of feathers turning the corner into the main lobby area.

I push my way through the horde of people. It's so much more crowded now, and I suddenly hate my size. 6'2, broad shouldered, and wide framed is great for security. Not great when chasing a petite, five foot nothing, professional ball kicker.

Rounding the corner, I peer over at the bar, then scan the room as I continue pacing toward the entrance. I don't see her anywhere, and when I face forward, I run straight into Hudson, who's grabbing me by the shoulders. He pulls me back, trying to get my attention, but it's nowhere other than surveying the room, looking for her.

"Did you see her?" I snap.

"Who?"

"Mi…the woman—the woman in white."

"Shay," he calls me by my nickname with concern. "What's going on, man?"

"Did she pass through here?" I shout, staring directly at him now. I'm fucking serious. Why doesn't he see how fucking serious this is? Aren't best friends supposed to be able to read you better?

"Yes, she was heading to the front door, I think she left." Now he tells me. For being a professional baseball catcher, he's pretty fucking terrible at actually *catching* things.

"Shit." I push him aside and run toward the front, circling around the waterfall barrier that separates the lobby from the club, and push through the double doors.

It's dark out, but the exterior lights are brighter than the interior of the club, and I'm momentarily blinded as my eyes adjust.

The line is longer now, the protestors are rowdier, and there are more police officers.

I realize I've missed out on everything happening at the club by her distraction, but I really don't give a shit. My eyes roam the parking lot, the mob of people, the paparazzi, and nothing.

"Fuck." I run my hands through my hair. "Fuck!" Shouting louder this time.

Stepping back I look through the entrance doors and see a couple checking in, showing their IDs. I glance back out to the crowd, and freeze.

She had to show her ID to get in.

I storm back inside and wave off the guy sitting at the computer he's not using.

With urgency, he stands and removes himself, his eyes looking everywhere but at me.

I observe the other girl who is checking in the couple. She scans the ID and a copy appears on her screen.

I can't help but internally grin recalling this suggestion that I made to Ember's team. Because of that, they require ID verification of members, and I'm internally patting myself on the back for it.

I cycle through the members that have all checked in, aggressively hitting the button as I skim over each ID that pops up. My blood pressure rises over the never ending review. ID after ID comes through, but none of them are her.

"If I don't fucking find her, I swear—" Then I freeze. My breath is quite literally ripped from my body.

Luscious, black hair, a bright, diamond-like smile and those gorgeous, mysterious, dark eyes stare back at me.

Relief blankets me until I see her name.

Naomi Masumi.

I never had her last name, so searching for *Mimi* was literally impossible. I tried every avenue when I gained any resource to do so, and still nothing. But now it all makes sense, because I never even knew her legal name.

Not even her real fucking first name.

"Naomi Masumi," I whisper to myself as I inspect her ID.

5'3, 130 pounds, and she lives right here in Seattle.

I snap a picture of the screen with my phone, and shut off the computer.

Alright *Naomi,* let's see what you've been up to.

3

SEAMUS

3 months later

Mimi was easy to track down once I had her *real* name.

I was furious to discover she lived less than thirty minutes from me in Texas when we were kids, but she moved right after she returned from summer camp.

That, I found odd. She had just turned eighteen and still had one more year of high school left, but for reasons that I haven't yet discovered, they moved to Seattle before the start of her senior year. There, she was homeschooled and finished her degree outside of high school.

She and her parents still live in Seattle. They are retired, and Naomi is a yoga instructor contracted by way too many studios to track.

I still tracked them and ran all the details on their entire business, obviously.

And of course, she's a goddamn yoga instructor. I could see it in the strong lines of her gorgeous body in that white dress that still haunts my dreams.

The address on her ID was up to date, so it was easy enough

to find her living comfortably in a small cul-de-sac right outside downtown Seattle. It was also easy enough for me to approach her neighbor, making an off market deal for their house they couldn't refuse.

Excessive? Maybe.

Necessary? Absolutely.

I've spent far too many years wondering what happened to her. Years searching for who I thought was a ghost, a figment of my imagination. Then she just lands back in my lap.

I'm not one to believe in *signs*, but that's a goddamn billboard if I've ever seen one.

With my government contacts, it only took a couple weeks to get all the details I needed about her and all of her neighbors, a day to make up my mind that I was moving to Seattle, and two long, excruciatingly painful negotiating weeks with the owners of the house next door to her to finally come to an agreement. Then once we did, they wanted a sixty day rent back to stay in the house for free.

I had no choice but to concede to their request, which put my plan back a couple months. A blip in the last decade, but still. I found myself impatient. And I'm *never* impatient.

Regardless, after nine cups of coffee, six bathroom breaks paired with gas tank refills, thirty hours of driving, and four hours of unloading, I've finally made it here, and the moving truck is officially empty.

"That's the last of it," I call out to Hudson from inside the back of the truck, as he carries the last box in the house.

It's too big for what I need, but I figure I'll find things to do with the extra space. It was originally a two bedroom, two bath home before the prior owners built a third loft style bedroom and added that on a second story. The floorplan is a bit strange, but the second story room is expansive and overlooks the backyard.

The owner told me he was a writer, and utilized the space as a sanctuary to write some of his best-selling novels.

I plan to use it as my painting room. A secret passion that no one knows about. I've never had enough space for all my canvases, but I will now with that addition.

I fold up the moving blankets that came with the U-Haul and place them in the corner, when Hudson walks up toward the back of the truck with a garbage bag in his hand. He trails the side of the truck, and as I hear the lid of the garbage can close, the brakes of a car squeak before an engine dies off.

"Shit," I whisper-yell. It bounces off the sides of this empty truck as I duck for cover.

I studied her goddamn routine for weeks, and she's never home at this time.

Realizing I have exactly zero places to hide, I rise to my full height, pressing my back into the side of the truck, attempting to blend in…with absolutely nothing.

"Hi, are you moving in?" Her angelic voice makes my heart stutter, or maybe it's the fact that Hudson might find out in mere moments what a complete lunatic I am.

He has no idea why I moved here so suddenly. He thinks it's for no reason other than I offered help to Ember at the club, and because I could. I know he knows me better than that, but I've never told him about Mimi and would rather not start now. Not like this.

Hudson rounds the back of the truck, peering in, double taking as he sees me standing like a goddamn stick figure, not even blinking, poorly camouflaged into the side of the truck.

"No, my friend—" And he points, he actually fucking points. I have no choice but to gesture *no* with my hand, cutting that shit off, right fucking now.

His wide eyes catch my drift, finally, but he still stammers through talking to Mimi.

"My friend is moving in but he…went…to…the store."

Je-sus, fucking Christ, he's a horrible fucking liar. Could he have stuttered anymore?

"Oh bummer, I'll have to introduce myself another time," she replies, buying his awful lie.

"Have I met you before?" He squints in her direction, studying her.

Shit.

Shit. Shit. Shit.

Her shadow is splayed out on the ground behind the truck. My heart races at the fact that she's inches from me, from finding out I'm her new neighbor. She will eventually, of course, but I need that on my time.

Her shadow displayed on the cracked cement of my driveway shifts as she moves her hair from one side to the other, then removes her jacket. The dark silhouette splays out on the ground, showing the petite profile of her frame.

There's a brief pause before she says, "No, I don't think so."

Hudson's hand trails over his face, as he smothers a smile. And I know, he knows.

Goddammit.

"Well, hey, it was great to meet you. I've gotta get the truck back to the rental company, but I'm sure I'll see you around." He peers into the truck, with a stupid—really stupid, big, smug ass —smile, grabs the rope attached to the sliding back door, and swings it down, slamming it closed. An astounding click echoes through the metal box, locking me in.

"Hud," I whisper-yell through the metal barrier.

It's pure fucking darkness in here. Not an ounce of light comes through, except a sliver between the corners of the cargo door.

Pausing, I try to listen for any more conversation. Pressing my ear to the side of the truck, I hear a goodbye, then the slamming of the car door before the truck roars to life.

This motherfucker.

He steps on the gas, making me lose my balance and I fly toward the back of the empty truck with nothing to grab onto.

My back slams into the accordion panels of the cargo doors, and I let out a long groan before screaming at the front of the truck.

"You fucker!"

He slams on the breaks and I roll all the way to the front. *Jesus Christ.*

This goes on for twenty goddamn minutes.

I just roll, back and forth—back and forth—in the back of a goddamn moving truck. Fortunately, I've been in far too many military trucks on dirt roads with no suspension to get car sick, but never have I rolled around like a sack of potatoes hitting the side of metal walls over and over again.

Finally, after what feels like an eternity, the cargo door opens and sunlight blasts into the truck, blinding me instantly.

"I'm going to fucking kill you." I place my hand over my face, shadowing the light. My voice is raw and my entire body is probably bruised beyond recognition, but it won't stop me from strangling him.

"You deserved that," he's still wearing that stupid smile, "plus, I realized I'd never have that chance again, so I took full advantage."

He places a foot on the back of the truck step and leans forward reaching out his hand to help me. Grabbing it, he pulls me upward, thank God, because I don't think I'd be able to, at least not right then, anyway.

"You're losing your touch, Shay." I can't argue with him on that. I have been since the moment I saw Mimi again.

So I just agree and nod.

"Anything to do with the Hawaiian princess of a neighbor?" he asks nonchalantly, because I know he knows, but he wouldn't dare call me out on it, directly,

I remain quiet for a moment as I step out of the truck and pull out my phone to schedule an Uber.

"She's Japanese. And yes," which is all I can seem to say.

Without looking my way, he tips up his chin in a languid, slow nod.

"So, who is she?"

Normally, he wouldn't inquire so much, knowing I don't talk about that kind of shit. But he knows something is off.

I glance up at him and back down at my phone, then open my mouth to reply. But I have no idea how to respond to that.

Someone who stood up for me as an awkward teenager.

The girl whose virginity I took.

Someone I've pined over for the last decade.

The girl who made me believe in love.

The one that got away.

I know he would understand my actions. Of all people, he would—especially after his behavior the moment he met Ember —but I still can't seem to bring those words forward.

"Someone from my past," I simply say, which does her no justice, but I'm not ready to share everything she did for me—to me. How she changed me.

Hudson just gives me another slow, hefty nod, knowing me well enough to know I'm not ready to talk about it, then pats me on the back, hard. I hide my wince.

Dick.

"I will get you back for locking me in a truck," I tell him without even looking at him.

"I know. I'm looking forward to it."

4

NAOMI

"Inhale, circle your arms up."

"Exhale, forward fold."

"Inhale, place your hands to your mat, lengthen—halfway up.

"Exhale, forward fold."

"Inhale. Right leg steps back, left leg steps back. Exhale, chaturanga."

"Inhale, upward facing dog. Exhale, downward facing dog."

I repeat my class's sun salutations five times before going into chest and hip openers today. I teach this class at one of the local tech companies three times a week, and try to incorporate this specific flow at least one time out of those three sessions.

Most of the students who take my class aren't active yogis by any means. This is just a reason for them to get away from their desk for an hour, but it's a good reason. They need it more than most. Especially for people who work on a computer all day long and hardly get up from their desk.

Slouching in today's society is the biggest problem when it comes to posture and body health. Their shoulders are slumped forward, necks are dipped down, and legs are in the same position for a majority of the day. Opening up the chest and hips is what they need most. Oh, and those painful neck and forearm stretches that everyone always whines over.

It's a pleasurable pain, at least in my opinion. Either way, they need it more than anyone.

I started taking yoga in my last year of high school and it saved me, both physically and mentally. It challenged me both on and off my mat to continue to push myself. Some days it inspired me to push further in my career goals, in all the things I wanted to strive for.

Other days, I had to teach myself to just put one foot in front of the other and get through the day. It taught me to find the balance of being happy all the time, and just being okay some days. It got me through the hardest time of my life.

So, getting my certification to teach was an easy decision to make, knowing how much it positively affected my life and how much it continues to help me grow.

I got my first two hundred hour certification ten years ago. I've since expanded, receiving another five hundred hour certification and traveling the world to the most beautiful places. Fiji, Thailand, India, and my personal favorite, Bali.

I always come back home to Seattle, bringing my teachings here, because this place will always be a safe haven for me. Somewhere I have always felt secure.

"Stay grounded and draw power from your core. Breathe through the pose and as you exhale, twist just a little deeper," I remind my students as I stroll between the mats.

I glance around the class, and the man in the far corner catches my attention. The front of his body is facing the opposite direction. I see the strong lines of his back through his damp, black shirt, pulled tight from the pose that he's holding. His tousled, dark hair contrasts the milky completion of his skin that shines with a layer of sweat. His corded muscles flex when he releases the pose he's been holding, and my heart kicks up a notch.

I blink out of my trance, realizing I had the students hold too long, and quickly turn my head away. I continue to guide the class through the next pose before glancing back to the corner. This time, his face is angled toward me, looking down at his mat as he twists into this pose, and my body deflates.

I keep seeing him. But it's never him. *My Seamus.*

Even though I tell myself I never want to see him again, I still do. My subconscious is killing my willpower.

Ever since the night at Afterburn, he's everywhere.

Because now I know he's alive and out there somewhere, close. Too close.

Oh, and let's not forget, really irritatingly good looking.

I decided to check out the new club to see if it would be a good place to teach Tantric yoga classes. Currently, there aren't any studios locally that offer them, and I haven't been able to find a location that is willing to. So, my certification for Tantric teachings has been going to waste.

Afterburn would be the perfect place for it. An open, non-judgmental space to tap into your sexual energy.

But now, knowing Seamus is there, or could potentially be there? Hell no. Tossing that stupid idea straight out the window from the tallest building I can find.

And as for Afterburn, I haven't been within a mile of the place in three months. I can't say I haven't been tempted. Not just for the potential of teaching some amazing classes there, but for the sexual openness and possibility of meeting someone.

Originally, I became a member of the X-Connect site to research what it was all about and register for the opening night of the club. I wanted to connect with the owners about my services to see if it would be something they would be interested in. I never had the chance that night and, well, yeah that's been shot to shit.

If there is anything that has come out of this, I've realized one thing: as much spiritual healing as I've done, there's still a part of me that hasn't forgiven him.

No. I forgave him. A long time ago. But seeing him has opened old wounds, and now I realize that part of me still needs closure.

My faded memories make me doubt myself, but I know we had something so special.

We were special.

It was a short time in our lives, but there was no denying what we had. Giving him my virginity felt natural, good.

Then he just left.

Now, I don't know what to believe. Did we have something as special as I thought? Was he just lying to me the entire time?

I shake my head at incessant thoughts that keep roaming in that direction. The negative, bitter, resentful thoughts that want to rear their ugly heads. They have been for the past three months, and I need to do something to stop it.

"Pull your knees into your chest and slowly lower your back flat against your mat, giving your spine that nice little massage we love. Inhale," I exaggerate my inhale, "take a commanding breath deep into your lungs, open your mouth…exhale. Allow yourself to melt into your mat and release any tension you feel in your shoulders, arms, and fingertips. Allow your breath to guide you through the release."

Savasana is always a class favorite, and I give my students extra time here. Sometimes I walk around or sit on my mat and observe, wondering what plagues their minds. Today, I accept that mine is completely infected and there is no amount of savasana that will heal this.

I need to find him. Address him. Get the closure I didn't know I needed, and move on.

As my students find the stillness and peace they are searching for, I pad my bare feet over to my phone, unlocking the screen to search for something myself, starting with trusty ole' Google.

Typing in a name I've allowed myself to forget for the last decade.

Seamus Matthews.

5

NAOMI

So, Seamus Matthews is an apparent ghost and appears literally nowhere.

I searched every social media platform, every search engine, and zilch. I felt like a traitor to myself and the thousands of dollars I've spent on therapy every time I typed in his name on a different site. I got more and more frustrated with each dead end, which just fed more into the desperation that I've paid so much to manage.

You'd think with my go with the flow, *love the one you're with* attitude I'd be carefree and loose about this whole thing, but no. I've opened up the floodgates and now I can't stop.

I know I need to go back to Afterburn. I need to go back and ask for him. He'll get the message. I know he will.

So just stop, Naomi.

As I scold myself and put my phone down, I recall the way he said my name. The name I haven't gone by since that summer.

His voice was laced with so much confusion, a little happiness, and even lust, maybe.

Mimi.

I always loved the way he said my name. It wasn't unlike how everyone else did, but the way he said it was with such adoration and appreciation.

Okay, stop.

I am literally a trained professional at clearing my mind, but here comes Seamus Matthews, making an appearance for fifteen seconds—after a decade of being non-existent—and I'm that seventeen-year-old, insecure girl again.

It's official. I am triggered. Seamus Matthews is my trigger.

I finish my morning green tea and open the sliding glass door to step into my backyard.

My serenity.

No matter how many places in the world I've been to, this quaint little space in my own backyard provides a peace my body craves daily.

The back fence is lined with lush trees that rival the deepest forest green color palette. The cul-de-sac my house is on is sheltered from the hustling, downtown Seattle commotion, and the large outdoor bird bath with a waterfall fountain provides a stream of nature's white noise.

It's nothing extravagant, but it's my private oasis. I spend more time out here than I do inside my house.

Rolling my mat onto the patio, I hand brush it flat, clearing away any debris, then step out of my flip flops while simultaneously grabbing the hem of my crop top and pulling it off. I toss it on one of the lounge chairs then tuck my thumbs into the elastic waistband of my harem pants, letting those fall easily to my ankles, before kicking the loose, flowy fabric onto the same chair with my shirt.

The cold, crisp air kisses my exposed skin and sends goosebumps down my entire body.

It's not officially winter yet, but after Thanksgiving, there is a distinct shift in the weather here. Almost like it knows

Christmas is coming. And although it doesn't snow in Seattle, we have cool, wet winters, and it's one of my favorite seasons.

Well, they all are. I love the changing of them. The colors, the sensation in the climate. The shift of the drier, more dense air, to the cooler, humid air.

I suck in a deep breath and circle my arms over my head, pushing my fingers toward the sky, giving myself a full body stretch before kneeling down at the back of my mat.

It's natural to go through my warm up stretches, circling my wrists, arms, neck and ankles. Then moving into back arches and rolling my shoulders and hips side to side.

The breeze floats around my skin like a comfort blanket, and I recall the first time I did yoga out here. It was the middle of summer, and I had on leggings and a tank top that felt like a thermal turtleneck. It was hot, restricting, and I hated it. So, I stripped down to my sports bra and underwear, and I've never gone back.

It's my own personal space, no one can see me. So, why not?

I flow through my poses, holding each one as long as my breath will allow. Moving fluidly between each. Sometimes I have a plan, using this time to create a class flow in my head, and others I just move wherever my body needs to. That feels most natural and easy.

As I step to the top of my mat, I open my eyes and glance at the neighbor's house. My previous neighbors had lived there when I moved in and, to my knowledge, had no plans on moving. Until one day, a moving truck appeared in their front yard. They said they just decided it was time, packed up, and left. They didn't even give me any contact information or tell me where they were going.

Now, a mysterious—and very large—Ford Raptor has been parked in the driveway since the day the new neighbor's moving truck showed up. The friend I met, who was helping the neighbor move, seemed nice enough, but it's been days later and no sign of the new neighbor.

I personally think it's imperative to know your neighbors, so I have every intention of knocking on the door every day until I do. I know I can be a lot, with my overly bubbly and friendly personality, so I'll give them a few days to get settled in before doing that.

I cycle through a few sun salutations, and as I arch deeper into my upward facing dog pose, my eyes peer over the fence line to the second story window. It overlooks the neighbor's yard and, inadvertently, mine, as well.

It catches my attention because that window has always had thick, horizontal blinds that were *never* opened.

But right now, they are wide open.

I squint, trying to adjust my vision, and suddenly a shadow shifts in the background and the blinds slam close all at once.

Shit.

I push back onto my heels and glance down at myself, then back up to the window.

It's not like I'm dressed in anything worse than a swimsuit, but that's not the first impression I wanted to give my neighbor. I hope they just so happened to be looking out the window and weren't actually staring the entire time.

Well, shit.

I roll up my mat and grab my clothes from the chair, stepping back into the house.

I need to plan to meet my neighbor sooner than later.

6

SEAMUS

This is twice now. Twice she's almost seen me, and twice I've ended up trying to blend into a goddamn wall.

I crane my neck to peek out between the drawn blinds of the window. I can only see her lower half as her feet shuffle into her flip flops and then she steps inside her house.

She must have seen me, or at least the silhouette of someone watching her, otherwise she wouldn't have stopped.

She does yoga in her underwear.

She does yoga…in a dainty bra and barely there panties.

In her backyard.

I glance around the surrounding houses and, fortunately, none have a second story, so no one has the same view I have. I can't decide if I'm happy about the fact that I chose this specific house or really fucking pissed off about it.

It's a torturous temptation.

She stretched and moved her body flawlessly through every pose, and I couldn't keep my eyes off her.

It was like her own personal dance that was a show just for me.

My cock, normally not influenced by something so basic as a

woman in a thong and sports bra, was standing full salute the entire time.

Jesus, Hudson is right. I am losing my touch. I have no control over my body or my incessant thoughts of Mimi.

I was going to give it a little more time before I dropped myself back into her world, but I'm tired of waiting.

If I can just reconnect with her, clear the air between us, figure out what happened, I won't feel so conflicted and unruly. I've never felt so out of control in my entire life, and I need some of it back. All of it, preferably.

But if our meeting at Afterburn is a precursor of how she'll respond to me when she sees me again, I have to plan the next one perfectly.

I move to the other side of the room and peer out of the blinds into the bay window that looks into her kitchen. This has the perfect view of the sink that sits in front of the window and the kitchen island behind it.

She's sitting at the edge of the counter as she pulls her hair out of the messy bun she threw it up in when she was working out. It falls over her bare shoulders with only the straps of her sports bra between. She's holding her phone face up, presumably the call on speaker, and the genuine smile she's beaming into it is real and comforting. I tilt my head and squint as I focus my attention on the lit screen.

It's a picture of an older woman with dark hair and a smile that mirrors her own.

Shifting my gaze, I watch Mimi's lips move as she talks.

What are you and Dad up to tonight?

So, it is her mother. She keeps her eyes on the screen as her mother continues to talk.

That sounds fun.

Mimi flips her hair over to one side and leans her chin into the palm of her hand.

No, I don't have any classes today, but I do have a date later.

What. The. Fuck.

Not with that guy, he was pretty dull. I haven't met this guy yet. I've been talking to him on the site I told you about.

I know, Mom. I know. I always give Penny the profile information for the guys I meet online and I share my location with her the entire time I'm out.

Mimi rolls her eyes.

Mom, I'm super safe.

Her mom continues to talk, and Mimi listens with impatience written all over her body.

Yeah, okay, okay. I gotta go, though.

She hangs up the line, clearly irritated. A feeling I can completely relate to at this very moment.

I should expect that she would be dating, knowing she wasn't married and attended Afterburn on opening night. But now that she's here, next to me, so fucking close, knowing she's going out with another guy, has me seeing fucking red.

I'm in complete control, on the outside, not showing a single emotion, but I am raging on the inside.

Mimi gets up from the stool, takes a swig from her water bottle, then disappears from view.

I wasn't planning on making my presence known for a little while, but it looks like I have a date to crash tonight.

7

SEAMUS

17 years old

"*S*o, why have you never come here before this summer?" Mimi asks.

The first day of camp was interesting, needless to say.

She saved me from what was probably going to end up a fist fight, then we spent the majority of the day together with her showing me around the grounds after finding our cabins. She's absolutely gorgeous, in every way, and I find myself lost in her whenever she talks about, well, anything.

"I had never heard of this place, until my mom mentioned I was going. She just felt like it would be a good break for me this summer." I keep it simple and change the subject away from me. "How long have you been coming here?"

"Oh gosh, forever it feels like. Since I was seven, I think," she replies with a smile. "Yeah, this will be my tenth year. I met my best friend here, and this is the first year she couldn't come."

"Ah, I see, I'm a pity friend. The temporary replacement," I reply, nudging her with my shoulder.

"Well, I mean, I sort of did pity you. You were totally going to

get beat up by Tweedledee and Tweedledum at check in, so I had to do something." She nudges me back.

"For the record, I would have taken both of them on…easily." I clear my throat and sit up a little taller.

"Oh, I'm sure of it, Rambo."

"Rambo, huh?" I chuckle. "He has the best one liner in the history of all action movies, so I'll take it."

"Which one is that?" she asks, and I assume she hasn't actually seen any of the Rambo movies, so I recap the scene.

"The bad guy in the movie, he's all shocked by John Rambo's abilities, because he's killing off all his men and finally asks him through a walkie talkie, "Who are you?" I say with an accent, "and Rambo replies, 'your worst nightmare.'" She jinxes me with the quote as she says it with a deep voice at the same time I do, and my head snaps in her direction.

She's got a wide smile, and giggles at my shock.

"My dad is a huge Arnold and Sylvester movie buff. So, he'd probably challenge you to a one liner competition. I've seen all of them, and I would say that Arnold holds the record for that."

My face falls and I stare at her in complete shock. And excuse me while I fall immediately in love with this girl.

There's an awkward silence, like she knows it, and I have the urge to lean in and kiss her. Before I can, she interrupts. And I'm grateful for it, because I don't want to make things weird on the first day.

"The seniors, the campers who are here for their last year, we're having a sort of homecoming party at cabin one tomorrow. You should come."

"Eh, I'm not really coming home," I air quote with my fingers, "so to speak. I'll probably pass." Because nothing sounds worse than spending an entire night reuniting with people I don't actually know.

"I'll be there and you can hang with me," she replies smoothly. I steal a glance at her and I love that she's so carefree

and easy going. Everything she says is effortless, and kind, and I can't help but smile. No one has ever just made me smile.

She holds her fist in her palm and says, "Let's Roshambo for it?"

I glance down at her hand, then up to her adorable face. Her eyebrows raise and my lip turns up in a lopsided smile. Well, I can't say no to that.

"Okay," I concede, holding my fisted hand in the palm of my other, "on three." We pat our palms and she covers my rock with her paper, and beams a bright smile.

"Ha, I win! Mimi one, Seamus zero. You're coming." She rests back on her elbows, staring out onto the lake, and I can't suppress my stupid smile even though I just lost to her.

"Okay, sunshine, you win." I'm smiling, even though I lost.

"Sunshine?" she questions.

Yeah, you're radiant and everything about you screams happiness. *At least in how she makes me feel. So yeah, sunshine.*

"Yeah, sunshine," is all I can manage to say.

I peer out at the moon's reflection shining off the ripples of water in the lake. It's so clear out here, I can easily spot Orion, my favorite constellation, making its presence known against the night sky. It's a peace I rarely feel, and I don't know if it's the lake, the sky, or the girl next to me. The combination is overwhelming, in the best way, and I'm craving more of it.

A horn sounds, indicating it's time to get back to our cabins for the night, and I feel disappointed. I want to stay here with her.

"Looks like we have to head back." I stand up, holding my hand out to help her up.

She places her hand in mine and jumps to her feet at the same time I pull her up, creating more force than needed, and her body falls flush against mine. I freeze for a moment, holding her, and I'm tempted to pull her even closer. I reach up and tuck her hair behind her ear. She looks at me, blinks, then backs away and I realize I may be reading her all wrong. Maybe, she is just being friendly.

"So, I'll see you tomorrow," she replies as she steps completely out of my grasp. She turns, skipping toward her cabin, but not before yelling out, "Stay out of trouble, Rambo."

8

SEAMUS

Present Day

I've been dressed and sitting in my living room for well over two hours. I have no idea what time her date is at but, regardless of that, I'll be ready. I've waited a lot longer for less meaningful things.

Just like some of my missions and assignments, there's been nothing but time for me to overthink. I get stuck in my head, mostly about whatever task I am currently required to accomplish and some of the things I've done over the years.

Some I'm proud of. Some, not so much.

Before Afterburn, my thoughts were random, sporadic. Flashbacks of my father and how he treated my mother. The years of abuse we both endured for far too long because of my inability to protect not only myself, but my mother.

The years prior to that where I was too embarrassed to bring any friends over in fear they would see my father at his worst. The only person who broke that was Hudson and his annoying persistence of us being friends. I smile and shake my head at the memory of his too big head for his too awkward body, following

46

me to and from the bus stop. Sometimes, he'd just be waiting outside my front door since it was on the way to the bus stop from his house.

Like an asshole, I would never wait if he wasn't there. But he would always catch up with me and continue talking my ear off while I just listened.

I never made friends, but Hudson did, and then his friends became my friends, and that small group is the only family I have. They *knew* about my home life, my father and his ways, even though I attempted to hide it as much as possible. But they never questioned much, judged, or otherwise, making me explain anything.

However, they *would* question every sane cell in my body if they knew what I was doing right now. Buying the house next to the woman I fell for at seventeen, who I haven't seen over a decade, following her, studying her schedule and lifestyle while sitting in my living room with nothing but my rampant thoughts as I wait for her to leave for her *date*.

Fuck, even I'm questioning my sanity.

Of course, I justify my actions. Why? Because Mimi was different.

Mimi *is* different.

She branded herself to me, so quickly, so easily, and I have no idea how she did it. Was it just a vulnerable moment in my life during that time or was clinging to her like she was my lifeline, truly meant to be that? Because the moment I saw her again changed everything for me. Like that lifeline came back to me.

A seventeen-year-old going to camp for the first time, not knowing anyone, should have been the worst, most awkward experience a teenager could have. But, she made it...everything.

It was the first time in my life I truly felt happy, relaxed, and just content with day to day life.

It wasn't something to get used to, because it was short lived. But it wasn't camp, the lake, or the environment that made me feel that way. It was her. I've been chasing that same feeling for the past decade, and come up short every time.

There hasn't been another woman who makes me feel how she makes me feel. Not that I've ever cared to try. I've never had any type of serious relationship with a woman, just hookups between active duty or during breaks, which were empty and ultimately unsatisfying. My extended periods of active duty trained me to not need sex or desire it as often as I probably should, and jacking off was purely for relief out of necessity.

But the moment I saw Mimi, that desire for her resparked the dead ashes from the fire she created so many years ago, and I can't stop fucking thinking about everything I want to do to her.

The light in her living room dims, ripping me from my thoughts as I see a car pull up to the front of her house.

The pink Lyft light in the windshield indicates she's getting a rideshare tonight, which is interesting. She either plans to drink or use that as an excuse to have him drive her home.

That thought pisses me off, but I shove it aside as I watch her exit her front door. She turns to lock it, then proceeds to scurry down her driveway toward the vehicle.

The wind forces her dress back, hugging the front half of her body as the flowy fabric whips behind her. The contour of her hourglass shape is fully visible, as is her cleavage on display from the top of her low cut dress.

Christ.

She looks like a gorgeous, tempting sin, leveling the little bit of sanity I have left.

As the car pulls away, I'm already two steps out the front door and getting into my truck.

9

NAOMI

I fake a smile back at my date as I force myself to listen to another story about disc golf.

As a chronically single woman, I've realized a very important fact about dating.

Every date will not be a home run, but there is always something to enjoy out of it. The process, sure, it can be redundant, but it can also be fun. It's part of the journey, getting to know someone, listening to their story, and finding pleasure in their company. The less you look at it like a date with the intent to find love, the more we find enjoyment in all the little things.

We can find flaws in anyone, that's easy, so I make it my mission to find the things I like about them.

Other than the fact that he talks incessantly, he's a *nice* guy. I mean, I probably share the same amount of chemistry with a garden gnome, and even though he's not half bad looking, there is zero happening in the attraction department. In fact, he seems a little pompous and conceited.

A total turn off for me.

I have yet to answer any questions about me, because, well,

he hasn't asked any. And he can't stop talking about himself. He's talked about his job as a general contractor, his love for stand-up comedy, and disc golf. So not only do we lack chemistry, but we lack anything in common.

I continue to smile and nod as I try to give him my undivided attention while I appraise him, studying his dark features. His thick jawline and high cheekbones pair well with his dark brown eyes and slightly curly, shaggy hair.

He's handsome, but all I can envision is him with a bandana and he'd look like Rambo. I smile at the memory of my own personal Rambo, and yet hate how much the memories of our moments feel as happy as they do painful.

I peer over the shoulder of wanna be Rambo, and flinch as I see *him* again—his eyes meet mine and I feel his presence all the way to my bones. A shiver runs through me as I blink hard. I position myself in front of my date to avoid staring at a stranger that I *think* is him again.

My date is still talking about disc golf…I'm still unsure how there is so much to say on the topic, but I distract myself by tilting my head to peek over his shoulder again.

The table is empty.

Of course, it's empty, because I'm going crazy.

But, he felt so real that time. *So real.*

"Would you excuse me for a minute, Jeremy?" I interrupt my date's topic of lighter versus heavier frisbees, and the importance of their use in game play.

Standing, my chair scoots back and I place my napkin on the table, then head straight to the women's bathroom.

Fortunately, it's empty and I'm able to give myself a moment to splash some cold water on my face.

I've never been one to wear much makeup. In fact, I never do when I teach, but on nights like this, I do wear a little foundation and mascara. I avoid splashing any over my eyes so I don't end up looking like a raccoon for the rest of the night.

God, I'm really losing it. Seeing him tonight, *feeling* him like I just did…*that* has never happened before.

Puffing my cheeks and blowing out some excess air, I realize now, I really do need to go back to Afterburn and ask for him. I need to confront that part of my past.

Patting my face dry, I toss the damp paper towel in the garbage and open the door to exit. I jump back with a gasp as I'm hit with a wall of flesh. My eyes trail up his torso, to his chest, and over the snug, charcoal colored shirt he is wearing under his sports jacket.

His jawline is smooth and tight, and then my eyes meet his. The ones I thought I knew so well, once timid and amiable, now look more experienced and confident. I always felt like Seamus was wise beyond his years. He was more mature than all the other guys his age, chivalrous and attentive, even back then.

As my eyes bounce between his, it's the same old soul but *different*.

My brows furrow as I realize…he's actually here.

The anxiety I was feeling earlier at the thought of him morphs into something else…frustration. The mix of his presence and my imagination has my mood changing in a kaleidoscope of emotions.

"What are you doing here? Are you following me?"

"We need to talk." The deep bass of his voice vibrates through me.

So not only did he have to grow up into some god-like structure, but he also sounds like Zeus on steroids.

"I'm a little busy right now." I cross my arms over my chest and his eyes flicker, oh so quickly, to my cleavage that's now pushed up from my forearm shelf.

"Lose the date." His deep voice isn't angry, it's factual. Like he already knows I'm going to listen. "He's going to bore us both to death."

My eyes widen as my eyebrows hit my forehead, and my shocked face is an understatement.

The audacity he has.

And how the hell does he know how boring he is? He's not wrong, but still.

After all these years, here I am seeing ghosts of him, wondering if I've lost my mind, and now he's appearing out of nowhere, coming at me like a bullet train with no brakes.

"Mimi." He cocks his head at me like, he can't believe I'm not obeying his stupid, bossy order.

"Well." I clear my throat while switching my purse from one shoulder to the other, purposely hitting him with it on the side swing. "You of all people know how I respond to bullies." I creep up onto my tippy toes and lean in close to him to whisper in his ear.

"I take the other guy home." Leaning back to look at him once more, I give him a fake smile then squeeze between him and the door.

I can hear the frustrated breath he sucks in as I walk away and head toward my table.

My confused state has me in a completely different world by the time I sit back down.

I glance back to the hallway where the bathrooms are, but I don't see him. My eyes search the restaurant, and nothing.

Maybe he actually listened.

And I'm confused, and pissed, that I feel disappointed by that.

I turn back to Jeremy and realize how uninvested I am, knowing I just need to call it a night.

"So, ready to go back to my place, babe?"

Ewww, *babe*. My nose scrunches at the nickname.

"Well, that's very presumptuous of you." My tone is friendly, but factual.

He shrugs. "I bought dinner, so how about you treat me to some dessert…in my bed."

He wiggles his eyebrows.

Oh my God, this guy.

"Come on, it'll be fun." He reaches over, gripping my hand a little harder than he should, but I yank it back, accidentally hitting the wine glass between us. The deep red liquid splashes onto the table and a few drops splatter onto his shirt.

"You bitch!" He stands, throwing his hands out like I just threw a barrel of gasoline on him.

My jaw is slacked as I stare up at him, towering over me at the table.

It was just a little wine, and it was an accident.

"Sit down." Seamus' deep voice cannons through us both as he steps up to the table.

Jeremy eyes him up and down, confused. "Who the hell are you?"

Seamus glances down at me, an almost invisible smirk ticks on the corner of his lips, then he looks back over to my date.

"Dude…" Jeremy's arm reaches out to push Seamus away. Seamus knocks it away then cups his hand along Jeremy's collarbone, right where it meets his neck, and grips him hard.

Jeremy's legs fall from underneath him and his ass plops down onto the chair.

"What the hell?" Jeremy appraises himself, like he's unsure why his body did what it just did.

My jaw drops open as my eyes bounce between the two men.

"Let's go." Seamus holds his hand out toward me.

You've got to be kidding me.

I roll my eyes and open my purse. Grabbing a twenty dollar bill, I toss it on the table. I hate feeling like this man thinks I *owe* him something. Twenty isn't enough to cover my portion of the bill, but it'll do for my conscience at least.

Plus, that's like the universal, *I'm definitely not into you* sign, so hopefully Jeremy never calls me…ever again.

Standing, I tip up my chin, saying nothing as I turn to walk out of the restaurant.

Glancing back over my shoulder, because clearly I'm addicted to the drama, Jeremy attempts to follow me. I see Seamus hold out his palm to him, calling a command like an owner to a dog. "Stay." Then he turns to watch me as I round the corner of the entrance door.

Ugh! Why is he here? How is he here? Coming out of the woodwork, bossing my boring date around.

I pull out my phone, open the Uber app, and call for a car. Fortunately, there is one available within four minutes.

I should have driven, but I hate driving at night, and I never drive even if I have one drink.

Standing on the side of the curb, I glance up and down the street, looking for the silver Toyota Camry that is surely nowhere nearby yet.

"Do you know how much restraint it took not to reply with *your worst nightmare*." His voice is deep velvet, and even mocking Rambo sounds like cashmere to my ears.

My back is to him, thank God, because I have to press my lips together to stop my smile and suppress my giggle.

Damn him. My goofy Seamus. The one I remember so well.

Then I remember I'm mad at him.

"Seamus," I turn to face him, "what are you doing here?"

"I had to see you."

I scrunch my nose and screw up my face. "How are you even here?"

"I saw you."

"Did you follow me?" He remains quiet.

"Do you live here?" I ask.

"Yes."

"Where?"

"Seattle."

I huff and roll my eyes as I look away from him. Yes, that's where *here* is. Ugh.

"We need to talk. That last day...what you think happened, didn't happen like that."

"Seamus, stop." I avoid looking at him. I can't do this, I can't listen to him telling me what I should think when *I know* what happened.

"I know what happened, Seamus, I was there. I know *exactly* what happened." I divert my gaze down at my phone, anywhere I can look except on his gorgeous, tight body and stupid, beautiful face.

At seventeen, he was cute. A soft, smooth jawline with far too much hair on his head that didn't fit the frame of his face, but he still had a strong, lean build.

Now...Now his body looks hard and sculpted with a jawline that could cut glass. My eyes briefly roam over his thick arms that fill out his clothes to tailored perfection, and I've never found myself staring at a man's ass, but Seamus' is a sight to be seen, like he spends all his spare time sprinting for the Olympics.

I need to get the hell out of here. I sneak another peek at my phone. The Uber is just around the corner and can't come fast enough.

"You need to give me a chance to explain." He steps toward me.

I step back and he stops, feeling my discomfort.

"Mimi, that night—"

"That night you took my virginity and then you left!" I shout at him, and he recoils. "You left, without a word. Nothing!" I yell even louder. The back of my throat is heavy with boulders. I swallow thickly and fight back the tears that begin to pool in my eyes.

"Your ten years of silence has said it all."

The car pulls up and I take a couple steps back toward it.

His body stiffens and his brows squeeze together, expressing a painful confusion. Like he's dumbfounded I would feel this way. But how could I not?

Then my stupid heart flutters at the possibility that he's hurting. That my words hurt him.

"What happened, happened," I say, defeated. "We're done, we can move on and it's okay."

It's okay…the Mimi melody I play on repeat and theme song of my life.

Grabbing the handle of the passenger door, I swing it open and hop in, closing it swiftly behind me.

Seamus stands frozen in place as he watches me. His eyes find mine and they're…broken, but there's something behind the hurt. A drive, a desire, a need.

And it's all too much.

I slam my eyes shut. It's so fucking painful to look at him, to see him. After all this time, you'd think I'd be over it. That I wouldn't care what happened between us, more importantly, what it ended up leading to. But somehow, all my old wounds are open again and fully exposed.

The car finally pulls away and my lungs decompress.

I rest the back of my head on the headrest as my Uber driver comes to a stop at the light.

Unable to stop myself, I turn and look out through the back window. Seamus is walking away from the restaurant with purpose, and down the row of cars parked on the street.

Reaching into his pocket, the lights flicker on one of the parked cars and he opens the driver's side door and jumps in.

The light in front of us turns green, and my driver accelerates at a snail's pace.

"Um, excuse me, can you drive a little faster?" I squeak out.

"No way, lady, I do this for a living. I can't get a ticket or pull some *Mission Impossible* car driving stunt just to get you away from your broody boyfriend." He glances back at me in the rear view mirror and studies me for a moment. His eyes soften a bit. He doesn't say anything, but I feel the car go a tad bit faster and it turns the corner, out of sight.

I stare out the window at the Seattle skyline, recalling the moment I saw all the towering, downtown buildings. I didn't want to move here. I didn't want to leave Texas where all my friends were, and experience my last year of high school in a brand new place.

Everything was so foreign, and it made everything hurt so much worse. I felt lonely, insecure, and the nightmares I had…I shake my head, attempting to clear my thoughts. My body inhales a deep breath, as if it were automated, needing a hefty dose of oxygen.

His presence is stirring up all the feelings I've spent years masking, and now I wonder if I ever really *truly* got over everything or if they were just lying dormant.

Tomorrow is a new day. I tilt my chin up and silently pep talk myself. Something I've done my whole life, but I need it now more than ever.

What happened…happened.

That's all I can say. That's all I can do. It wasn't his fault. Deep down, I know he didn't cause what happened to me.

My getaway driver pulls up to the front of my house and I thank him, making sure to give him a tip on the app for going a few miles over his desired speed limit, and exit the car.

It's cooled down substantially in the last twenty minutes, and I take in the humid but crisp air as I tilt my head toward the sky. It took a while to get used to when I first moved here, but now, one of my favorite things about this place is the weather.

Sure, the sun is great, and I love the feeling of the heat on my skin, but rain—the rain is cleansing. There is something special about being able to smell the rain coming.

Padding up the walkway, I take the two steps up onto my porch and dig in my purse to grab my keys, when a car pulls around the corner into the cul-de-sac. I glance over my shoulder at the empty driveway of my neighbor and my heartbeat kicks up a notch.

Finally, I'll get to meet him or her.

The headlights of the over-sized truck beam through my front yard as they turn into their driveway. Blinded for a moment, I squint and raise my hand to cover the flare of the light as it hits my pupils.

The truck stops and sits idle for a moment, and I decide that I'm not going to let them avoid me. I turn fully and stand at the top of my steps. A lone silhouette sits in the driver's seat, and it appears to be looking my way. There's a brief pause when the engine finally shuts off, killing the lights with it, and the driver's side door pops open.

A man steps out, and my breath catches in my throat as my brain registers everything in slow motion.

Seamus.

He stops, stilling between the car and the open door, resting his elbows on either side, as if he knows I need this minute to catch up. Those dark, driven eyes sear through me. Studying me. Testing me.

I blink, questioning my sanity, and look away, then look again, and he's still there.

Fuck.

He steps back, shutting the door, taking a few steps forward, aligning himself in front of his truck, still saying nothing.

This can't be right.

I look at his house, my house, then back over to him. I can't help but huff out a laugh.

I've always been a believer in fate, signs, karma, and anything else you want to dress up as coincidence, but this… This is the worst prank of divine intervention that could ever happen in real life.

I gesture my arms up from my sides, in a silent *what the fuck.*

My shoulders slouch as my arms fall to my sides. Defeated. I feel defeated.

Unmoving and frozen, I gaze over the yard between his house and mine as he pulls the sports jacket off his shoulders and shrugs it down his arms. The long sleeve shirt underneath fits him like a glove, wrapping around his corded arms and broad shoulders like a second skin.

Stepping over the white, knee-high fence that separates our homes, he begins making his way toward me.

As he crosses the lawn, nothing has been said between us. The silence thunders through the air and I have no idea what words even make sense at this point.

His face is level with mine as he steps onto the bottom stair, aligning his body directly in front of me.

His colossal size on just the bottom step of my porch is over-whelming. His physical presence is commanding, taking over the space around me and stampeding through my emotions simulta-neously. The same feeling of security and adoration wraps around me, and I hate that I feel so comfortable so easily.

"Hey, sunshine." He says it slowly, like he's savoring the syllables that have been waiting a decade to be spoken.

I glance back over to my neighbor's house and recall the urgency in which they left, the off market sale, and sudden *need* to move a couple months ago. It wasn't even a month after I saw Seamus at Afterburn that all of that happened.

Holding my eyes closed for a moment as I take a deep breath, I blink before turning back to face him.

"It's not a coincidence that you're my new neighbor, is it?" I ask, although I already know the answer.

I stare at him, appraising his body, his face, and studying his beautiful, dark eyes. Recalling all the moments I got lost in them. A drive, a desire, a need burns through them like wildfire, unafraid of consuming everything in its path.

"Why are you here?" I ask.

"I wasn't done loving you yet. And I'm here to prove it."

I gasp in shock at his confession. My lips part as I open my mouth to fight back, to say something, anything. But nothing comes out.

He looks down at my mouth, and as if on instinct, his tongue darts out, licking his bottom lip. It catches my attention as my eyes bounce between his eyes and mouth. A lopsided, barely there smile replaces his tongue, and then he reaches up, using his thumb and finger to caress my chin.

It's the first time I haven't backed away or flinched at his touch. My entire body is heated, not just from the tiniest touch of his skin on mine, but from the raging inferno of everything that I'm feeling.

I want to be pissed, but somehow, he's suppressing it, extinguishing it with one simple touch along with his stupid, gorgeous face and dangerous eyes.

His thumb traces my bottom lip as he tilts his head, studying the way my body responds to his touch.

Stupid, traitorous body.

He smirks, because he knows. He knows what he does to me. What he's always done to me.

"Goodnight, Mimi," he says, pouring ice cold water on the mood of the moment. Stepping down, he makes his way across the yard, the same way he came, and I watch, still in absolute shock.

He grabs his jacket and reaches into his pocket, pulling out a small set of keys. Walking up the steps of his porch, the metal key zips into the keyhole of his door handle, the sound echoes through the air between us.

He pauses and turns to look at me, still frozen in the same position he left me in. He shoots me a blinding, gorgeous smile, then steps through the threshold of *his* house, closing the door behind him.

What the fuck.

Still dumbfounded, I glance down at my rooted feet and shake my head.

Seamus:1

Mimi: 0

You win that round, Rambo.

10

NAOMI

17 years old

"*W*ho was that guy you were with yesterday, Meems?" Shane asks before taking a big bite off the corner of his pepperoni pizza he has hovering over his mouth.

I didn't see Seamus all day today. He must have made friends with the guys in his cabin and found something to do. I hope that's the case, because I couldn't imagine coming here for my first time as a senior in our last year at camp.

"Who, Seamus?" I reply like a guilty person when they think they did something wrong, and I instantly regret my words. Like I'm defending my choice to hang out with him already, solidifying the fact that I like him.

Shane side-eyes me, chewing the doughy pizza and replies with a chuckle, "Yeah, I guess if that's who you were hanging out with all day."

"Oh. Yeah. Seamus. I met him at check in, it's his first year here. I was just trying to help him out," I say, brushing it off to not make anything too obvious.

Although, Shane and I have been friends since the first year he came to camp, a year after me, so I know he can sense my awkwardness.

Glancing around the room, there are quite a few seniors here tonight—the ones who have come almost every year since we were old enough to.

It's bittersweet.

Seeing everyone again has been great, but knowing that most of us will probably never talk again after this summer is a bit depressing. We'll go through our senior year of high school, graduate, and the only ones who will come back here are the ones who will volunteer to lead the younger camp groups.

I don't know of any of my friends that are doing that, and since I want to backpack through Europe and take a gap year before settling into college life, I know I won't be back here to see anyone again. My parents don't love the idea, but they're supportive of my decision.

The door opens and I steel my spine, anxious to see if it's Seamus. Instead, it's Nathan and Wes, the termites from check-in. I huff out an annoyed breath as I sink back into my chair.

"Ladies and gentleman, the party has arrived!" Wes shouts, holding out his arms like a messiah. Someone tosses a garlic knot at him and others whine or shout profanities. A couple of other guys hoot.

I roll my eyes because, ew.

"Oh hey, Mimi. Where's your new friend?" Nathan asks as he plops down in the one person chair I'm sitting in, forcing me to shift over so he doesn't squish me.

He wraps his arm around me, pulling me into his side, and I lean as far away from him as possible.

"You're annoying, Nathan. Get your own chair." I push at his shoulder, but he doesn't budge."

Everyone is talking, eating, and playing some card games when Wes comes up, popping some peanuts into his mouth with one hand while holding an empty glass bottle in the other.

*"Come on, Mimi. Let's play Spin The Bottle, roulette style,"
Wes states without question. Nathan stands, grabbing my waist
without asking, then pulls me up to my feet.*

*I slap his hands off my body and shoot him a nasty look as I
run my hands down my shirt, straightening it back out.*

*We've all played Spin The Bottle plenty of times in past
years, but never 'roulette style'.*

"What's roulette style?" I ask.

*He places two Folgers coffee tins in the middle of the table.
They both have a bunch of folded up pieces of paper in them.*

*"This canister," he points at the green one, "has locations
written on little pieces of paper. Things like, on the couch, in the
circle, on the pool table, outdoor picnic table…" He looks over
at the kitchen area then writes down another, saying aloud as he
scribbles, "In the pantry."*

*Daphne, another senior, takes a blank piece of paper, writing
as she says out loud, "Against a tree," placing it in the green
container.*

*"This container," he points at the red can, "holds pieces of
paper with different actions written on them. Truth. Dare. French
kiss. Over the pants handsy." He lists out a few others as he
passes around more pieces of paper to some of the other seniors
that walk up.*

*"You guys can write down anything that comes to mind and
place it in the jar." He leans down, pressing his pencil to the
paper, "BJ," he says as a couple of people look at him wide-
eyed. Some look curious and worried, others curious and
interested.*

"No. That can't be in there," I spit out.

*"Sure it can be. Each person gets to write down whatever
they want. Doesn't mean they will get their own, but someone
could. So, the spinner will pick out of the location jar first,
seeing where it will take place. Then they will pick the action,
then you spin the bottle picking your partner at random. Every-*

*body plays, no exceptions." He taps the pencil to his chin. "I guess I should write down, "head" or "*make me come*" instead, since a girl can't give a girl a BJ." He shrugs since he already put BJ in the container. I glance down as I see him write,* make me come, *on another before throwing it in the canister.*

"Girl-girl, guy-guy. No matter who it lands on, you have to play," Nathan announces to the group.

My jaw slacks as I look over at Shane, and by the expression on his face, he's also worried about how this is all going to go down.

Nathan slides his hand over my waist, pulling me closer to him. He leans down and whispers in my ear, "Get your mouth ready, gorgeous," as he shows me what he wrote down: lick my balls.

Disgusted, I attempt to pull away when the bell on the door pings through the room. I look up and Seamus is standing in the doorway. His eyes land straight on mine, then bounce between Nathan, me, Nathan's hand still resting on my hip, and back up to my eyes again.

He steps through the door and shuts it behind him, his body tense and rigid.

Wes clears his throat. "You're not invited, semen."

"I invited him," I spit out, slapping Nathan's hand off me.

I walk toward him, meeting him halfway between the front door and where our circle is grouped together, holding out my arm, inviting him. "Come on, Seamus."

He glances behind me at everyone gathered in a circle around the bottle and two containers, then slowly takes a step toward me.

"What are you getting me into, sunshine?" he asks under his breath so only I can hear him.

I should have let Wes kick him out and not rope him into this shitstorm waiting to happen, but I did actually invite him, and it would be totally messed up if I didn't stand up for him.

Plus, I oddly feel comforted by his presence.

"Nothing you can't handle, Rambo," I whisper back as we line ourselves up with the others in the circle.

My eyes bounce around to everyone here. There's only ten of us, and there are more guys than girls. A few others are playing darts, and Wes is yelling at them to come play, but they hold their hands up at him, shaking their head profusely.

Exactly what I should be doing.

Wes recaps the rules and I sneak a peek over at Seamus, since he wasn't here when he said them before.

"Green jar picks the location. Red jar picks the action. Then you spin the bottle and whoever the narrow side points to is your partner. Everything is random and left to chance. We'll go clockwise, starting with the oldest here, which is Nathan. And like I said, your race, gender, religion, or any of the other shit doesn't matter. Whoever you land on, is who you get."

Seamus' eyebrows shoot up to his forehead as he turns slowly to look at me.

If looks could kill. I would be dead.

I bite my lip and throw a lopsided smile at him, my eyes squinting an apology that I can't verbalize.

His chest rises and he huffs out an annoying breath, and now that I think about it, I feel terrible. I would hate it if he pulled me into this.

When no one is looking, I slide my hand over his exposed forearm, giving him a tender squeeze. He looks down at where my hand is touching him, giving me a close lipped smile as his hand cups mine, telling me it's okay.

Nathan reaches into the middle of the circle, grabbing a piece of paper from the green container. My eyes scan over everyone in the circle and their reaction is as still as mine. We all follow the paper as he unfolds it.

"On the pool table." He flashes the paper up in the air before flicking it down on the table.

Then he reaches into the red container. "Hell yeah, lap dance," he reads aloud before tossing that one ahead and reaching into the circle to spin the bottle.

Lap dance. Oh God, I can't dance. My eyes bounce around the circle and I wonder who else is freaking out internally like I am. I guess it could be worse, but still. A lap dance, on the pool table, in front of everyone.

A flick of his wrist has the bottle spinning, the sound of the glass grazing circles on the wooden table vibrate through the room as everyone holds their breath.

It slows down, slowly, then slower, finally landing on…Wes.

The jaw dropping smile that crosses my face could be seen across the entire state of Texas.

A few hollers and hoots leave the group as Wes palms his face and Nathan throws his hands up. "What the fuck? Really?"

They joke and banter while Nathan wants to back out, but Wes forces him over to the pool table, reminding him, and all of us, that if you play, you play. And there is no backing out.

I glance over at Seamus, and he is smiling a tight lipped smile. I think he's happy with the turn of events.

Wes takes his phone out of his pocket and taps the screen a few times, then the familiar beats of the Thong Song *by Sisqó blare through his tiny speaker.*

Wes, being the idiot that he is, ended up half stripping and making a joke about the whole thing, shaking his ass and humping Nathan's leg. It was more humorous than it was sexual, and when it's all done, we all clap and give Nathan a hard time for appearing flushed.

He claims that he was embarrassed, we obviously think he probably liked it.

After that's all done, they return to the circle and the tension has softened.

Okay, maybe this won't be so bad.

"Mimi, baby, it's your turn," Nathan calls out as he takes a

sip of his water, looking directly at me with determination in his eyes.

"Not your baby." I reach into the green canister, showing more confidence than I actually have and pull out a piece of paper.

Unfolding it, I say out loud, "In the bathroom." I screw up my face, because yuck. But at least it's private. Although, there's probably only one person I'd be comfortable being alone with.

I sit to my full height and take a deep breath as I reach in the red jar, withdrawing with the folded note between my pointer and middle finger, then unfold it.

I gasp as I see the two little letters.

BJ

"Shit," I whisper to myself. Seamus stares at the diabolical piece of paper then looks up at my face, his expression is completely unreadable.

Anger, maybe. Uneasiness, definitely.

"Hell yeah!" Nathan shouts. "That's mine. Come on, Mimi, spin. Land on me, baby."

Fuck. I'm having an internal fucking meltdown and my heartrate is through the roof.

"What happens if the bottle lands on a girl?" Daphne asks.

"Same, same." Nathan rubs his palms together as he eyes the bottle. "Come on, Mimi, go."

"There is no such thing as giving a girl a BJ, so it's void if it lands on a girl. Even Wes said so himself earlier," Shane replies, coming to my defense.

Everyone nods in agreement.

I shift my gaze to Shane with a thankful look.

"Fine, just spin," Nathan finally agrees impatiently, then tips his chin at the bottle while he looks at me.

I glance around the circle once again then peek up at Seamus. His jaw is tight and he's completely uncomfortable, looking anywhere but at me.

I'm completely frozen, nervous, and my body is in full shut down mode.

Wes whistles, ripping me out of my own head, and my eyes snap over in his direction.

He wiggles his eyebrows, and just his expression makes bile rise to my throat.

I take a deep breath and finally lean in to grab the bottle, but I can't, I just can't. I pull back again and palm my face. "Oh my God, I can't do this."

"Mimi, do it…you have to follow through," Wes says, matter of fact.

"You can't back out, we didn't," Nathan reminds me, and the entire group.

My cheeks puff out as I release a long breath.

I reach in, flick the bottle aggressively, and it spins fast. The air around all of us is thick, and no one is breathing. It's like we're all frozen in time and the bottle is the only thing in our subspace that moves. After a lifetime, it finally begins to slow, slow, slow, and stops.

Pointing directly at Shane.

11

SEAMUS

17 years old

*"*S*hit," Mimi whispers, echoing my thoughts as the bottle lands on some random guy I've never seen before.*

She looks over at him as he looks wide-eyed back at her. He glances around the room, a few hacklers and people hollering, while Nathan is running his hands through his hair, pissed it didn't land on him.

I've only been around Nathan twice since camp started, and both times I want to choke him with his own tongue.

He's a prick, an entitled rich kid who bullies others around him. This version of spin the bottle is the exact reason I hate other people and have hardly any friends. Because it's stupid shit like this that leaves people with long lasting trauma.

"Shane, Shane, Shane," a couple of guys chant. Shane's face shifts into amusement as he stares back at Mimi. They both stand at the same time, still watching each other move, then Shane reaches out, grabs her hand, and leads her down the hallway.

My fists clench at my sides and I'm fucking burning inside. Fury rolls over my body like lava and my face heats as I go to stand and take a step in that direction, before forcefully stopping myself.

Mimi glances back over her shoulder at me, her lips in a tight, timid smile with eyes full of guilt.

I have no claim on her, no reason to feel the way I do. Still, I hate this. I hate this more for her than I do for myself.

They turn into the bathroom and a resounding click is all that's left in the now empty hallway.

"That's bullshit," Wes says, flailing his arm in their direction.

He grabs the bottle and starts spinning it. It stops, and he repeats.

"What are you doing, man?" Nathan asks.

"Practicing. I'm going to time this fucking perfectly so it lands on Mimi when it's my turn."

"Knock it off." I flick the bottle off the wooden slab as it falls onto the floor. Wes stands, instantly getting in my face.

"Fuck you, Semen. You shouldn't even be here." Spit mists over my face. I stand my ground, staring back at him, unmoving.

Do not swing. Do not punch him. You are not your father.

I repeat to myself as I find every inch of willpower to stop myself from killing him for being a dick, playing this stupid game, and putting Mimi in the position she's in now.

I get that it's her choice. She could just back out, but there's too much peer pressure and people like Wes and Nathan make it impossible to say no. She would be at the forefront of bullying if she backed out now.

"Is this the only way you can get anything out of a girl?" I ask Wes, taunting him. "Spin the bottle?"

"Fuck you, sperm." He palms my chest, pushing me back. But it's all just a front for him. If he really wanted to fight, he would have just swung. Instead, he pushed me in an attempt to look like the bigger man. I'm well versed in the action, at least in taking them.

A click of the door captures both of our attention as we separate from each other.

Shane steps out of the bathroom first. His hair is a little more disheveled than when he went in there, and a light sheen of sweat coats his forehead.

Fuck.

He steps back into the circle saying absolutely nothing. As he sits down, he glances around the group with a smug as hell look on his face that I'd like to pour gasoline on and light on fire.

Mimi steps out a second later, and her cheeks are flushed pink. She hangs her head in shame, staring at her feet as she walks back to the circle. Her eyes glance up to me and I tilt my head so my eyes can connect with hers, but she looks back down too quickly before sitting on the opposite side of the table from me.

"Shaneeeee, come on, spill the beans. Was it good? Did she swallow?" Nathan's way too inappropriate questions make Mimi cringe, and I'm seeing fucking red.

"A gentleman never tells," he replies, picking up the bottle and handing it to the person that was sitting next to Mimi. "Your turn."

I need to get the fuck out of here. But I refuse to leave Mimi here.

I squat down and take a seat, still trying to find her eyes, but she's just staring down at the center of the table.

Some guy I don't know pulls from the green jar, then the red, and the bottle spins landing on the girl I know to be Daphne, who he guides outside to the picnic table. I was too focused on Mimi to hear what he pulled out of the red jar, but by the way he's grinding on her, it was either some sort of dance or dry humping session.

Wes' turn is up now. He places his hand over Mimi's shoulder and says, "I hope you're ready."

I hope you're ready for my fist in your face.

She rolls her eyes, pushing his hand off of her. He uses that same hand to pick out of the first canister.

On the couch.

Then he picks from the second.

He reads out loud, proudly. "Hand job."

Everyone oohs and hollers.

A small shake of my head is my only display of annoyance.

Wes doesn't waste any time as he spins the bottle with a calculation similar to how he did when he was practicing. He stares at Mimi with a bright smile, like he knows exactly where that bottle is stopping.

It begins to slow as it comes up on Mimi. Her eyes follow and I watch the entire scene play out in excruciatingly slow motion. Her jaw slacks and her brows pinch together, but her tense shoulders and held breath release as it slides an extra inch past her, pointing at Shane.

"What the hell?" Shane belts out.

Everyone falls silent. There is no getting out of this one. No making fun with it, doing a joke of a lap dance and being the class clown or just dry humping a leg.

Shane's task is to make Wes come on the couch using only his hands.

In front of everyone.

Shane was an innocent bystander when it was Mimi's turn, so a part of me feels a little bad. But then I remember that smug look when he came out of the bathroom and that guilt diminishes quickly.

Wes, though. Whose face is currently disgusted and drenched in irritation.

Well, let's just say karma has a great sense of humor tonight.

"Fucking Christ," he spits out.

They both get up slowly, making their way to the couch. And I'm honestly surprised he didn't use every excuse to try and back out.

They sit in synchrony and everyone remains quiet. Shane goes to move, but Wes holds out his palm facing him.

"Just sit there for a second," Wes says angrily. He looks around the room and shakes his head. Someone I don't know, the one who had to dry hump Daphne reminds Wes this was his idea and he can't back out. A few people burst out in agreement, talking over each other, putting immense pressure on him.

"Fuck you guys." He flips the room off.

He huffs, throwing his head back, mutters something inaudible, then begins to toss his neck back and forth, giving himself a pep talk. While he attempts to hype himself up, Shane keeps stealing glances at Mimi, and it's pissing me off.

"Okay, just sit there. And don't do anything until I tell you," Wes reminds Shane, who seems more at ease than I would expect, but maybe he's like me and he hides his emotions well.

Wes unzips his pants and dips his hand into the front of the splayed denim as he begins palming himself. He rubs himself as his head falls back, resting on the top of the couch. His eyes are closed and he starts moving his hand back and forth.

Shane slowly reaches over, lifting Wes's shirt, but his head pops up as he swats his hand away. "Don't fucking touch me. Just give me a fucking minute," he spits out.

Shane pulls his hand back and holds it up in surrender.

Everyone in the room watches with stalled breath. The air in the room has grown thick and dense. Some are pretending to cover their eyes while peeking through the slits, others seem to be enjoying the anticipation of what's going to happen.

Wes's head falls back again, his eyes squeeze shut as he pulls out his cock and begins stroking it.

He's big, so I'm not surprised that he's confident being so exposed, but I can tell he's nervous. His breath is choppy and he's not fully hard yet. Most of his dick is hidden behind his fist that's fully wrapped around it as he continues to stroke with shaky hands.

Another minute goes by and his cock grows beyond the size of his hand as he continues to stroke and rub himself. One hand pulls the front of his pants down while the other rubs back and forth over the shaft. His eyes still squeezed shut, but his chest is rising and falling heavier with the sensation he's providing himself.

Shane watches. His eyes move between Wes' cock and his face, but I don't miss the shift in his seat and the quick lick of his bottom lip.

I don't blame him. Watching anyone do this is stimulating, even if it is the prick Wes doing it. I think everyone in the room is feeling the same way right now, because I'm quite certain most of us have only seen ourselves do this.

"Okay, do it," Wes breathes out.

Shane blinks quickly, frozen still, unsure of what he should actually do.

"Just do it," Wes says again more forcefully, making Shane lurch forward. He reaches out, but pauses, and glances up at Wes, giving him a curious look.

"God, you're such a pussy." Wes grabs Shane's hand and presses it to his cock. Shane's hand wraps around the shaft and begins to pump.

"Ah, fucking Christ," Wes whisper-grunts as his breath hitches, but he hides the initial pleasure by biting his lip and dipping his head back. His hands are at his sides, fisting the loose material of his pants.

Shane's hand continues the stroking motion as his chest heaves and his lips part. His body shifts again, moving slightly closer to Wes as desire clears the fog in the air.

I don't miss the whimper that leaves Wes' mouth when Shane releases his cock, spits in his hand, then returns and wraps it back around the length of Wes' cock.

"Oh fuck," he hisses as his hips pump into Shane's hand, and there's an unspoken lust that fills the room.

Shane's jaw is slacked as he watches himself continue to jerk Wes off, moving his hand from base to tip. He palms the thick, pink crown using the precum as lubricant that leaks from the tip.

Wes' breath is unsteady as inaudible sounds cast out from his throat. Unable to hold back, he groans, swears under his breath, and finally forces his head upright even though his eyes are still screwed shut.

"Look at me, Wes," Shane whispers.

Wes shakes his head, so subtle it would be easy to miss.

"Look. At. Me," Shane repeats in a whisper as he leans in closer. Wes' head snaps over to him. A look crosses over Shane's face that I can't read as his tempo changes, going wilder as he loses himself in the action.

Wes' eyes widen before he screws up his face, a low whine, a hidden whimper then he fails to hide a grunt that rolls into a series of moans and curses. Ropes of cum spurt out of the tip as he pumps his hips, staring at Shane through his entire release.

There is a long, awkward stillness in the room. Even the air is dense and unmoving.

"Dudeeee." Nathan elongates the word, breaking the silence.

Wes blinks out his daze and looks around the room in dumbfounded shock, then back to Shane. A brief look of shame crosses his face before he catches it, and his typical smug face returns as he tucks himself back into his pants. Pulling off his hoodie, he uses it as a towel as he cleans himself up. Shane sits like an ice sculpture next to him, staring at his hand that is drenched with Wes' cum.

Wes tosses the dirty hoodie at him. "Thanks, buddy." He pats him on the shoulder and stands up laughing, trying to play off everything that just happened.

"Who's next?" he asks, taking a swig of water.

I look at the table and realize, it's me. I'm up next and I want to throw the goddamn bottle against the wall, shattering it to a million pieces, and just stop the game. But I'm the last person and the only one who hasn't spun yet.

I want nothing more than to just walk out of here. I don't owe these people anything. I've been here for twenty-four hours and don't know anyone. I could do that and spend the next two weeks by myself, not caring what they think of me. But when I look over at Mimi, the shame blanketed over her feeds my desire to keep going.

I don't want to leave her alone in what she's done or make her feel even worse by leaving.

I keep my gaze on Mimi, watching her breath stall as I pull out one from the green jar.

Against a tree.

The awkwardness in the room finally starts to fade now that the attention is on me.

Still not diverting my gaze from Mimi, even though she still hasn't bothered to look my way, her breath hitches as I pull from the red jar.

I unfold it and I can't help but spit out. "You've got to be kidding me."

Make your partner come.

"Who the fuck wrote this?" My voice is laced with irritation. I throw the paper down on the table as people squeeze in to read it. Mimi's eyes widen as she realizes what is written and she palms her face, covering her mouth.

"Remember, girl, guy, or otherwise, you have to follow through," Nathan reminds everyone with a sinister smile as he pats Wes on the back, like he's some champion hero for following through with his dare.

God, he's such a dick. He's completely unfazed by what just happened.

Mimi finally looks up, her eyes are drowning in guilt. The corner of her brows are pinched together, almost as if she's in pain for me.

I can't find myself being mad at her, so I wiggle my eyebrows and give her a tight lopsided smile, attempting to relax us both.

Grabbing the bottle, I flick my wrist and turn the bottle. The empty glass spins over the wood panel of the table, and the patterned sound taunts everyone in the circle. It's deathly quiet as it begins to slow and the kneading sound of glass on wood fades.

Mimi's mouth drops open and my eyes flicker down to the bottle that's pointed directly at her. As her eyes meet mine, I remain impassive and expressionless. I'm stoked it didn't land on someone else, but the worry in Mimi's face has me on full alert. We have to do this outside against a tree that everyone will witness.

"Oh come the fuck on!" Nathan yells, stomping his foot like a three-year-old.

I stand and hold out my hand to her.

She slides hers in mine and I guide her up. We head toward the front door, closing it behind us as loud shuffling and a couple verbal snips muffle behind it.

My jaw is clenched as I recall when she was walking to the bathroom with Shane, and an inferno begins to light deep inside me.

"Did he hurt you?" I ask, generic as hell, but I can't seem to say anything more specific.

"Who?" She cranes her next to look at me. "Shane?"

Clenching harder, I nod.

She giggles, actually giggles, then shakes her head.

"No. God, no. He's…" She pauses looking over her shoulder at the cabin. "He's a really good friend of mine. We just faked it."

The tension in my face releases and I can't help but smile.

She glances up at the monstrous redwood tree and I study the lines of her smooth skin between her jaw and collarbone. She swallows thickly as I see the muscles of her throat constrict.

I step toward her as she turns around, leaning up against the bark.

I place my arms on either side of her head, caging her in entirely so they see as little of her as possible.

"Well, now that you've got me here, what are you going to do with me?" she says, playfully, assumably trying to make this whole situation less awkward.

"I'm going to pin you up against this tree. Put my hand down the front of your pants, and pretend like I'm touching you. You have to fake it...again."

She snaps a quizzitive look back at me.

"You don't want to...I mean..." She tucks a stray strand behind her ear as she shifts her weight between her feet.

"You don't want to do things to me?" she finally asks.

I huff out a chuckle and move closer to her.

"Oh I do."

I lean in even closer.

"You have no idea how much I want to do things *to you."*

She swallows audibly.

I intertwine my fingers in hers, stroking the channels in between them, giving us a sense of calm we both need as I stare into those gorgeous, almond-shaped eyes. They're dark with need, mirroring my own.

Getting turned on by the events of the night was inevitable, but Mimi staring back at me, my body inches from hers, with lust-filled eyes have me feral in a way I've never felt before.

I look between her lips and eyes, then peer over at the cabin. The window panes are full to the brim of everyone's faces, trying to squeeze in for a view of us.

I turn back to look at Mimi.

"I'm going to kiss you. But not here. Not in front of them. Because it's all I've thought about since we met and they can't have it. That's going to be mine, and mine alone." Her breath hitches at my confession.

I circle my hand around her wrists and bring her hands over her head, pinning her to the tree just like I promised.

I lower my head into the nook of her neck and she throws her head back, giving me easy access to the soft skin of her neck.

If rainbows and butterflies had a scent, she would be it. Like sunshine after the rain and the perfect spring day.

Unbuttoning the front of her pants, I ask, "Is this okay?" I shift my hips away from Mimi's body so she can't feel my dick growing impossibly hard.

"Yes," she replies, breathlessly.

Dipping my hand into the front, I realize I'm not going to be able to avoid touching her without it being obvious what we're doing. I take a step to the right, concealing her body from everyone else, then appear to drop my hand further between her legs. My body skims up against hers with the movement, and her eyes widen as she peeks down at my hand, then back up.

"You're hard." Her tone is both surprised and curious.

I can't help but chuckle that she is surprised by this.

"How could I not be?" I lean back into her, this time pressing my lips against her neck. My hips roll against her on instinct.

She moans, then whispers my fucking name, making my cock twitch like it's never heard a better sound in its life.

"Touch me, please."

What the fuck? I lift my gaze to meet hers. My cock jerks this time harder and I can feel the knowing sensation of precum leak out of the tip.

I've only ever done this once before, and I wasn't even really interested in the girl. It happened at some random house party I was at. I had no idea what I was doing. I was turned on because of the action and everything that was happening, not because of the girl.

Mimi has both my mind and body reeling, and I honestly have no idea how I'm still in control of either at the moment.

I look back over my shoulder at the cabin window, then back at Mimi. She's biting her bottom lip, desire filled in her gorgeous eyes. She implores further. "Please."

"Jesus." I dip my hand into the front of her panties as my middle finger trails down her center. Wetness engulfs my fingers and the pad of my fingertip grazes the peak of her clit.

"Holy shit. You're so wet."

She gasps, bucking her hips into my hand as her leg rubs my impossibly hard cock.

My eyes roam her tormented face. Her parted lips and pinched brows give away her desire as her chest heaves and hips roll into mine. I look at my hand dipped inside her pants and move my finger back and forth. She throws her head back against the bark with a loud moan.

I can't help but lean into her. My cock needs to feel something more as I rub my body against hers. "Seamus." She says my name like a prayer and my dick, with no guidance from any part of my brain, convulses uncontrollably.

"Fuck," I spit out. My teeth bite softly into her neck and I grunt.

My climax hits me and I moan loudly in her ear.

"Fuck. Fuck. Fuck."

My cock pulses multiple times. I groan and pump my hips through each one because I've lost all power over my traitorous dick.

The warm liquid spills over my cock, coating the inside of my underwear and I've completely drenched myself.

I just fucking prematurely ejaculated. In. My. Pants.

I stay completely still and I know Mimi knows. Her body is completely frozen and she's still holding her breath.

"Oh my God," I can't help but mutter. "Shit."

I am never going to live this down. Everything is moving a million miles an hour in my head. I'm ashamed I couldn't control myself in front of Mimi, and even more embarrassed this happened in front of everyone. The moment I step back and they see the tent in my pants and the overly saturated wet spot on the front, I'll be the laughing stock of the entire camp for the next two weeks.

My eyes slowly side-eye to her as I lift my head just enough to inspect the shock on her face. Although she looks surprised, there's only a smirk to her lips and a playfulness in her eyes.

Everyone else probably doesn't know what just happened, but I do and Mimi sure the hell does. But the moment I step away, everyone will figure it out. Not only did I come in my pants, but I didn't get her off, either.

I need to get the fuck out of here.

I glance around, trying not to make my movements too sudden, as I attempt to find an escape route.

Suddenly, Mimi begins to buck her hips and groans loudly, surprising me and waking my unreliable, traitor dick back up. "Oh, God." She bucks her hips into my hand. "I'm coming," she gasps, followed by more moaning.

My mouth is slacked open as I come to the realization of what she is doing.

She lifts her head back up, a smirk on full display with lust in her eyes after putting on that Oscar worthy performance. She stands to her full height and I release my grip on her wrists pulling my other hand out of her pants.

Still in shock, I step back, but she grabs my shirt and pulls me into her, whispering in my ear.

"Mimi, two. Seamus, zero."

Oh, this brat.

She smiles, leans into me, giving me a quick kiss on the cheek as she buttons up her pants.

I watch her and she saunters back toward the cabin with everyone scattering out of the window with a few hollering and cheering like a bunch of idiots, and I'm beyond thankful for the humiliation she just saved me from.

12

SEAMUS

Present Day

These past few mornings I've been waking up with a renewed vigor on life. I succeeded last week in the goal of making my presence known and why, but still managed to play a little hard to get, knowing that will probably pique her interest. Keeping my distance this past week, although painfully difficult, is needed to maintain that enigma.

I sensed her attraction to me, just like it's undeniable to control mine when I'm around her. But seeing the way she looked at me, her eyes slightly softening behind the angry squint, as I walked over the front of her house was a silent acceptance of my presence here.

Sure, she might be pissed I moved in next door, and she might be upset at how things ended between us—which we clearly have two different viewpoints on—but her body can't help but react to mine. I could feel how much she wanted me that night.

I should have leaned in, kissed her, and made her remember how good we were, but I wouldn't have been able to stop once I started. Plus, the patience I've learned over the course of my life is my signature trait, and I want her to give in to me first.

Can't say she isn't testing me, though. I would have assumed she would have been knocking on my door by now.

But fuck, she's as stubborn—or driven—as I am.

Walking upstairs with my coffee in hand, I head straight over to the window that overlooks the backyard.

At first, taking a moment to enjoy the view was just something I did out of habit. Something I've always done in any home I've lived in.

After spending years in barracks or living in tents in the most undesirable locations, I appreciate when I have a view through a window. Regardless of what that view is.

Seattle isn't known for sunny, blue skies and great weather. In fact, it's pretty fucking drab. The sky's the most depressing shade of gray, sprinkled with clouds that rival the same color palette. And although the downtown skyline is pretty spectacular, you can only see the buildings on a clear day, which is few and far between.

However, the view from this window?

Priceless.

Worth every overpriced penny I paid for the off market offer I made for this house.

Why? Because a certain goddess who brings her own sunshine into every living, breathing moment, practices yoga in her backyard wearing nothing but a sports bra and lace underwear.

Every. Fucking. Morning.

Sometimes it's ten minutes. Sometimes it's an hour. I suppose it's based on how much time she has.

Do I watch her the entire time?

No, of course not.

Not the entire time.

I mean, I do have to blink.

Regardless of how long her practice is, my jerk off session mirrors hers.

Every morning I watch with appreciation. The way the lace disappears between her ass cheeks. How her breasts push together in certain poses. The way her chest rises and falls with each breath. Observing her strong arms hold her body up in these gorgeous displays of balance and strength.

What starts as a mesmerizing display of physical art turns into a desire I can't control. I grip my hard cock, stroking it from the base to the tip, rounding my hand over the sensitive tip. And, as usual, she gets me there way too fast.

As unpredictable as her schedule is, it doesn't matter if she spends ten minutes stretching or an hour. The moment I can sense that her session is over, I allow for the full pleasure to consume me and take myself over the edge.

There are passing moments when I realize how ridiculous my behavior is.

But like I said, passing moments.

The only time she saw me was the first morning when I was unaware of her daily morning backyard ritual. I've since remained out of sight to avoid any awkwardness, plus I'm not insane. I know my behavior is embarrassingly unacceptable.

I simply justify it by the pure fact that I recognize it.

She's changed her angle today. Her back is facing me, which is excruciating because every time she does that down dog pose, her round, apple-shaped ass pushes back into the air. The pose shows off her muscular legs, smooth skin, and gives me a preview of what she would look like bent over in front of me.

She's petite, so she doesn't have long, lanky legs or a prolonged torso.

Her curvy body is strong and fibrous in all the best places. I could watch her bend and move all day long.

Kneeling on the mat, the muscles in her back contract and she circles her arms over her head. The heels of her feet press into her ass as she leans forward in a grateful bow, giving me a teaser of the lace that disappears between her gorgeous cheeks.

She always ends her practice that way, bowing with her hands at her heart.

So I stroke myself faster, envisioning her on her knees looking up at me, mouth wide open begging for my cock. The thought sends me spiraling.

"Goddammit, Mimi," I grit out.

Fireworks explode behind my eyes, and I let out a groan of pleasure as white ropes of cum paint my abs and spill over my cock.

Jesus, every time is better than the last.

Her shoulders lift and her chest rises in a hefty breath before peeking down at her watch. Then scurries, gathering the items next to her mat as she rushes inside the house.

She is obviously in a hurry. But I've noticed that about her.

If she isn't rushing or running late…well, come to think of it, I don't know if there is a time I have seen her at any other pace.

It drives me crazy to watch from afar, because nothing in my world operates that way. I know exactly where I'm going and what I'm doing at all times—and I always have ample time to do whatever it is that I need to do.

I am as predictable as the Seattle weather.

She, on the other hand, is like betting on dachshund racing.

In any other person, I would immediately cut them off and not give any shits about it.

With her, I find it…endearing.

God, help me.

She is going to drive me to drink, and I don't even drink.

Not only do I hate the loss of control, but steering clear of anything my father loved has been my *how-to-make-it-through-life* guide. It's the only thing he ever taught me. Inadvertently, of course, because that man didn't actually try to teach me anything good.

Using a rag to clean myself up, I wash my hands before grabbing my mug and heading downstairs.

Finishing my coffee, I rinse the cup out in the sink and place it in the dishwasher.

I'm already partially dressed, wearing only jeans—which I inspect to make sure I didn't make a mess on myself and, thankfully, I'm good.

I walk into my room and click on the iron. It quickly heats up and I press the button to release a spritz of water and steam as I run the base over the shirt on the ironing board.

I hate wrinkles.

Not only is it ingrained in me—fifty pushups for every one wrinkle—but it looks like shit.

Grabbing the shirt, I shake out the stiffness and throw it over my head, then finish getting dressed.

I peek out the window and I'm surprised to see Mimi walking out of her house not wearing her normal yoga outfit. She still has on leggings, but it's dressed up with an oversized top that hugs her waist and flows over her upper body. She paired with the deep navy leggings and black leg warmers that wrap around her bottom half. They start at her knee and trail all the way down, hugging the back of the heels she is wearing.

She's not teaching in that, so where the hell is she going?

I'm suddenly irritated that I have my meeting with Ember at Afterburn today. I should consider canceling, but I know I can't.

The moment I found out Mimi lived here, I offered myself up for Ember's permanent security team for her large events, and she immediately took me up on it.

We have an event this weekend that we need to plan for. My team is meeting me there to go over the logistics and prepare for anything different based on the theme of what she has planned.

Dammit.

You can't follow her around everywhere she goes, I tell

myself, but I would rather punch myself in the face than listen to that guy.

Step away from the window, Seamus.

I do it reluctantly.

I'll see her later. I know I will, but my obsession is verging on dangerous, and I hate that she hasn't given in to her curiosity and made her way over to me yet.

She's more stubborn than I thought.

After I get back home, I'll conjure up some way for her to *have* to come and see me.

AN HOUR LATER, I'm parking my truck in the same spot I always park in, on the side of the building of Afterburn. The vast difference between the club at night and the club during the day is quite literally, night and day.

Seeing it now, virtually empty and desolate, is a complete one-eighty from the nighttime chaos of the reporters and the members who are practically begging to get in on a nightly basis. The protestors still show up on event nights, which is why Ember has my secondary security team for those, as well as the weekends, too.

Rounding the corner to the front entrance, I slow my steps as I inspect the white Mini Cooper that's parked near the front.

There are a lot of white Mini Coopers, I remind myself as I continue to walk.

But as I get closer to it, I peek through the windshield and my legs stall. Yoga mats are rolled up haphazardly in the back, a sweater thrown over the top of them, a couple bottles of water are resting in the center console, and other random crap spread across the front seat.

I snap my head in the direction of the building, then back at the disaster of a car.

What the hell is she doing here?

Unable to stop myself, I stalk to the front entrance, pulling the heavy doors open with ease. Walking through them and around the front lobby desk with purpose in my step.

The waterfall isn't on like it normally is, so the quietness of the vast space is deafening, which is a dramatic change from the customary nighttime ritual. It's open and so empty you could hear a pin drop.

I make my way to the bar, passing it as I head to the stage area. I hear voices echoing through the hallway of the staircase that leads to the second floor.

Stopping, I crane my head back in that direction and the sight shocks the hell out of me.

Ember is hugging a clipboard against her chest, smiling from ear to ear and talking to Mimi.

My Mimi.

She's awfully comfortable, like they've known each other their whole lives. But, I know that can't be the case considering Ember is from Missouri and has lived in Seattle for less than a year.

I don't realize how long I'm frozen—and staring—until Ember looks my way. She calls out my name excitedly, waving her hand, gesturing for me to come over.

My eyes bounce between the two of them as I head in their direction.

I know my face is unreadable, other than the chronically pissed off look that I always have. Mimi's face matches mine, even though she fakes a smile as I step up to their circle.

"Seamus, you're early…well, I mean I guess you're always early." Naturally, my eyes snap over at Mimi with a snarky raised brow, because she's never early, and I feel like I should win points for that.

Instead of saying anything, I huff out a grunt. I have no

words. I had no idea she would be here, and I hate fucking surprises.

"Naomi, this is Seamus. He is in charge of my security team. He's grumpy," Ember says fluidly, like it's part of my name.

My neck swivels in her direction and I pin her with a grumpy look to match her ridiculous introduction.

"Oh, don't I know it." Mimi giggles at Ember, then says, "Hi, Seamus."

Goddammit. I hate how my name on her lips affects me. It's like an instant shot of adrenaline straight to my dick.

I turn to look at Mimi again.

It's like I'm watching a tennis match, as my neck pivots between the two of them, as I'm trying to break down this scene and decipher what the hell is going on.

I would ask, but less is always more. Most people give you all the information you need without even having to ask.

"Do you guys know each other?" Ember's brow furrows as she looks between us, but my gaze is still focused solely on Mimi's gorgeous face.

Her pouty lips are a glossy pink tint, and she's wearing minimal makeup, showing off her naturally gorgeous features.

The normal blanket of dark, luscious hair is pulled up in a messy bun with wispy strands framing her high cheekbones.

"Yeah, we do, actually." Mimi cocks her head to the side with a slight raise to her eyebrows. If her facial expression were words, they would say something like, *test me asshole.*

Since I'm not interested in that, I remain quiet. I'd like to see what she is going to say, so I pin her with a reflection of her own expression.

What is she going to say?

He's my neighbor. *Fine.*

We met as kids at camp. *Okay.*

My first love. *I fucking hope so.*

So, I raise my eyebrows back at her with a smirk, testing her back.

"He takes my yoga class every morning." She looks at me deadpan.

My face drops.

That… I was not fucking expecting.

Her gorgeous, smug smile is on full display, and only I can read the hidden smirk behind it.

"Seamus, you do yoga?" Ember's exaggerated tone is as accusatory and shocked as they come.

What? Because I'm a large, muscular guy with military experience and no facial expressions, I can't enjoy yoga? I would ask her why the judgment, but I don't feel like getting into that now.

Crossing my arms over my chest, I attempt to calculate my response. I know there is only one way to go here.

Keeping my eyes locked on Mimi's, I finally reply.

"Favorite part of my day."

"Well, aren't you full of surprises?" Ember replies, then asks, "Not that I need confirmation, because I can tell she's fabulous and I'm already going to bring her on, but how are her classes?"

"Amazing," my reply is instant. "I experience the ultimate release during her practice." Her eyes are unable to hold mine as she looks away. Her cheeks flush and she bites the corner of her lip, and it takes all my willpower not to yank her into one of these private rooms immediately.

Wait a minute.

I cross a look over to Ember. "What do you mean, *bring her on*?"

Ember's smile is a mile wide.

"Naomi is going to teach specialty yoga classes and tantric massage here," she says excitedly.

I glance back at Naomi, whose smile mirrors Ember's.

My first reaction is to be irritated by this. Her being here in my space, co-mingling with people in my circle, when all I want to do is keep her to myself. But in reality, this is good.

"What type of *specialty* classes?" I ask.

"We haven't fine-tuned the schedule yet, but I'm thinking she'll teach once a week and we can see how it goes from there. No other studio offers Nagna yoga, so we'll start with a co-ed class, maybe couples only, then see if we need to expand depending on everyone's comfort level," Ember replies, talking to Mimi the entire time, like they are still negotiating what her schedule will look like.

"Nagna yoga?" My brows furrow at the name.

Not that I know any kind of yoga classes, but this one sounds especially weird.

"Naked," Ember replies, "naked yoga."

My neck snaps over to Mimi. "And what do you wear?"

"Nothing," she replies, her voice soft and seductive.

I clench my fists as I suck in an annoyed breath.

"Don't worry, Seamus, you can have any of your guys monitor during that time. It'll be couples only to start, and we won't be planning any playtime after. So no need to have too much security staffed during that time," Ember assures me, like that's the reason I'm annoyed.

Over my dead body I'd schedule anyone else on my team for that class.

"I'm always here for any special events Afterburn has, including these moving forward," I reply with a clenched jaw.

"Okaaayy…" Ember elongates the last bit as her eyebrows hit her hairline. She glances back at Mimi. "As you can tell, we have very passionate people who care about everyone's safety and comfort here."

"For the comfort level of the students, I would prefer that security not be present in the room during class," Mimi adds.

I open my mouth to vehemently object, but Ember replies

first. "I completely agree. We will work out the logistics on that later." Ember makes a note on her clipboard.

"Great," Mimi replies with a smile, then pins another look at me while I bury my eyes into her.

My eyes drop to her neck, and I stare at the diamond shaped beauty mark that rests right at the base of her collarbone. Recalling how many times I would inspect that part of her with my lips. Kissing her neck was one of my favorite things to do, because I would be able to touch her soft skin, taking in the scent that is so distinctly Mimi.

Back then she would easily open up for me. She would expose her neck so I could graze my lips over her skin. So many nights of just kissing and caressing, and that was all I needed. It wasn't about sex, at least not until that last night.

Bitterness sweeps through me. Not just at the memory of what happened after, but the fact that she's closing herself off from me now.

I may have gotten pulled out of camp early, but she's the one who disappeared.

So many years wasted, when I didn't know where she was or what happened to her. I'm determined to find out what the hell happened.

Mimi runs her palm over the base of her collarbone, interrupting my gaze and rampant thoughts. My eyes meet hers and those dark chocolate orbs are swimming with lust, mirroring my own. I know she's thinking about the same thing I am. The sexual tension is thick, and I want nothing more than to band my arm behind her waist, tug her into me, grab her face, and kiss her like my life fucking depends on it.

Ember looks over her clipboard as her eyes bounce between Mimi and I with furrowed brows. Even though I'm only seeing her through my peripheral, I don't miss the slight squint that tells me she's suspicious of us.

Ember's face suddenly softens into a look I've only seen when a certain someone is around.

Goddammit.

13

NAOMI

"Hudson." Ember's voice pulls me back into the moment.

Running into Seamus here was even better than I imagined. Even though his stoic face is mostly unreadable, I can tell I've hit a nerve. Or maybe it's the fact that the guy who helped him move in is walking up right behind him.

Seamus is clearly frustrated, which again is a shock considering reading him is like reading a brick wall. I'm trying to figure out if it's by my presence, the other guy, or if that's really just Seamus nowadays.

The Seamus I knew was not nearly as grumpy or obscure, and I find that raising my curiosity more than my own concern about him being here.

Since my date with Jeremy that night—when Seamus showed up again out of the blue and I found out he bought the house next door—I've had more than enough time to think. Plus, a couple of last minute sessions with my therapist has helped me see this as an opportunity to heal.

I didn't go through a decade of therapy, years of practicing spiritual discipline—both on and off my mat—to allow the pain and suffering of what happened to consume me.

95

And he didn't come back into my life by chance. I don't believe in that.

Somehow, we found each other again and he made a point to make his presence not only known, but a permanent fixture.

I wasn't done loving you yet, and I'm here to prove it.

Do I believe that? I'm not sure. I've had too many years of telling myself otherwise to accept it that easily, but after the last few days of pondering everything, I am willing to listen.

At least I'm going to try.

Ember, and the man who I can only assume is her husband, pull out of an embrace. Well, Ember does. Hudson has his arms wrapped around her, holding her body to his like he'll never have the chance to do it again.

Her face is flushed while she sneaks a glance in our direction. She looks shy and embarrassed, which is a far stretch from the woman that just interviewed me about her sex club while we talked about naked yoga and tantric massage.

She told me all about how Afterburn was birthed into reality. A small idea from the X-Connect website that led the CEO of Ford Enterprises assigning her the great task of making this club a reality.

Her ambition was easy to see, and she holds a passion that I could relate to the moment we met. Although she holds a high end corporate position at Ford Enterprises, and oversees more things than I can even imagine, she remains to be a huge part of the decision making processes and day-to-day workings of the club. And, she *loves* this club. You can tell by the way she speaks about it and how much she supports the exploration of all things in sexuality.

So, naturally, she loved the proposal I had about bringing yoga into the mix. We both love the sensuality of the human body and the openness of that display. This is just another way to bring that to the masses.

"Hudson, this is Naomi. Naomi, this is my husband, Hudson," Ember introduces us.

Hudson forces his gaze away from his wife and his mile-wide smile drops when he sees my face. His eyes bounce between Seamus and I while his faded smile fights to return.

If reading Seamus is like reading hieroglyphics, reading Hudson is like crayon on construction paper.

Hudson's suspicions are on full display, and he's more than holding back giving Seamus shit about it.

"Great to see you again," I reply with a smile.

"You too." You can hear the knowing smirk in his tone.

"Wait, you know each other, too?" Ember's tone is laced with confusion.

"I met Hudson the day Seamus moved in next door to me." I stare at Seamus, his face completely unamused, unlike mine.

"Wow. What a small world," Ember says with surprise. "I think you might already know everyone in my circle of friends."

"No, she does not." Another voice rings out from behind me. I turn to see a leaner, and slightly tanner, Clark Kent look alike wearing a suit and black rimmed glasses with pure perfection.

"Cruz, you're late," Ember sings songs playfully.

"Better to be late than arrive ugly." He fiddles with his glasses before he holds his hand out to me. "I'm Cruz."

"Naomi." I slide my hand into his with a giggle.

Hudson pats Seamus on the back in some internal bro-code. I can't tell if he's giving him shit or trying to console him silently. Either way, I'm completely amused and Seamus is obviously suffering from crowd anxiety.

"Just so we're clear. If you want anything related to baseball, Hudson is your guy. If you want someone to disappear without a trace, G.I. Joe here is your man." He points at Seamus and I don't miss the slight wince in his expression. It hits me that I've learned nothing about what Seamus has done since we saw each other last, and I hate that I know nothing about him. "And for anything else, I'm your guy. Jack of all trades, master of none, at your service." He finishes with a head bow.

"Great to know, I'll keep…all of that…" I glance between Hudson and Seamus, "in mind." I can't help but relax around this group. It's apparent they are close. Well Hudson, Ember, and Cruz are. Seamus is still as legible as a brown paper bag, but I'm finding my anger and bitterness of the past years begin to fade and warp into a curiosity of sorts.

"Em, our afternoon meeting moved up an hour, so I'll be joining you for lunch with Hudson—because I'm not functional when I'm hungry, and I need to eat," Cruz says factually.

"Oh, but I still have to give Naomi a tour and coordinate her schedule," Ember replies as she takes out her phone.

"I'll do it." Seamus' response is lightning speed.

The group falls silent and everyone looks at each other.

"Come on." Seamus doesn't give anyone else a chance to rebuttal as he steps outside our circle and holds his arm out toward the back of the club.

I pause, looking at the gap that Seamus has opened up, and then back at Ember. A part of me wants to continue to play hard to get, like I've been the last few days, but I'm tired of ignoring his presence and my curiosity is way too strong.

"Will that be okay, Naomi? I can call you later to work out the details of the schedule?" Ember asks, a bit unsure.

"Absolutely, it's no problem at all." I step over and give her a hug. It's inappropriate for an interview, but I'm a hugger and I'm over all the handshakes. "Great to meet you guys." I step back and wave to Hudson and Cruz as I walk past Seamus.

"I see you still can't resist me, Rambo," I say playfully, but loud enough for the group to hear. Because giving Seamus shit is going to be my new favorite hobby.

His gaze lasers through me as I walk by. Is he angry? Absolutely. But that desire that drives him is brighter than the lights in

Times Square, blaring through to every cell in my body. A shiver runs down my spine and goosebumps erupt all over my body.

A tiny part of me is worried I may be playing out of my league with him right now, because figuring him out won't be like it was when we were younger. If I've realized anything since the moment I saw him again, is that he's had more life experience in the last ten years than most people have in a lifetime. I can see that in his stoic expression, the apprehension of his demeanor, and the way he carries himself.

"Did you just call him *Rambo*? That's the most accurate thing I've ever heard in my life." Cruz has zero filter, while Ember and Hudson are speechless as I retreat. I smile over my shoulder and wave again, because I know his nickname is perfect, and I hope with everything I have they use it on him now, too.

I head toward the back of the club and arrive at the first glass window that overlooks one of the voyeur rooms. I remember this from my first time here, and I remember being completely mesmerized by the couple on the other side of it.

The room is now sparkling clean and empty, but a tingling sensation rolls over my body from the recollection of what I witnessed behind it.

Speaking of tingling, I don't need to look behind me to know that Seamus is right on my heels. It's the same feeling I've sensed since he has arrived back in my life, like he's unable to stay too far away.

My eyes catch his reflection in the expansive, sheen windows. For a brief moment, I see the shadow of the boy I knew years ago, and I can't help the small curve to my lips from forming as I recall how awkward he was. But even with those lean, lanky limbs and shaggy, out of control hair, there was something about him. A will, a drive, an undeniable pull.

It feels the same now.

I've come to the conclusion that Seamus is in security, being that he runs it here at Afterburn, but Cruz referred to him as a G.I. Joe, and I feel the need to dive into that.

"G.I. Joe, huh?" I insinuate the question, turning around to face him.

"Don't listen to Cruz."

"Is he right?"

"Not really."

"What does that mean?"

"That I'm not a G.I. Joe."

Well, yeah. I roll my eyes because he's not a green plastic stick figure or a boys' version of a Barbie doll. Although he would make a pretty hot military Ken doll.

I digress.

"Okay, but you were in the military?" I ask cautiously, because I know while some people are proud, others can be bitter.

He nods, but doesn't reply.

I cross my arms over my chest. "The Seamus I knew was an open book, we talked about everything." I pause, staring at him, waiting for him to say something more. "Work with me here."

I study the features of his strong jawline and high cheek-bones. The same lines I studied under the stars next to the lake as we discovered everything about each other. Our likes and dislikes, quirks and cues. I feel the depth behind his midnight eyes and wonder about the story behind his barely-there scar that runs over his eyebrow.

I revel in the fact that I never thought I'd get to see him again, yet here he is in front of me, wearing the last ten years of experience like an impenetrable mask. I can still see my Seamus behind the façade, and I want more. I want what we had back.

"You've gotta give me something," I practically beg.

He can't come flying back into my life, drop a bomb, tell me he *wasn't done loving me yet*, then remain a mute during conversation.

His jaw clenches as his head tilts up, looking at the ceiling. His Adam's apple bobs and I see the strong lines of his throat flex. How is it possible that even his neck muscles have muscles?

He returns his gaze, heated this time, desperate in a way I've never seen. And I can feel it to my bones.

The moment passes at a glacial pace. Time stills and it's just him and I and all the unknown thoughts between us.

Still, he remains quiet, and all I can hear is the whooshing of my own heartbeat in my ears.

Come on, say something.

I huff out a small breath.

I give up.

I shake my head and take a step forward to walk around him.

His arm shoots out, palming the wall behind me, preventing me from moving that way. I step in the other direction and his other arm does the same, trapping me in between his colossal frame and the glass window.

My gaze travels down his body and back up to the arms that are caging me in. His forearms are threaded with muscles, twitching as he presses harder into the glass behind me.

"Well, now that you've got me here, what are you going to do with me?" I say playfully, reminding him of how he's held me like this before.

"Don't tempt me, Mimi." His face leans in closer to mine. The scent of his aftershave wafts around me like a comfort blanket. It's rugged, and manly, and smells exactly like I imagined grown up Seamus would smell.

"Why not?" I'm feeling frisky.

"Because we have an audience." His lips graze my jawline as I look over his shoulder behind him. The distinct outline of three heads peer out from behind the corner. Cruz's glasses catch the light as he moves before he dips back behind the wall.

"So, you don't want them to see you come in your pants, either?" My smile is a mile wide at the playful jab.

He lifts his head back to look at me, pauses as he inspects me, then gives me a slow, sexy, incredibly dangerous smile.

Shit.

"Oh, you're gonna get it, sunshine."

He leans down, dipping his shoulder into the crease of my hips as he wraps his arm around the back of my leg. In a swift move, he lifts me up over his shoulder and half my body is hanging behind him.

"Seamus!" I scream. "I'm going to fall."

"No, you're not," he replies without a hitch in his breath, even though he's carrying an entire human.

"I'm too heavy."

"No. Nice try."

He walks past Ember, Hudson, and Cruz standing in the corner, and they are all beyond shocked with the view as we pass by. Me upside down, squealing as Seamus walks by like nothing is weird at all.

Cruz moves out of the corner, wide-eyed with his jaw to the floor. Even with his upside down form, I can still read his expression like the cover of a non-discreet romance novel.

"Like I said, play with fire and you're gonna get burned," Cruz says to Ember and Hudson after we pass, and I can't help but wonder if he's right.

14

NAOMI

I'm still kicking and screaming as I hang over his shoulder when he pushes the entrance doors open and exits out of Afterburn.

He doesn't stop, or appear to be struggling, as he carries me around like a zero gravity duffle bag. Making his way down the front steps, he turns toward the parking lot, then continues walking past my car.

"Where are we going?" I ask, louder than necessary.

No response.

"Are you going to say anything or just continue to establish your dominance by sheer force?"

No response, again. Instead, he slaps my ass.

I squeal moan, surprised at the slap, and I feel it in more places than just my ass.

"You really are a caveman, you know?" I smack his ass right back, being that I'm only inches from it.

I hear the click of a door handle, then my body's momentum changes and I fall back into a seat. His large truck is slightly lifted, so gravity doesn't change much when he places me down and moves my legs inside the truck.

"Wait, I drove here," I said, pointing at my car.

"I'll bring you back later." He shuts the car door and I watch him as he walks around the front of the truck. He side-eyes me as he passes by. His pupils are blown out—desperate with desire, but there's a playful threat behind them, and I can't help but want to challenge both.

He gets in the truck, starts it, then reverses out of the parking spot. As he pulls onto the freeway, I finally ask, "Okay, so where are we going?"

Shocking, no response.

Apparently, he only speaks if *he* deems it necessary. Great. I'm next door neighbors with a partial mute who watches me do yoga every morning. Oh, and apparently pleases himself while I do it.

My cheeks flush at the feeling of when he told me that. I knew he had been watching, but I had no idea *that* was going on. I find myself shifting in my seat at the vision.

"What are you thinking about?" I jump, because…well, he spoke.

"Nothing," I snip back quickly.

He glances down at my hips, then back up to my face. A slight smirk crosses his face.

Hiding my internal eye roll, I realize I need to maintain some power here.

The heat is on low, but it is still warm enough for me to take a layer or two off.

Leaning forward, I take off my jacket, folding it in my lap.

I skim over the outfit I chose to wear today; it's the least sexiest outfit to strip out of, ever.

Leggings, an oversized, baggy shirt that hangs over my shoulder, with leg warmers and heels.

Nothing about this outfit screams sex.

Oh, fuck it. I have a tank top on.

I strip off the oversized shirt, pulling it over my head and folding it on top of the jacket that still lays on my lap.

Seamus's eyes flicker my way for a split second before returning to the road.

Hm…Got his attention.

Without the extra layers, it's much colder and my thin bra does nothing for support or protection from puckering. Giving myself another once over as I shift in my seat, I can't help but notice my taut, erect nipples peeking through my top. I pull on the fabric, giving it a bit more friction and add to their pert demeanor.

I lift my chin and tilt slightly toward him. His eyes flicker to my face, down at my chest, then back to the road. His hand grips the steering wheel with white knuckle force as he blows out a steadying breath.

As he turns into the cul-de-sac that I know so well, he parks in my driveway and my face falls in confusion.

He gets out urgently, slamming the door behind him, and I can barely turn to follow his movements when my door flies open and he grabs me the same exact caveman way he did at the club.

He takes the clothes I held in my lap, then I yelp as he flips me over his shoulder again.

"Seamus, what are you doing?" He stops, glances around again, then heads to the side yard gate between our houses. He kicks it open, breaking the clasp.

"You savage animal! You didn't have to break it, you could have just flipped the latch."

"I'll fix it."

So, not only does he act like a caveman, he sounds like one, too.

Walking through the side yard, he turns into the open back-yard and passes by my yoga mat that's still laid out on the patio. I was in a rush this morning and left it out. My sweater and jogger pants are draped over the patio furniture, and I blush again with both arousal and a little embarrassment that he's had his vantage point on my life that I don't typically share with anyone.

He tosses my jacket and shirt that haphazardly lands on top of the left over clothes already there, as one tumbles over itself onto the ground.

I feel myself falling back again as he leans down and places my feet on the ground. Before I can turn around, he presses his body against mine, caging me in between his extended arms, and I'm backed up against the oak tree in my own yard.

Memories flash behind my eyelids of a younger Seamus, standing like a fortress in front of me, attempting to shelter me from the watching eyes of campers.

He stood so strong and so proud until I begged him to touch me, and then he completely fell apart.

I want that Seamus.

"Why did you bring me here?" I tilt up my chin in a bit of defiance.

"I owe you an orgasm."

My eyes widen at his response. "Here?"

"The girl I knew was always up for a challenge."

Oh, he is baiting me right now.

"If it turns out anything like the first time, it won't really be a challenge," I bait him right back with a smile.

That slow, sexy smile returns, like what I said was the equivalent to shaking a red flag in front of a bull.

He leans into me, completely engulfing his body over mine. The tip of his nose trails over my jawline and down my neck. His breath is hot against my skin, and even though he's hardly touching me, I feel him everywhere.

"Can I touch you?" he whispers over the shell of my ear.

Apparently, I'm up for no challenge and he's already won since, I nod without a second thought.

"And…Is *this* okay?" His fingertip moves up my arm, around my collarbone, and trails down the peak of my breast with a barely there graze over my pebbled nipple.

"Yes," I breathe out.

"Can I kiss you here?" His lips explore my skin again, this time planting kisses along my collarbone.

I nod again, tilting my head back, exposing more of my body to him.

His fingers tuck into the strap of my tank top, pulling it down, exposing my nipple to the frigid air, making it harden even more.

"And what about here?" Leaning down further, he wraps his lips around the peak, pulling my nipple into the warmth of his mouth.

"Oh, God. Yes." Jesus, I'm already a puddle.

I can hear his smile in the moan he releases. It infuriates me, but not enough to make him stop.

My hand reaches around the back of his head, and I grip his hair between my fingertips, holding him in place as his tongue circles around my nipple. His hand trails up my other arm until he finds the strap and pulls it down, exposing me fully.

He moves freely between both nipples, giving them shared attention. Goosebumps break out all over my body when he leaves one for the other as the crisp air coats the sensitive tips, giving me a secondary sensation my body is completely unsure of.

I moan, tossing my head back and close my eyes as he teases me, and I realize he's completely undone in a matter of a minute.

Bracing myself, I hold one hand against his arm while the other has a white knuckle grip on his hair. The bumpy tree bark scrapes my skin as my body presses into it, but nothing can overpower the feeling of his mouth on my body. His tongue feels like magic against my skin and his hands hold me like I'm his sole source of air.

It's been so long since I've felt a connection, something deeper than just the physical sensation. It's like he knows exactly what I need and he's spent a lifetime studying for it.

Every touch is sensual.

Every kiss is personal.

Every look is pleasurable agony.

I squeeze my eyes closed, attempting to hide the emotions that rip through my body. His passion, his desire, the desperate need is adding to my sensual state and I question my emotional wellbeing.

Changing pace, he grabs my wrists, yanking them over my head, and presses me hard against the tree.

My breath hitches as my eyes snap open, and I panic. My body bucks in dispute, as I look up at his hands holding me in place. My chest heaves as my breath quickens, and I'm unable to hide my fear.

He squints as he appraises my expression, looking up at where his hands are covering mine then back down at my face. He lets go immediately, taking a step back, tilting his head, giving me a look of uncertainty and confusion.

He goes to take another step back, but I reach out and grab his hand, placing them on my hips.

I'm not scared of him. I don't want him to stop. In fact, I want him more than I can admit. But he can't do *that*, not here. I don't know how to tell him or if I ever want to, so before he can ask I pull him in flush against my body.

"What was that, Mimi?" he asks anyway.

"Touch me," I say, ignoring him.

His questioning eyes inspect me with concern.

"Please," I beg, pulling him closer. "It's been a really long time for me," I embarrassingly confess.

He growls and leans back into me.

I tuck my hands underneath his shirt and run my hands over his body. I can feel the hard ridges of his muscular torso and I lose count of how many abdominal muscles my fingers roam over.

I push my hips into his, feeling the length of his hard erection behind his jeans.

Sucking in a breath between clenched teeth, his hips roll into mine, and I can't help but moan at the sensation, at the idea that he's losing a bit of that control he holds onto so tight.

Releasing my hip, his hand stretches the waistband of my leggings as he reaches inside. The pads of his fingers swipe through my wet slit and he groans in approval.

A whimper escapes me in response as his finger finds my clit, and he rubs circles around the tip.

My body grinds against his, asking for more—needing more. It's been so long, too long.

"Do you have any idea what you do to me, Mimi?" His lips graze my ear.

"Parading your body out here every morning, fighting with myself to stop watching you. Begging myself to step away from that goddamn window." He nips at the lobe.

"And every morning, I lose all the willpower I spent my life building, because you strip it away like it was nothing. Like I didn't spend years practicing, giving up everything, sacrificing everything. Yet somehow, one look from you and it's ripped to fucking shreds."

"Oh God," I whimper as my body begins to tremble.

For someone who has barely said a full sentence since he came back into my life, that was *saying* something. I never really figured out what my love language is, but based on what he said and how I'm feeling, maybe it's words of affirmation.

"I'm so close," I confess as my hands grip tightly against his body. I bite my bottom lip, attempting to smother any confessions.

"That's my good girl. Fall apart for me like I do for you."

Yup, I'm officially a words of affirmation girl, because I erupt instantly.

I toss my head against the tree and I gasp through explosive orgasm. I feel myself practically trying to climb away from him as his fingers continue to wring it out of me. I'm desperate for him to stop, but somehow still begging for more.

A minute goes by, an hour, God who knows how long before my breath finally evens out. His forehead is leaning against mine as he pulls the straps of my top back over my shoulders, it covers my chest, but my shoulders and arms are cold to touch and covered in goosebumps.

He kisses my temple before stepping away, and I instantly feel the emptiness. The cold air wraps around my body and my eyes shoot open to see him walking away toward the side yard entrance. That same sensation I felt that night overwhelms me. Seeing his back as he walked away, feeling on top of the world just to never see him again. And never realizing it was the last time I was ever going to see him.

Pain bites my back as I fall to the ground, the husk of the tree scraping my skin as it trails over the bark. My head falls into my palms, ashamed of myself, disappointed that I repeated this again. Then a strange sensation of fear blankets me as the memories after flood in.

I lift my head and look around. My head turns frantically to the left and right, behind me, and I can't help but look around.

I'm in my backyard. I'm in my backyard.

I coax myself, wrapping my arms around my bent knees and rocking into myself.

It's okay. No one is here.

"Mimi?" Seamus' voice rips me from my thoughts as my head snaps in the direction of my name. My old name. His tone is laced with so much worry and concern.

Seamus stands a couple feet away, frozen, with my shirt in one hand and jacket in the other.

He wasn't leaving, he was grabbing my clothes.

"What's going on?" he asks.

His questioning look gives his concern away as I attempt to gather myself.

"That's not my name. I haven't gone by that name in years." I stand up, running my hands down the front of my body before wrapping my arms over each other, contradicting my lifted chin in a fake confidence.

"That's not what's bothering you," he deadpans. As if he knows, because he does. I swear he's a goddamn mind reader or something. That's what he must have spent the last ten years doing.

"I have to get ready. I have a class." Without meeting his gaze, I step forward grabbing both items of clothing from his hands, then sidestep to move around him. He catches my arms softly with his hand and dips his head in front of mine, searching for my eyes.

I look in the other direction, avoiding him.

"Mimi…"

My neck whiplashes back in his direction. "I'm not Mimi anymore," I spit out as he releases my arm.

He flinches at my tone, but steps back, allowing me space to move around him. "Okay, sunshine. You win."

I pass by him and walk into my house through the sliding door, leaving him in my backyard.

I wish I could call that a win.

15

SEAMUS

I walk toward my house, my mind reeling from what just happened. I'm still high on the feeling of touching her, feeling her against my body for the first time in a decade, wrapping my lips around her perfect, pink nipples while drowning in the sensation of how she makes me feel.

I can still smell her on me, which does nothing for my pissed off, rock hard erection that doesn't want to relax nor accept that it's not getting a release right now.

Because as I recall the look on her face when I pinned her against the tree—the sheer panic stricken response she had—I've lost all desire for anything more than to figure out what the hell is going on. Especially after seeing her response to the aftermath of her orgasm when all I did was walk away for a high-speed second to grab her clothes.

And she must be absolutely crazy if she thinks I'm not going to call her Mimi. I have no idea why she all of a sudden doesn't want to be called by the name I've always called her. Other people can call her Naomi, but she's my Mimi, and I won't call her anything different.

I don't understand what the hell is going on with her and why she completely fell apart after. None of it makes any fucking sense.

Walking through my front door, I pull out my phone.

Seamus: I need a security clearance background check. Full details.

Rocco: On who?

Seamus: Naomi Masumi.

Rocco: The yoga instructor that you had me look into a few months ago?

Rocco: Is she gonna be teaching yoga to the president?

Seamus: Roc...

Rocco: What do you want to know?

Seamus: Everything.

16

SEAMUS

17 years old

"*Lineup in alphabetical order by your first name. It's been a week, so by now you should know everyone's names, but if you don't, ask and introduce yourself, then get into line,*" *the camp leader announces to all of us as we stop in the middle of a wooded area surrounded by trees.*

"*Are we in kindergarten?*" *Wes spits out as he walks to the back of the line.*

"*You're just pissed because you're always at the back end,*" *Nathan yells, with a chuckle at his immature joke, as he takes his place in line right next to Mimi.*

He bumps her shoulder playfully, then leans in closer to talk to her.

There are only a few people between us, but it's enough that I can't hear what he is saying. My jaw tightens as I watch him talk to her, all smiles with his cocky personality taking full flight. She seems interested, but I find that Mimi always makes everyone feel good by listening, engaging with them, and making them feel like the only person in the room.

I know because it's how she's made me feel since the moment I got here.

I have to admit it's been nice, not having to worry about my dad or what's going on at home. I worry about my mom, but I always worry about her. I'm trying to do exactly what she wants me to do and just have fun.

I've befriended my cabin mates, and we've been staying up after lights out just shooting the shit about almost anything, playing cards. And it's actually been...nice.

Our group leader rallies in front of us, whistling to get our attention. "Alright, everyone, starting with Wes at the rear," Nathan chokes out a laugh, "break out in groups of four. You three," he points to me, Shane, and Toby, "follow Wes to obstacle number one."

We head that direction, stopping at the wooden sign staked into the ground with the words OB-1.

Appraising the area around us, it's expansive, wide open, and lined with trees and huge rope displays. Between the trees are ropes criss-crossing over each other, secured in different places between them that completely surround us. Some have ladder style ropes, others are just one lone rope with vertical hanging ones that look like you can use as a grip.

I've never seen anything like this, and it's clear that the guys haven't, either.

"This is like American Ninja Warrior *but for lumberjacks, man," Wes says. "This wasn't here last year."*

Mimi's angelic voice rips my gaze away from the rope course as I look over my shoulder and see her group walking by.

She glances in my direction, her eyes meeting mine almost instantly, and she gives me that gorgeous smile of hers. It sets my fucking soul on fire that she went out of her way to look for me and I can't help but smile back.

"Group three to obstacle course three, baby. Let's go!" Nathan yells out to...well anyone that was listening, which really

wasn't anyone. He skips up behind Mimi and wraps his arm around her shoulder, pulling her into his side. Our eyes break apart as she turns to push him away.

I seriously hate that guy.

Everyone in my group goes through the rope course. We help each other as we talk through the balancing, foot placement and grips, trying to refrain from falling through the more difficult parts of the obstacle course. Wes is actually helpful and we're all getting along shockingly well.

I glance over to the other rope courses, craning my neck as my eyes bounce around trying to find her.

"She likes you, you know." Giving myself whiplash, I turn to look over at Shane who's staring up at Wes and he takes slow, calculated steps over the rope course's final leg.

"Who?" I ask, attempting to be coy.

Looking over at me, he huffs out a laugh, shaking his head.

"Just don't be an idiot. She's a good person with a good heart."

"Are you guys good friends?" I ask, since he's just cutting through the bullshit.

"Yeah, just friends, though. She's been there for me through a lot. We talk throughout the school year and always see each other here."

"Have you guys ever been anything more than friends?" I hate how ridiculous and jealous I sound.

He looks over at me, eyeing me for a moment, and it looks like he's sizing me up.

"Nah, man. She's uhh...not my type." His lips thin out as he presses them together. His eyebrows raise in a knowing look and...ah. I get it.

That explains a lot about that first night at camp, with Wes during spin the bottle. His comfort level. How he handled everything.

My eyes bounce between him and Wes, his eyes never leave him. Hm. Interesting.

"Well, that's probably the only reason why someone wouldn't be into her, I suppose."

"Isn't that the truth." He laughs, pausing for a brief moment. "That's not really public info, though, like I don't talk about it. So if you don't mind…"

He doesn't finish before I place my hand on his shoulder. "I get it." I use my other hand to imitate a zipper crossing over my lips.

He returns a tight lipped smile before returning his gaze back to Wes.

"Alright campers. Switch!" our camp leader yells out.

And, we're on to the next course.

AFTER A LONG ASS day moving through the obstacle courses, we start our trek back to the cabins. I'm fairly athletic, in decent shape, but this kicked my ass. Even with the lethargic feeling that weighs over me, I keep stealing glances at Mimi who's walking directly ahead of me, near the back of the group.

Her ponytail bounces with each step, and even though we just spent a majority of the day in the blazing heat running obstacles, she still has that addictive, radiant energy.

I glance ahead to the front of the group. Everyone is either focused ahead, ready to get to their cabins, or they're looking down, just zombie walking with the group.

There's a small path ahead that veers off behind a row of high bushes and even taller trees.

Fuck it.

Right as we come up at the hidden dirt crossroad, I gently wrap my fingers around her elbow and pull her into the small path hidden behind the shrubbery.

"What are you doing?" she whispers as she ducks, but then peers over the top of one of the bushes.

"Meet me tonight. After lights out." I have no idea where that came from or why I said it. I just want to spend more time with her.

"What? We can't." She peeks again, watching the group as they move further away.

"Meet me by the lake. Tonight." I plead with both my eyes and my tone.

She bites her lip as her eyes skim over my face, and a small lopsided smile appears. "I'll try."

"Yeah?" I reply with more excitement than I should.

"I said I'll try," she presses her palm to my chest as she replies playfully. My hand folds over the top of hers, keeping her in place as my eyes roam over the face I've been obsessing over since I first laid eyes on it.

I wrap my fingers around the back of her neck and pull her face close to mine. Our lips create a channel between our bodies, as the mountain air moves between us both. I look into her gorgeous, chocolate eyes and back down at her lips, pausing to breathe her in. No one has ever made me feel like she does. Feral, desperate, so goddamn needy.

I press my lips to hers and she purses hers against mine. It's awkward for a moment until we both part our lips and our tongues collide in perfect rhythm. My heart is pounding out of my chest and I feel the thumping all the way to my bones.

I've kissed a few girls, but nothing has ever felt like this.

"Wow," she whispers as we pull apart. My eyes are still closed, living the dream that is all Mimi.

"Mimi?" a voice calls out, ripping us out of the moment.

Shane steps into our line of sight and peers down the pathway we are hidden behind.

His eyebrows hit his hairline when he sees us together before his head snaps back to check if anyone else is near.

"Come on," he waves, "they're counting heads."

Our legs shuffle to keep up as we duck through and catch up to everyone just in time.

"Go clean up. Dinner's in thirty, then we'll have a little time before lights out." The camp leader finishes, then everyone goes different directions as Shane gives us the stank eye with a smile.

I turn to Mimi.

"Meet me by the lake. Tonight." I step backwards as I remind her.

"That's a bad idea," she whisper-yells back.

"Are you backing out of a challenge?" I hold my fist in my palm, challenging her to rock, paper, scissors.

She immediately matches and we battle.

My scissors cut her paper.

The glare she pins on me could rival Hades.

I can't help but smile.

"An hour after lights out. By the lake." I turn and head the other direction, not giving her a chance to respond.

17

NAOMI

Present Day

"And how does that make you feel?" Penny asks before she takes a bite of her blueberry pancakes.

"You're therapizing me," I reply with a half-smile, because Penny just can't help herself sometimes. I've shared with her a few details about Seamus moving in next door, and she continues to pick at questions and make comments. I know she's worried, but it's exhausting.

"Oh sorry, girl. Occupational habit. I'll stop." She holds her hands up in surrender.

Penny is a brilliant family therapist and my best friend. She was one of the first people I met after I moved to Seattle. I spent the majority of my senior year at home, finishing my high school diploma and getting home schooled by my mother, then went to community college as a default because I had no idea what I wanted to do.

I took a few courses including a sociology course, where Penny and I met and bonded pretty much immediately.

It didn't take long for me to realize that I had no idea what wanted to do with my life. But, it didn't involve me sitting in a classroom getting a degree for something I knew I truly didn't want, nor would be useful in the future.

So, I dropped my classes and started my CYT training to be a yoga instructor. Starting with a two hundred hour certification course, then a year later completing the five hundred hour course. Being on my mat, teaching, guiding and sharing that love with people was exactly where I wanted to be.

"Speaking of, what *did* Sabrina say?" she asks.

"Nothing," I reply, looking up to see Penny's brows furrowed together in confusion.

"I didn't tell her. I mean…I haven't told her yet." My tone drips with guilt because I know my *actual* therapist is the first person I should be telling these things to. "I'll tell her, I just haven't had a scheduled session since I realized it was Seamus that moved in next door."

Penny's lips roll over each other before she looks around the restaurant, attempting to smother what she really wants to say. I look around awkwardly, following her lead.

This is our favorite place to eat. She loves their pancakes, and I love the egg white omelets and their never-fail, perfectly cooked hash browns.

The carafe of the seasonal fruit flavored mimosas are a pretty decent selling point, too.

"I don't want to be the one to point out the elephant in the room, but you have to be careful here, Naomi. A man from a very distressing part of your past moves in next door, and he's determined to *love you*." She air quotes with her fingers. "If that past didn't have so much underlying trauma, it would be romantic, but you do see how this is actually very problematic, right?"

"I know." I nod in agreement. It's all I can muster to say, because I know she's right, but she's mentioned it a few times and I'm emotionally drained by all of it.

I need her to be my friend, not a therapist.

I'm thankful I didn't share all the details with her, like him watching me through his second story window and the caveman stunt he pulled at Afterburn.

That was a few days ago, and I've been a professional dodge-ball player since, avoiding my backyard and rushing in and out of my house when I leave or come home.

I completely shut down after my—I don't know what to even call it, emotional breakdown? Of course, it was post that mind blowing orgasm, so I'd like to blame my unpredictable hormones and overly stimulated endorphins.

Oh, and the fact that another man hasn't made me come, since—well him—ten years ago.

My trust issues with men run so far deep I've never been able to open myself up sexually or otherwise. I've only been able to please my partners by giving hand jobs or oral sex, but the moment they attempt to touch me, I completely shut down.

I've always played it off that I like to be in control, telling them I like giving pleasure instead of receiving it. At first, most of the men were fine with that, thinking I was just some lighter version of a dominatrix.

Ironically, that couldn't be further from the truth. I want to be able to give in, give up control and I want to fully trust someone with my body. I've fantasized about being tied up and blind-folded, allowing a man to take control of me, giving me the most erotic pleasure.

Yet, I can barely stand when a man touches me in real life.

I've tried with other men, but panic, almost immediately with the slightest touch. The guys would get immediately frustrated, and then I'd spend weeks blanketing myself in shame.

Because someone like me shouldn't crave that kind of sex.

Penny knows about my history with men, which is why I'm opting to leave out the tree incident that happened in my back-yard. She'll Sigmund Freud that half to death.

I'm not even a therapist and *I'm* overanalyzing the fact that

Seamus has been the only man to successfully get me there, yet he was the originator of a large part of my trust issues.

"Penny for your thoughts?" Penny asks, with a dorky giggle.

I smile and change the subject.

"I have my first tantric massage class at Afterburn this weekend," I say instead as I take a bite of my veggie omelet, ignoring the big fat elephant.

"Ooh, it's all confirmed?" she asks with that buoyant tone I usually hear from her.

"Yeah." I nod, swallowing my food. "The first class is couples only, and we've already had so many signups that Ember had to move the class from one of the rooms to the open space stage area." My smile is a mile wide as I tell Penny.

"That's super exciting," she says with little excitement. "Will Seamus be there during that class?"

I drop my fork.

"I've got it handled, Penny." My exhausted tone radiates annoyance.

"I'm just worried. It's natural," she replies.

"I know, but stop, please. Just…be my friend right now."

"Okay," she relents as she reaches out, placing her hand over my forearm. "Just promise you'll talk to me if you need to, or if there is something more going on that you are not telling anyone. You wear fake happiness like a non-peelable face mask. It's okay to do that sometimes, but don't let that turn into a permanent fixture on your face until it's too late and you break down completely."

"I get it. I do. But I'm good. I promise," I say, folding my hand over hers.

"Okay," she says, granting me a half smile, and I can see she's finally dropping it.

We finish up, pay, and hug before we head out. Usually, I feel light and happy after our brunches, especially with the over-sized mimosas running through my body, but everything still feels so heavy.

My body craves movement and I need the time to clear my mind.

I haven't been able to get Seamus out of my head, and even though the logical part of me wants to, my body and soul scream something different.

Because he was *always* different.

The connection I had with him was unlike anything I've ever felt. Sure, I was young and inexperienced, but even after all these years, nothing has compared to what I felt when I was with him.

And I fucking hate that.

It's been ten years and more dates, attempted relationships, and set ups that I can count, and still, nothing has come close.

Was it the fact that we had to sneak around after lights out? Was it the excitement of getting caught? Was it the limited time we had together or knowing there was an expiration date? The forbiddenness of it all?

I believe in soulmates, I always have. But am I blinded to think that there is only one perfect person out there for you.

I think back to all the nights we laid by the lake together, counting the stars, talking about anything and nothing, while we shared our dreams with each other. We were young, naïve, and had more ambition in life to achieve these unrealistic, silly goals than we did common sense.

Life hadn't hit us yet.

I guess that's the thing about love.

You just can't help it. Love is involuntary.

Seamus Matthews only had two weeks of my twenty-eight years, and still, I've loved him my whole life.

Closing my eyes, I inhale the crisp, cool air and force out all the oxygen that feels like bricks on my chest. It's cold enough that my breath fog is thick as it leaves my lips, but evaporates quickly as I continue on my walk home.

In my current quest to avoid my backyard, I haven't practiced in days other than the classes I've taught—which doesn't count when it comes to what my body needs, because I feel stiff everywhere. My legs are sore from *not* working out, and as I roll my neck back and forth, the tight muscles whine and scream in protest.

I know I can't avoid my mat any longer, and I don't want to. If Seamus is home, he's just going to have to deal with the show. And I need to force the idea that he could be watching out of my head.

18

NAOMI

17 years old

"I don't see it," I whine, squinting my eyes at the sky as I search the stars for some pattern relative to a man shooting a bow and arrow. "I see three bright stars lined up." I point to the sky as Seamus aligns his head next to mine, getting the direct line of sight to where I'm pointing. "The rest of it gets lost after that."

He brought a blanket from his cabin, and the night started with us sitting under a tree next to the lake. We've been here since and it's been hours. It has to be well after midnight at this point, and he's been trying to show me where all the constellations are.

Mind you, I've only succeeded in finding one constellation, the Big Dipper and a planet, Venus. Until now, I had no idea you could see Venus with the naked eye.

"That's it, now trail your eyes up to see the other three stars spread out above it, the two stars on the corners of his torso are brighter than the others," he explains, pointing at invisible spots in the sky.

My eyes bounce over the dark, vast sky. It's dusted by the gorgeous glittering of stars that just look like far away fireflies. They look nothing like patterns to me.

"I just don't see it." My shoulders deflate.

"Hey…" Seamus rolls his body closer to mine, placing himself flush in front of me.

"Some nights are easier than others. We'll try again tomorrow night." Using his thumb and forefinger, he tilts up my chin to meet his gaze. "Will you meet me again?"

There's such a vulnerability about Seamus that I noticed he doesn't share with everyone. Actually, I don't see it with anyone except when he's talking to me.

He's soft spoken and caring, and somehow, even when he's not near me, I feel his presence. Like he's protective of me, of our friendship, or whatever this is that's happening between us.

I nod, as his lips inch slowly into a smile.

Even though the color of his eyes are pitch black, they shine bright with happiness at my response, and I'm mesmerized by the contrast. A darkness is embedded in their depths, not just in color, but in the abyss of emotion that hides behind them. Yet that small smile lights up something inside his irises that makes my stomach flutter. The way his gaze drinks me in, showing his admiration and loyalty without words.

"How do you know so much about the stars?" I ask, curiously.

"I just like them." He shrugs.

That's his tell, I've noticed. Sometimes he responds openly, and sometimes I ask him a question that he responds with the most generic of answers while his shoulders lift up in a shrug.

I give him a hard squint, pinching my brows as I question his reply.

"That's the answer you give a stranger," I tell him as he blinks and looks away. His eyes take in the lake, and his lungs

take in a deep breath before turning back to me with a tight lipped smile.

He rolls onto his back, placing his arms behind his head. A glacial pause passes in the silence before he finally speaks.

"I climb out of my window at night and sneak up to my roof. I can spend hours just searching the sky," he admits.

"What are you looking for?" I ask.

"Peace," he says quietly as his eyes continue to graze the vast skyline, like he's asking now.

"Sometimes, it's quiet. Sometimes I hear my father yell at my mother. I used to hide up there. Things would break, he would yell, and I would just hide, because that's what my mom told me to do. She would tell me, hide until all the noise goes away, then it's safe to come out. *I never really understood what was happening, until one day it all just clicked. I couldn't keep hiding, so, that day I climbed down through the window and stood between him and my mother."*

Shifting his gaze, he looks over at me briefly without making eye contact, then turns back to the stars. "He still drinks and he's still angry, all the time. But at least he doesn't take it out on her anymore."

I just stare at his profile, unsure of what to say, unsure of what to do. I swallow thickly, attempting to find words to comfort him, to soothe him. I wish I could say something profound and meaningful, that he could take with him and remember when he needs it. But there is nothing. There is nothing one can say to comfort something so physically debilitating.

So, I stick with the facts.

"You're the bravest person I know." I interlace my fingers in his and give his hand a loving squeeze.

He turns on his side to face me as he brings my hand up to his lips. His warm breath coats my knuckles as his lips wrap around the peak, and just that sends shivers down my spine.

"People are brave when they have to be, not by choice."

"That's not true." I turn to face him so we're laying with the blanket on one side and the stars on the other. We gaze into each other's eyes, and nothing about it is awkward or weird. It's simple and meaningful, and so much passes between us in the silence.

"People are forced into making a choice, but not everyone has the courage to choose the selfless, brave one." I give him a sad smile. "I think you're a hero. I know you are in your mom's eyes."

That makes him smile, and I can see how much he loves his mom. Like that comment makes him proud.

A few minutes pass, maybe longer. And we're stuck, happily in a world where it's just us for a moment in time. Gazing into his suffocating eyes, layered with pain, yet dare I say peace—at least for now. We lay in silence when a shooting star skims the horizon.

"Did you see that?" I say excitedly as I sit up and point to the sky.

"Make a wish." He props himself up on his elbow, watching me as I close my eyes and silently make my wish.

Laying back down, we're flush with each other again.

"What did you wish for?" His mouth is turned up in an adorable smile as his eyes take me in. He could easily make fun of me for acting like a ten-year-old, wishing on shooting stars. Instead, he looks at me with appreciation asking me my wish.

"Your peace." His face falls at my confession and I wonder if I said too much, but I don't regret telling him that truth. I wish for him to feel peace. "What was your wish?"

"I wish I could kiss you." A giddy smile spreads across my face. I can't help but bite my bottom lip as I look at his.

The kiss he gave me earlier today was quick and rushed, but it was magical. There was so much passion behind the short lived moment, and I want nothing more than to recreate it.

Keeping my eyes locked on his, I lean in, bringing our lips as close together as possible without touching.

Starting at my waist, he sweeps his hand up the side of my body, over my arm, to my shoulder then cups my cheek. He gently pulls me in closer as our lips collide, and I squeeze my eyes shut as I attempt to decipher a hundred sensations at once. His arm wraps around my back, pulling me closer, like our bodies are two puzzle pieces that finally found their home.

Our tongues dance together and everything feels so perfect. The sound of the lake, the wind rustling through the trees, the crickets echoing through the night. It's a dream kiss for a girl, and when he finally pulls away so we can properly breath, my heart is fluttering, feeling so full, I swear it could explode.

He dips his forehead to mine. "Now both our wishes have come true."

19

SEAMUS

Present Day

Using my angular brush, I swipe the mixture quickly over the canvas. As I flick my wrist, the tertiary colors blend together, making some combination of beige that reminds me of the shade of Mimi's tank top the day I took her against the tree.

That was the first time since that I followed the out of control emotions I've been suppressing. I finally let them take over, completely giving in to the loss of control whenever she is near.

And it completely bit me in the ass.

The terror that blanketed her face, the fear that enveloped her body, was as blinding as the desert sun. The overwhelming sensation of confusion I've had since the moment I pinned her arms up, and how she responded after, has been loitering in my mind for the last few days.

There is so much more that she isn't saying, that I don't know, and it's bringing me to the brink of insanity.

So, naturally, she's ignoring me and I'm dropping flowers at her front door everyday… twice a day.

It's not excessive. It's persistent.

Plus, let's be honest. I'm well past stalker-ish behavior.

My most trusted ability to read people is totally failing me when it comes to her. I'm left so goddamn confused after spending any amount of time with her, it makes my brain feel like an unsolvable Rubix cube.

Rocco is still digging up information and hasn't found anything that makes any sense.

Usually, my daily therapeutic trips to the shooting range is what I need to feel clarity, but that's not even working. The only thing I've been able to do to get my head on straight is paint.

I'm torn away from my thoughts and the gaze I had on my canvas by the knock at the front door.

I look down at myself, holding a brush in one hand and a palate in the other. My dark denim jeans hang low on my hips and a few color streaks paint my bare abs and arms. Putting the brush down, I slip my hand in my pocket to grab my phone and check my Ring app, to see Hudson is at my front door.

Shit.

Did we make plans today?

Maybe we did and I completely forget, which is entirely possible with the distraction of a certain neighbor.

I haven't actually seen him since our run in at Afterburn, and I'm certain he's here to give me shit.

I prepare myself for the verbal Armageddon as I put down my palate and throw a towel over my shoulder that I use to wipe off the excess paint from my fingertips.

Walking downstairs, I step to the door and open it to Hudson with a smug smile and a questionable look in his eyes. All of a sudden, Dane pops out from the side of the house and comes barreling into me like a goddamn untrained dog, practically knocking the wind out of me.

"Dane. Jesus, man," I huff out as I pat his shoulder.

"I told him that it was a risk to rush in and tackle you like that. I'm surprised you didn't shoot him," Hudson says, as he steps into the house, kicks his shoes off—because he knows better—then goes to the kitchen to grab some beers.

Hudson and I have been friends since we were in kindergarten, and he knows me the best out of our group of friends. Well, I should say *his* group of friends. Because I never knew our current friend group until Hudson introduced me to all of them.

Hudson and I spent our entire childhood together, practically inseparable. Then he went off to college, staying close to home, going to the University of Houston because the local baseball scouts wanted nothing more than the local baseball hero to go to their university.

It was a good investment for them considering he played for them for four years before getting recruited straight to the major leagues, until an injury set him back in his career for a few years.

Although those years were tough for him, now he's back in the MLB playing for the Seattle Smashers and loving every bit of his professional baseball life with his wife Ember, and I'm so fucking happy for him.

I still remember the motto the university gave him after they announced his recruitment and full ride: *Hudson Byrnes—Texas grown*. Giving him shit about that was probably my favorite thing to do. Especially since I was overseas, on active duty, living in the most obscene conditions, seeing some of the most painful things.

I had never planned to go to the military until my senior year when I was left alone with my dad, leaving me with no other option.

Bootcamp was difficult, but once I got through that, I didn't hate it. Being athletic my whole life, a fairly healthy eater, and my natural personality of enjoying routine made adjusting to the military lifestyle easier than I expected. Then it became second nature, and it felt like something that was a bit of calling for me.

I didn't have much at home, so it never felt like I was missing much.

I think Hudson had a harder time with me being away than I did.

He went out of his way to write me letters, just to keep me updated on life and everything happening in what used to be *our* world. I know he did that more for him than he did for me, but those letters kept me sane. He kept me connected to reality, because it was easier to disconnect and disassociate my emotions than process all the pain and suffering that was happening around me and my squad.

Either way, he always kept tabs on me, and whenever I would return home from being deployed, Hudson would *always* be around. So, naturally, his college friends became my friends. I didn't really need them, or want them—the more people you care about the more people you risk losing—but Hudson is a stubborn prick who refused to not let me get to know them.

Needless to say, I'd do anything for any one of them now.

Dane included. Even though he has the attention span of a squirrel and is as predictable as a raccoon.

When I first met him, I was unsure how he even got accepted into a university. Then I found out he was on a full academic scholarship because he's brilliant. Beyond brilliant—Einstein brilliant.

During his time in college, he felt that the communication process between the university, students, and professors lacked, well, everything it should. So, instead of doing what every other normal human would do and complain about it to the school board or suggest change, he did something about it.

He created a platform that fed all the information the students needed to know, from the moment they applied to the university, to the acceptance process, and building out your college career for what you wanted to pursue. It was like an automatic built-in school counselor, that walked you step by step through the orientation process and followed you through your entire college career.

It also connected the students and teachers, and allowed for a tracking system that could be shared between community colleges and universities, so there wasn't a lag when transfers happened—because that was also a frustrating thing for some of the students.

It integrated grant and scholarship platforms, providing up-to-date information to all the students who were applying with any type of financial assistance, allowing them to take advantage of programs that they might qualify for based on the parameters they provided when applying.

There was some type of smart code that he created on the backend of this platform that was really the beginning of an "AI" type of technology.

The entire system was fully automated, integrated, and so far advanced for its time.

So, pretty much, if Dane is presented with a problem he doesn't like, he fixes it.

You would think he would be a total 'Type A' personality and completely rigid, like myself. But he's the exact opposite.

Slap a surfboard in his hands and you'd confuse him with a beach bum that spends his days on the sand, basking in the California sun.

His bright, blue eyes are never not smiling and his shaggy, dirty blonde hair has never changed. Actually, I think he cuts it himself when he's bored.

The basic white T-shirt and cargo shorts he currently has on pair well with his beige flip flops and backwards cap, even though I doubt he had any thought of what he was wearing when he got dressed this morning.

You'd never know it by looking at him, but he never has to work again due to selling off not only the platform he created, but also, the rights to the code behind it to one of the most prominent tech companies in the world.

He's an unpredictable jokester with a genius IQ, and half the time none of us know what country he is in or where he's living.

"Dane, man. What have you been up to?" We finally pull apart in a brotherly hug as he kicks off his flip flops, and it reminds me of how Mimi does it before she steps onto her mat. Actually, come to think of it, they are almost identical in many personality traits.

I haven't seen her practice this week and that…Well, frankly, it pisses me off. Not only have I come to rely on my daily *yoga* sessions, but I hate not knowing what she is doing, *how* she is doing.

"I just got back from Italy, spent some time in Rome. The hostels there are wild, man. Wild."

"Out of all the places you can stay. Hostels, really? Why don't you at least get yourself a short term flat or something?" I ask as I pad my way to the kitchen where Hudson is holding a beer out to me.

"Because it's fucking crazy fun. You can meet people in bars and some of the nightclubs, but hostels, hostels are where it's at. You guys have to come with me sometime." He wiggles his eyebrows, and all I can do is shake my head and laugh as I tap the neck of my beer with Hudson's and take a swig.

Hudson is married now and would never look at another woman sideways, much less join Dane on one of his *trips*.

Me? Fucking kill me before I sign up to backpack through Europe, staying in shared rooms with random ass people.

"Never, not happening. Ever," I reply, taking another swig of the excessively hoppy, bitter beer.

I don't drink often, but whenever the guys get together, I let loose a bit. Especially with Hudson around, because I trust him and know he's always got my back.

"So, how's the obsession with your neighbor going?" Hudson asks.

I retract my previous statement.

Prick.

"You're obsessed with your neighbor?" Dane echoes back in the form of a surprised question.

"No," I lie.

An awkward beat passes, as we all take a sip, then another.

Dane glances between Hudson and I like there's a secret we're not telling him.

There is, but Hudson doesn't even know about the history, either.

I've been in love with her since I was seventeen-years-old.

"Okay, come on, Shay," Hudson finally says, his tone pleading, yet forceful.

He doesn't usually push too much, but it's been too long that he's questioned the situation with Mimi, and I know I can't hold him off any longer.

"Do you remember that camp my mom put me in the summer before senior year?"

Hudson looks up to the ceiling, his eyes bouncing around for a moment. "Oh yeah, that two week sleepaway camp you went to. The one you told me to ask my parents to sign me up for, but I couldn't do it because I had baseball."

"Yeah, well…I met her there." I glance out the kitchen window, in another attempt to see if she's walking by or if I can steal another look at her. I know she left this morning and don't think she's back yet, but the knowledge doesn't help my brain searching for her, even when I know she's not there.

"Wait a minute," Dane jumps in. "You moved here, bought a house, and it just so happened to be next door to a girl you went to camp with?"

Hudson smiles. "No, he saw her at Afterburn months ago, stalked her, then scared off her neighbors with a shit ton of money, buying their house so he could place himself next door to her."

"That's not…" I trail off…Well, I guess that *is* sort of how it happened.

"That's not *entirely* how it happened," is all I can respond with.

"We're listening," Hudson replies, pulling up a barstool as Dane curiously peruses my living room, looking at the bare essentials of decor and the very few photos I have placed out around the room.

I relent and share the details of meeting Mimi, telling them how she stood up for me the first day when I was totally by myself and honestly, a bit nervous about being there. I tell them about that stupid spin the bottle game—leaving out the tidbit of my premature ejaculation mishap. I shared with them the details of all the nights after the day camp events, when Mimi and I would sneak out and meet up by the lake. Every single night.

"Then the last night there, we had sex. It was perfect. One of the happiest nights I've ever had. Afterward we saw some of the camp leaders walking to my cabin, and we panicked. She was finishing getting dressed and told me to get back so I wouldn't get in trouble, so I raced back to my cabin. That's when they told me about the accident and pulled me out of camp right then and there to go see my mom." My eyes meet Hudson's and I see his face fall when he understands the timing of all of this.

"Did you ever see her again after that?" he asks, his eyes telling me he already knows the answer.

I shake my head.

"As you know, by the time I got to the hospital, she had already passed." I pause. The overwhelming feeling of resentment and guilt for not being there for her has always weighed heavily on me. Over the years it's gotten better, or shall I say easier to accept, but finally admitting all of this to Hudson is cracking open some old wounds.

"There was so much confusion and chaos, it took a few days to get my head on straight. Once I did, I looked up the phone number to the camp and tried to get in touch with her, but camp was over for the summer." I later came to find out, the camp just stopped all its operations after that summer.

"I never asked her last name, never got her phone number, didn't even know what city she lived in." I take a long pull of my beer, remembering how defeated I felt all those years ago. How my heart ached for the loss of my mom—my biggest supporter, my biggest cheerleader in life—coinciding with the pain I felt realizing I was probably never going to see Mimi again, either.

I was broken. My soul was shattered.

Life conquered me in a matter of minutes. Stealing away the one person who cared for me unconditionally, while teasing me with the idea of another. Leaving me with the knowledge that she was out there, and I couldn't have her.

Hudson eyes me with caution. Because he knows me well enough to know the loss of my mother broke me, but now knowing this happened on top of it, his tightlipped smile says it all as he remains quiet. He doesn't apologize, because he knows I don't want pity. I never want pity.

I probably should have told him all those years ago, but I felt like if I hid it away, then I wouldn't have to admit that it was real. I could just pretend that it was all just a dream.

It was easier to accept.

"Well, you sure know how to make an entrance back into someone's life." He chuckles, attempting to lighten the mood. "How did she handle seeing you here for the first time?"

"Not exactly good," I squeak out. My lips lift in a half smile as I recall the look on her face when she saw me at Afterburn, and how she kicked me in the balls.

"Does she know?"

I shake my head. "No, she thinks I left her half naked getting dressed by a lake after I took her virginity, and just opted to never return."

"Hm." He nods, heavily and very slowly. "Looks like you got your work cut out for you, brother."

"I know," I agree with him. I have to open up to her and share things that I've emotionally locked away, and I'm totally unsure where to even start with all of that.

I glance around the room confused, because Dane is nowhere to be seen.

"Where did Dane go?" I ask, not surprised that he got side-tracked.

"Shay, did you paint these?!" His voice clamors from upstairs.

From my *private* space.

My eyes widen as I turn to Hudson. "What the hell is he doing up there?"

Taking the stairs two at a time, with Hudson trailing behind me, I land at the top seeing him inspecting a few of my canvases. *Goddammit.*

I palm my face as I walk toward him.

Another thing I haven't shared with anyone. The only one who remotely has any idea that I paint is Hudson, but he's never actually seen any of them.

"These are so good, Shay. Have you ever thought about selling them?" Dane asks, as he cocks his head sideways, appraising the one I just finished.

It's an abstract painting with no definitive lines. Just colors splashed over the canvas, but in the middle is the blurred appearance of a man and a woman. Both shirtless, the colors resembling just their skin tone, as he holds her waist and her head falls back while he kisses between the channel of her chest.

It's bright and vivid, regardless of the vague lines and blotchy undertones.

When I painted it, I just thought of every moment I had with

Mimi that first night. When I traced her body with my lips and caressed her skin with my hands. Her head would fall back on the blanket as her body arched into me, writhing under my touch. It was like everything felt whole for the first time in my life.

"He's right, Seamus. These are really good," Hudson says just as surprisingly as he walks over to the one I finished two days ago. That one is less colorful than the one Dane is looking at, with just the outline of a woman seated in the same position Mimi poses herself in when she looks like a pretzel; her arms are crossed over each other in front of her body.

It has enough color to be happy and light, but dark enough to give you the same feeling that she gives me right now.

Closed off, hidden. Unwilling to open herself up. But still managing to be the same Mimi that smiles to the world, making everyone else feel good about themselves and comfortable.

Because that's how she makes everyone around her feel.

Hudson pats me on the shoulder as Dane explores the other side of the room. He looks out the window and he gets a curious glint in his eyes.

Shit.

"So, did you know your hot neighbor does half naked yoga in her backyard?" Then he precedes to open the window, sticking his head and half his body out of it, shouting.

"Hey, yoga girl!"

20

NAOMI

"Exhale, press into your heels," I whisper to myself as I rehearse my queuing.

I've been going through my poses for twenty minutes, but the feeling I normally get when I'm practicing outside is missing.

That tingling sensation I have when I feel his eyes on me has been absent.

I've always loved my privacy out here, but now I crave his hidden presence.

It's a conflicting emotion. Like I shouldn't enjoy it, I shouldn't look forward to it. But I do, and I can't help it. He provides me with an overwhelming feeling of admiration and protection, something I've come to enjoy more than I'd care to admit.

I wish I could explain it, but if the last ten years have taught me anything in the realm of karma and fate, it's that sometimes there's no reasonable explanation for any of it.

The few men I've trusted enough to *officially* date were still short term, and even then, none of them made me feel as special or as safe as when I was with Seamus.

There is just something about him.

There was then, and it's still there now.

"Hey, yoga girl!" A booming voice startles me as I push back into a seated position and glance up to Seamus' window.

A very gorgeous man with a huge smile and shaggy, blonde hair is hanging halfway out of it, waving his arm back and forth, trying to get my attention, like he's miles away from me.

He might be the happiest man I've ever met from afar.

I look behind me and glance at my surroundings, because that naturally feels like the right thing to do, then glance back up to him with a questioning look.

"My best friend is obsessed with you!" he yells, and my jaw drops as a laugh escapes me.

"Is that right?" I yell back.

"Yeah, he's super crabby, but I think you could totally make him not crabby. So you should give him a chance to take you out." His smile is a mile wide.

"Are you asking me out for your friend?"

"I am, but I might not tell him and show up myself." He wiggles his eyebrows dramatically before his body jerks back and he grumbles something I can't hear. His head hits the exterior of the window as his entire body gets pulled back through it, like he was just sucked up by a vacuum cleaner. I hear a distant, *hey, ouch* and *knock it off,* then a *dude.*

I keep my eye on the window, unable to hide a smile. I find myself leaning forward to attempt to see further into the window, even though it's completely impossible from this angle.

Suddenly, a man with short, trimmed brown hair peeks out the window and I recognize him immediately.

"Hey, Hudson," I greet him as I give him a wave.

"Hey, Naomi." A loud crash breaks out from inside the room, making him turn to look into the room. He holds up one finger while scrunching up his nose before disappearing back through the window.

Some more rustling happens, a few profanities from multiple voices, then the blonde guy appears back in the window. His shaggy hair is a complete mess as he runs his fingers through it, pushing it away from his face.

"So, what do you say? Saturday?" His body jerks as he kicks something behind him.

"I can't, I have a class I'm teaching at Afterburn on Saturday." A curious look crosses his face, but he immediately fires back.

"I'll come to your class on Saturday, if you go out with Seamus after?" he says without a second thought.

"You don't even know what class I'm teaching?" I yell back.

"You don't know me, but I'm down for *anything*, yoga girl." His eyebrows hit the top of his hairline, like he's daring me.

Oh, he has no idea what he's getting himself into.

"You need a partner. Bring one with you on Saturday and we have a deal." I have a hard time not mirroring the smile he has, because he's adorable and looks like he has fun anywhere he goes.

"Yes!" He fist pumps himself as his body gets pulled partially back inside the window. "I got you a date, you broody bastard, stop it!" he yells into it.

There's a bit of grunting while he white knuckle grips the window sill, his head pulling in and out of the window like his entire body is being used as rope in tug-o-war. Finally his head pops back out the window. "Saturday, no take backs!" he shouts out, then he's ripped away again.

The window slams down shut echoing through the backyard.

I palm my face and silently laugh to myself as I finish my routine, holding a few static stretches before I lay down in savasana.

I allow myself time to clear all the chaos in my head, focusing only on my breath as I count each one, forcing myself to start over the moment my mind wanders to negative thoughts.

Does meditation always work? No.

But at least trying to get to a space with clear thoughts and a sharp, conscious mental state will help my overall mood and mindset.

I want to forgive Seamus. I know I do.

My head is telling me he didn't leave me by choice. I think I've always known that he didn't walk away that night knowing he'd never see me again. He definitely didn't leave knowing what would happen.

Regardless of all of those circumstances and however fate brought us back together, I need to be honest with him. I need to tell him everything. He might look at me differently, and that scares the hell out of me, but we both need to come clean if we're going to try this.

I've done an unnecessarily good job pulling back after every encounter with him, ignoring his flowers and kind gestures at every turn. It's time to put the past in the past, and move forward. Attempt a chance with him that was taken away from us for whatever reason, and not let those reasons hold me back any longer.

After an incredible yoga session, a bit of fun banter with Window Yelling Guy and way too long in savasana, I feel revived. Clear. Everything feels light, and for the first time in a long time, I'm giddy with excitement.

"I have a date," I whisper to myself, smiling as I roll up my mat and place it in the bin next to my backdoor.

I have some sequences to plan and playlists to finalize, then I'm going to go shopping to find an outfit for my date with Seamus. And I hope it makes me feel as irresistible as he does.

21

SEAMUS

17 years old

"*Happy Birthday,*" *I whisper in Mimi's ear as I hand her a small bunch of daisies I picked from a bush near my cabin.*

She glances down at the pathetic, floppy flowers and looks at me over her shoulder with the most gorgeous ear-to-ear smile.

"These little guys will have to do, until I can find a florist to send you a million roses." I want to tell her how much more it would be if we weren't stuck in log cabins in the middle of the woods.

"A million, huh? That's a little excessive, don't you think?" Her fingers wrap around mine as she grabs the small bouquet, lingering for a few moments longer than they should, sending shivers down my spine.

"Not for you," I respond back instantly.

"How did you find out?" she asks.

"I have my sources," I say confidently before shifting my gaze up to the camp leader as she gives us the details on tonight's event.

"Shane told you, didn't he?"

"Yup. His loyalties have changed, sweetheart. He likes me better than he likes you." I place my hands in my pockets as I roll back on my heels.

"So then, tell me. How do I know your birthday is tomorrow then?"

Damn him.

I pin her with a playful but dirty look.

"Fine, you win. But you have to promise to save me the last dance tonight."

Shane told me the camp leaders put together a dance every year. We only have two more full days until we leave on Saturday, and the dance is happening tonight. I'm hoping to spend the entire night dancing with Mimi before we sneak out to lounge by the lake like we've done every night this week.

The late nights with her have made this entire overnight camp trip worth it.

Most of our time there is spent talking, but last night we kissed for hours. I couldn't keep my hands off her, and by the end of the night, our lips were swollen. When we finally parted ways, I had a horrible case of blue balls. It was so bad I had to relieve myself in the bathroom before making it back to my cabin.

At one point, I debated coming in my pants again just to feel relief, but I had no interest in embarrassing myself for a second time.

I've been trying to find a way to talk to her about figuring out how to see each other after camp. I know she lives in Texas, and wants to stay close to her parents. She wants to be a teacher, so her plan was to finish school and apply at some community colleges near her home to start working on her degree and teaching credentials.

Maybe, I could make a plan around where she goes. So far, I've only applied at a couple universities—the same ones that

Hudson applied to—but I know he's staying in Texas, so this could work.

I want to bring it up without sounding desperate, and I want to talk to her about it tonight before I miss my chance.

"Just the last dance?" she asks, pinning me with an equally playful look.

I lean in, grazing my lips against her ear as I place my hand at the small of her back, making any excuse to touch her.

"I'll take all of them, if you'll let me." I secretly kiss her temple while no one is looking. The camp leaders call for us to break out in our curricular courses today.

We all had to pick three classes on the first day we started camp. They are all classes that teach skills revolving around wilderness and camping.

Shane and I have the same archery class, and it's been great getting to know him. He's down to Earth and easy to get along with. I can see why he and Mimi have been friends for so long.

The survival skills course I selected has been amazing in regards to content and what I've learned, but Wes and Nathan are in that class with me, and I swear I lose brain cells just being around them. Wes isn't half bad by himself, but when the two are together, it's a torture I wouldn't wish against my worst enemy.

Mimi and I happen to both select hiking, which is obviously my favorite. Not the hiking part. The Mimi part.

After the full day events, we head back to our cabin to get ready for the dance. I spent a majority of the day practicing my 'how to win Mimi over for life' speech, coming to the conclusion that I have no idea how I'm going to even start the conversation without sounding like an obsessive lunatic.

I just hope when the time is right, it comes out smooth and I don't sound like a blubbering idiot.

*S*HANE *and I stroll into the dance hall together. We decided to be fashionably late because Shane said that creates anticipation for girls if they are waiting on guys. I think he is entirely mistaken considering the entire camp is pretty much on the dance floor, not giving any shits about who isn't here yet.*

Will Smith's Gettin' Jiggy With It *blares through the speakers, and by the look of it, a lot of the kids—and some of the camp leaders—really* like this song.

I even see the camp counselor gyrating her hips to the bass as she rolls her head back, singing at the top of her lungs.

It makes me smile and, dare I say it, sort of happy that everyone is having a good time. The positive energy is contagious, even I *feel like dancing. And I never dance.*

My eyes graze over the crowd because there's only one person I'd like to spend my time with, and I'm a bit desperate to find her since Romeo here decided we should be late and I've kept her waiting.

My eyes catch her long, silky hair splayed messily over a bright, shiny pink dress and my jaw fucking drops.

The dress criss-crosses over her shoulders, exposing half of her back. The hem falls just above her knees, showcasing her gorgeous legs. And it's like she senses my arrival when she looks over her shoulder and catches me drooling.

I mouth, wow, *as she smiles, spins, then dips her head mouthing,* thank you *back.*

She twirls her finger in the air at me.

Is she asking me to twirl?

I glance around and then point to myself. She nods. So, I shake my head and crook my finger calling her over. Her eyes squint at me, scrunching up her nose in the most adorable way, and finally takes a step in my direction.

I swear it's like she walks on water, floating toward me like a fucking goddess.

I'm not sure at what point she stole my heart. Was it the inno-

cent look of sorrow when I got roped into playing spin the bottle? The way she kept my secret by the tree in order to save me from the most humiliating moment of my life? The easy conversations on every single one of our hikes?

Honestly, I think it was the first day. When her hands wrapped around my arm, pulling me away from check-in chaos. It's like she cuffed herself to me that day and threw away the key.

I don't want us to end when camp ends.

Because this is everything.

She is everything.

"Well, someone is late." She sounds seductive and playful.

"It's his fault." I hitch my thumb over at Shane and he rolls his eyes.

He leans over to me, whispering loud enough for both Mimi and I to hear, "That's when you say, 'Did you miss me'?" He shakes his head. "You have so much to learn, young jedi." He buttons his sports jacket, looks around the room, pats me on the back, then walks toward the punch table.

"You know, he wasn't supposed to do that," I say as I turn to Mimi.

"I don't think you're supposed to blame your wingman, either," she replies with a smile, and I realize how easy it is to be myself around her.

"You clean up nice," she says before I can reply.

Holding my arms out, I say, "Shane had an extra sports jacket because I had no idea there was going to be a dress up day. You almost had to dance with a lumberjack because all I had were flannels."

Her head bounces back and forth like it's a debate as to what would have been better. "I find lumberjacks sort of sexy."

"Hmmm, really? Good to know," I reply.

"Are you going to twirl for me now?" she asks, expectedly.

"Me? No. I don't twirl. But I'm happy to get naked for you later instead." My intent was to be playful, but I realize how

presumptuous that might have sounded. I open my mouth to retract, but she of course replies with a jaw dropping response.

"Oh good, I've been dying to see you naked. You've got yourself a deal."

My eyes widened in shock. "I was joking, Mimi."

"Shane's right, you need to work on your game. Try again."

This little minx.

I stare at her, taking in every single inch of her. The way her eyes shine with a brightness that could go to war with the sun. The way her hair falls over her shoulders, one side covering the front of her chest while the other is completely exposed, affording me a perfect view of her smooth, tan skin and the curves of her cleavage.

She is absolutely perfect.

"I'll show you mine, if you show me yours." My words smolder, and I'm even shocked at how sexy I sounded.

She bites her lip, and fuck, I wish I could kiss her right now.

"That was good. You'll have all the girls swooning when you get back home."

"I don't want any other girls," I reply quickly, leaning into her because I don't want to hold back anymore.

I wrap my arm around her back, pulling her flush against my body. Crooking my finger under her chin, I lift her gaze to mine because I want her full attention.

"In fact, I spent the entire day figuring out how we're going to continue this after camp. I haven't figured it out yet, but I'm not letting you go."

Leaning down, my lips are inches away from hers when a throat clears next to us. The camp counselor, fresh off the dancefloor, looking wild after her dance off with Will Smith, places her hands on each of our shoulders, separating us a bit.

"Six inches," she chastises, then she storms off.

Mimi giggles, and even though I just got cockblocked, I can't help but laugh, either.

"Come on, let's dance." She interlaces her fingers in mine, pulling me to the dance floor. I hate dancing, but since it's clear I'll do anything for her, I guess I'm dancing.

So, it turns out, I'm a horrible dancer.

Mimi is not.

Her body moves perfectly with the rhythm of the music, and I gave up trying after the third song where I pretty much just felt like a broken robot trying not to malfunction.

She's been at it for over an hour. She'll grab me when a slow song comes on, where I'll spend a majority of the time stepping on her sweet, dainty toes before exiting when the next upbeat song comes on.

It turns out Shane actually dances competitively, which just adds to his whole, already suave demeanor, and all the girls are drooling over him. I actually never paid attention until now, but he's pretty much got his choice of, well, all of them.

I've been keeping an eye on him, as I've been watching Mimi, and he's constantly sneaking glances at Wes.

Surprisingly, Wes is doing a bit of the same. He hasn't shared anything with me since that day on the rope course, but I'd bet my left arm something more has happened between them other than the night when we played spin the bottle.

Shane doesn't strike me as the kind of guy to pine over someone, but there's a feeling of animosity and expectation.

Wes pushes himself off the bench he's sitting on and heads over to the floor where Shane and Mimi are dancing together. Shane spins then stops, stunned for a split second as he sees Wes approach, then continues to move awkwardly.

They look at each other for a brief moment, then Wes grabs Mimi's hand spinning her around and bumps hips with her. Annnnnnd, now I'm heated. I shift in my seat, wanting to go to her, but she's laughing. So far it seems all very platonic, but I'm not sure I trust Wes' intentions.

Wes moves between them, placing himself in a sandwich between Shane and Mimi. And although Wes is facing Mimi, he's closer to Shane than he is to her. Shane's hand grazes the side of Wes's body, his arms hiding the touch from most angles except the one that I have.

Wes places his hand over Shane's, pressing his fingers in between Shane's, then let's go.

It was quick, milliseconds before he pulled his hand back, but that was definitely intentional.

He changes direction, stepping closer to Mimi and places his arms around her, rolling his hips into hers, but she steps back smiling kindly—like she always does—then pats him on the arm.

You got the pat, bro. Move along.

He lifts his hand up in a high five, and she gives him one before he walks off, stealing a glance at Shane while he does. That whole thing was…interesting.

I've had enough of trying to figure out people tonight.

Is This Love *by Whitesnake, comes on and I walk up to the dance floor, but Nathan beats me to Mimi.*

"Hey, Mimi. Dance with me," he demands as he grabs her hand and pulls her body close to his.

Where the hell is Ms. Six Inches when you need her?

"I was actually going to dance with Seamus." She looks over his shoulder at me as I walk up behind him.

He glances over at me with a sinister fucking smile. "Semen here doesn't mind sharing. Do you?"

"Actually, I do." My voice is deep and hostile.

"Come on, man. She'll like it, I promise." He pumps his groin on her as he wraps his hand around the back of her neck, and I see red.

But I'm not the only one, because Mimi steps out of his grasp and punches him straight in the nose, stunning literally everyone.

"You bitch!" he yells, holding his nose. She probably didn't hit it hard enough to break it, but it's bleeding and everyone is getting a good laugh out of it.

"Don't ever touch me like that again." She points at him, stepping back further.

"Come on." I interlace my fingers in hers, leading her toward the exit and leaving everyone else behind before we draw too much attention and never get the hell out of here.

22

NAOMI

Present Day

"Thank you, everyone, for joining me today." I welcome the class and introduce myself to the unexpectedly large group of people. Ember is standing at the edge of the open theater area, counting heads and looking gorgeous as ever with her long, red hair and sophisticated jumpsuit.

She's young, maybe in her early to mid-twenties, but wise, far beyond her years, exuding a confidence I don't see in many people. She's been able to coordinate this event in a short amount of time, and the promotion of it was so well marketed, that she shattered the original goal of ten couples and there is now a waitlist for the next class.

We had planned to have the class in the mid-afternoon, before the club officially opened so it was private and more inti-mate. That way we could use the open theater area instead of clearing out the private room with less space.

So, instead of teaching in front of a small class of people, I'm currently on a stage and I'm going to be guiding people through the sensuality of tantric massage.

I've never been nervous teaching, but this is definitely a whole other level.

We were able to comfortably get fifteen couples in here, some cuddling closely together holding each other, while some others sit next to each other holding notepads. It's easy to tell who will be more willing to participate or not.

This club is the perfect setting for this class, knowing the openness that people need to have during the session.

All of the couples are all members and none I recognize. However, I do spot Window Yelling Guy, who Ember introduced me to before class started as Dane. Apparently, he went to school with Hudson and has been friends with the guys for quite some time.

Even though I only chatted with him for a couple of minutes, we immediately connected due to his lighthearted, fun personality. He is definitely more easy going than both Hudson and Seamus, who both hold a more serious demeanor in different ways.

Hudson is professional and kind. Seamus is just…Seamus.

Especially right now.

Standing like a statue in the corner of the room, he looks extra cranky today. His dark eyes match his all black, fitted to perfection black suit, dressed like a secret service agent runway model. His broad shoulders hold the confidence of someone in his position, his body in full control, giving nothing away.

Still, he looks delicious and edible, and it's *so* annoying.

I'm unsure how it's possible that I was attracted to young, playful Seamus and now, I'm drawn to the older doppelgänger, stick-in-the-mud Seamus. They are night and day, two different people, which leads me to believe that maybe I don't have a specific type of guy. Maybe my type is just Seamus.

"Today we're going to be learning the art of Tantric massage. For those of you who are not aware—" I glance around and see Dane sitting, all smiles next to Hudson, and I snort out a giggle.

Ember definitely didn't give them details about what this class is, if Hudson agreed to be here as Dane's partner. "—Tantric massage is a sensual, full body experience."

Hudson's brows pinch together as he turns to look at Dane. Dane isn't fazed by this, giving me his full attention.

"You will begin by meditating with your partner. During this time, we will focus on breath-work, using only your sight and hearing to build a connection with each other. Once you reach the full height of sexual energy, we will focus on exploring each other with touch, allowing your partner to *feel* all of your senses together, as one." I wander slowly around the room as my soft, meditative voice radiates through the crowded space.

Seamus stands at the back, stoic and stern, with his arms crossed over each other. His typically unreadable demeanor appears to be slightly uncomfortable as he shifts his stance, his eyes bouncing over the room and back at me.

"Some of you may like to watch and observe, while others may want to participate with their partner openly in this room. I ask that everyone be considerate of each other's choices."

Hudson's eyes widen as he leans over to Dane, whispering something.

Seamus shifts his stance again, uncrossing his arms, then crossing them again.

"Before we begin our breathing techniques, I will demonstrate the Tantric massage techniques for those who would like to experience that while you are here with your partner in a meditative state. Again, I ask that everyone be respectful of those partners who would like to experience that here today, as it is all part of the journey together, riding with the sexual energy that you both are feeling."

I walk back up to the front so I can see everyone clearly.

"There may be some of you who have never done anything like this, and can't imagine doing it openly in public. However, when you hit that peak of sexual energy, it can be quite persuasive, and you may find yourself doing things you typically wouldn't do." Glancing around the room at a few timid couples, I give them a reassuring smile, because I've seen it before.

"Now, can I get a volunteer as my partner for the demonstration?" I announce to the room. Dane's hand shoots straight up. Seamus' arms drop to his sides as he looks around the room, then over at Dane.

"I'll be performing the massage on your body in order to teach the technique to the class, that way everyone has a visual example. So, before you agree, you need to be comfortable with that type of public exposure and consent to me touching you."

It happens all at once: Dane—with his arm still stretched in the air—switches from a seated position to a kneeling position, putting himself higher amongst the crowd. Hudson palms his face, and Seamus immediately begins to march over to where the guys are sitting.

"I volunteer. I volunteer as tribute!" Dane yells and the class chuckles.

I can't help my smile as I walk over to the class clown.

He's full of positive, but hyper energy. It may be difficult to get him in a relaxed and meditative state, but it would make for a fun class.

Squatting down in front of him, I glance between him and Hudson, knowing they wouldn't be able to partner up together, and it would probably be best for Dane to have an experienced partner.

I need to make sure he's fully aware of what this all entails. I ask just as Seamus comes up beside us, "Are you aware that a tantric massage is *full* body, including genital massage?"

23

SEAMUS

"Hell yeah," Dane says, unaffected.

"You can fuck right off," I tell Dane as I look over at Hudson, mouth agape.

"Seamus," Mimi scolds as she stands to face me.

"You are not stroking him off in front of a class full of people," I angry-whisper so only she can hear me.

"You can't come barging into my class, telling me what I can or can't do." She holds her hand out to Dane to help him stand.

"Sit the fuck down." I point at him. "Right now."

Glancing around the room, everyone is staring, confused at the turn of events. And fuck, so am I. Why the hell am I acting like fucking Tarzan right now? She makes me lose every ounce of control I have.

But I can't fucking help it.

The moment I saw her and she stripped off the jacket she was wearing over her tight yoga outfit, I immediately wanted to throw her over my shoulder and take her home, so only I got her undivided attention.

It should be a crime how goddamn sexy she is in her bright white leggings and that tiny, matching white sports bra. In fact, white should be banned for such an outfit—and I doubt the sports bra could be considered one at all. It has a criss-cross back and low cut front. There is nothing *sporty* about it. It's functional lingerie.

She eyes me with trepidation, still managing to shoot invisible daggers at me. Her cheeks are flushed—and not in a good way—as she clenches her fists at her sides, yet her brows pinch with worry.

Fuck, I don't want to ruin this for her. Ember told me that this was the first opportunity she's had to teach this class on her own because she wasn't able to find other venues to accommodate this type of *yoga*.

I didn't ask what was so special about it, and I didn't understand it then. Now I get why.

But I can't watch her jerk off my best friend in public.

Not a chance in hell.

"Seamus, this is educational," she says between clenched teeth.

I just shake my head, slowly.

"If you can't watch, then leave."

I continue to shake my head.

Her chest lifts in an exhausting breath. She turns to look out over the room, then turns back to me, opening her mouth to continue the fight.

"I'll do it," I spit out before she can say anything more.

"Hell yeah," Dane says.

"Oh shit," Hudson follows.

"What?" Her delayed response reflects the shocked look on her face.

"Dane already has a partner." Hudson flinches back as his jaw slacks, like he's shocked I would volunteer him for that. I raise an eyebrow at him, because he actually *is* Dane's partner in this venture.

As he goes to open his mouth to refute, I raise a pointer finger at him to stop him from speaking.

"I'll do it," I repeat.

She leans in, whispering so only I can hear her, "Seamus, this is serious. I need a proper partner who is going to be open-minded and fully committed to this."

"Oh, I'm committed, sunshine," I assure her.

"Are you sure?" The same uncertain look she had behind those gorgeous chocolate eyes when I got sucked into spin the bottle, stare back at me.

Placing my hand on her shoulder, I press my lips against the shell of her ear. Grazing them lightly over her skin.

"Tantric massage…on stage…with Mimi. I think I won the spin the bottle jackpot." Pulling back, I give her a reassuring look.

I've never enjoyed being the center of attention. In fact, I have vehemently avoided it in any way I can in all aspects of my life. But the thought of not being the center of hers is worse.

Plus, if I had to watch her give anyone else a fucking genital massage, I would end up in a padded jail cell.

A spark of light beams in her eyes and I see my girl again. The one who's not angry with me, who doesn't hate me for leaving. The one who trusted me with her body and soul.

Her hand slides down my arm and her fingertips roam over my knuckles. I immediately relax in the comfort of her touch. The soft caress ignites fireworks on my skin, sending shock waves to my cock, deactivating all of my brain cells. So, when she steps back, leading us to the stage, my feet follow mindlessly. And now I know I've lost my goddamn mind with just one touch.

I've been thrown into some pretty terrible situations in my life. Had to walk—literally walk—into a battle zone with nothing more than melee weapons and our wit, yet, the walk to this stage has me challenging the stress inoculation training I've mastered my entire life, and I'm completely losing my composure.

Mentally, at least. Physically, you'd still have no fucking idea.

I'm not sure if it's the knowledge that Mimi will have her hands scouring every inch of my body or if it's because I'll be naked in front of…a lot of people. Close friends included.

This is a goddamn fucking dumpster fire, but I'm all in.

24

NAOMI

I can't believe he agreed to this. Not only did he agree, he volunteered.

Stepping on to the stage, I cup my hands around his massive shoulders and turn him to face me. He follows my lead as his body stands flush with mine. With only a couple inches between us, my hands begin to roam over his clothed body.

And for the entirety of this time, his eyes never leave mine.

Not even when I run my hands over his chest, pushing his jacket over his shoulders, allowing it to drop behind him.

Not even as I unbutton his shirt, following the same pattern as the jacket as it pools on the floor.

Kneeling down in front of him, my eyes still a permanent fixture on his, I unbuckle his belt and unbutton his pants. His hands fist at his sides, mirroring the tight clench in his jaw as I lick my lips when his pants fall to his ankles.

He swallows thickly as I have him step out of leg holes, pushing his pile of clothes to the side.

His body is on full display with nothing but a pair of black Calvin Klein boxer briefs on.

It's my turn to swallow audibly as my gaze roams over his

thick, muscular thighs, past the V line where his torso meets his hips, and up the washboard abs with more ridges than the Grand Canyon.

Someone clears their throat, and it's a hard realization when I remember we aren't alone and I have a class to teach.

Although the slow strip did add to the tantric connection due to the sexual tension that's already been building between us, I still need to keep this educational and professional.

My eyes steal another look at his perfectly sculpted body and my cheeks flush without permission.

"What now, Mimi?" Seamus's husky question goes straight to my core, forcing me to press my thighs together.

I am a professional. *I am a professional.* I play on repeat in my head.

"Lay down." I don't mean for my voice to come out as raspy as it does. I clear my throat as I pat the neck pillow and run my hand over the blanket.

His chest rises in a commanding breath, as if preparing for battle. He glances at the mat, then back at me before he crouches down and rolls onto his back, lying face up.

Glancing around the room, I take in a lengthy breath to calm myself before starting to talk a little more about Tantric massage and begin to explain what I'm going to be demonstrating.

My gaze goes beyond the couples in the class to Ember, standing in her same spot at the edge of the theater room next to a gorgeous blonde woman and two other men. One I recognize immediately as Christian Ford, the CEO of Ford Enterprises who owns many things, including the X-connect app and this club.

I've only ever seen him in pictures, which does him no justice for what he looks like in real life.

My voice stutters briefly as I walk back over to where Seamus is laying and kneel down next to him. I quickly peek back up to where they are, hoping they've gone, but nope—still there.

Seamus reads my nervous energy without effort and turns to look around the room, spotting the group immediately.

"Jesus Christ," he whispers as his eyes roll annoyingly to the top of his head.

And there the guilt is again. The same guilt that I had when he got sucked into that stupid spin the bottle game, and I instantly feel like an insecure school girl who's learned nothing in her life.

All the impulsive choices I've made that have trailed into horrible, life altering decisions flash through my head. The ones I actively made not knowing the outcome, and the ones I've subconsciously made that have always drowned me in guilt.

My gaze turns down to the floor as I attempt to calm myself down. I haven't had a panic attack in years, and I'm uncertain why this is triggering one.

I am capable. I can do this.

I remind myself over and over again, but the forcefulness of my thoughts only make my nerves worse.

Seamus expertly reads me again, interlaces his fingers in mine, and pulls my attention to him.

His eyes have softened and they're full of nothing but admiration, and I see my old Seamus again.

"I need you to touch me, before I prematurely lose it and *really* embarrass myself for the rest of my life."

Pulling my hand to his body, his palm is flat against the top of my hand, trailing it over his chest.

He blinks slowly as a long breath leaves his lips, like he's been unable to breathe without my touch.

I'm instantly addicted to his reaction. His desperate need and desire for me outweighs everything else, and I focus on inhaling and exhaling that match the rise and fall of his chest.

My hands begin to roam over his body, using just my fingertips to caress it. Goosebumps form over his skin as a shiver passes through him, and I'm hooked at how easily he responds to me.

Somehow, I'm able to form words and explain more about the Tantric connection as I continue to explore his body. Everyone can see what my hands are doing, but really the true purpose of this is to feel the emotional reaction between two people and the energy that's shared.

Ours is undeniably contagious, as I see other couples begin to explore each other.

I hook my fingers under the waistband of his boxers and trail my finger underneath the seam, teasing him expertly.

His cock twitches behind the thin cotton, and there is no hiding the massive bulge behind it.

I side-eye a glance over to his face. Verbally, I don't need to say anything. I feel everything between us. The admiration, the respect, the unrelenting desire, the craving our bodies have for each other. The undeniable connection that we've had from the first moment we saw each other all those years ago, that reignited the moment I saw him again.

Without saying anything, he lifts his hips slightly, giving me the permission I already knew I had. Slowly, I strip the last article of clothing that protects him. Exposing him completely to me, to his friends, to the entire class watching us.

And the entire time, his eyes never leave mine.

25

SEAMUS

My cock springs free as she pulls off the last article of clothing I had on, and a rush of cold air wraps around my cock, attempting to pull me out of heaven.

I know we aren't alone, but I don't care where we are or who the fuck is watching. I have her full attention and she has mine, so honestly, I care about nothing else.

Even seeing Christian, Jake, and Elena show up didn't faze me. Of course, they *had* to be here. I figured they would since they are so involved in everything that relates to the club. I just didn't realize I'd be in such a compromising position.

Regardless, I have no regrets offering myself to her. I'd rather her touch me than anyone else. And I damn sure would rather be exposed with all eyes on me, than witness people watching her.

If that happened, I'd end up in jail—for ripping everyone's eyeballs out of their sockets.

Her fingertips brush lightly over the thin skin of my achingly hard cock, as it lays erect on my stomach. The sensation pulls me out of my thoughts and my eyes back on hers.

She looks at me behind hooded eyes as she bites the corner

of her lip, and wraps her fingers around the base. My abs flex at the touch and everything is so sensitive.

I've never experienced the sort of sensations like I am now. Pricks of pleasure at every corner of my body, it's like a stroke of lightning passing through me when she grazes my skin, and it sears me to my core.

She's verbally explaining every touch and every pressure point as she begins to lightly massage my cock. Her hand cups underneath my balls as she puts pressure at the base behind them.

"This is the perineum. Gently, very gently, I'm making circular movements with light pressure to assist in more blood flow to the area," she tells the class.

An uncontrollable groan leaves my lips as my cock hardens even further. Precum leaks out of the tip and drips down the side and I moan again. Clenching my fists at my sides, I press the back of my head into the floor, which by way of physics, pushes my hips up slightly, allowing her better access to my fucking traitor perineum, forcing more precum out of my backstabbing cock.

"Fuck," I breathe out with a stutter.

I tilt my head to the side, looking over the crowd and instantly regret it.

Dane watches in awe and curiosity, eating up every word that Mimi is saying. His full attention is on my cock as he visually takes in all the techniques that she is describing.

Because it's Dane, I internally chuckle to myself that this is what it takes to get his undivided attention.

Hudson's palm is covering half his face, with his eyes peeking between his fingers.

Ember's flushed face is peering from over her clipboard— and it's interesting to see her demeanor in this situation, considering I know she likes to take control of Hudson in the bedroom.

Speaking of taking control, Mimi's teasing, languid strokes

change pace as she squeezes me with more pressure. Perfectly timed with a twist over the crown of my cock, an animalistic sound reverberates from my chest, echoing through the room.

What the fuck.

My whole body tenses as I uncontrollably arch my body toward Mimi. Squeezing my eyes shut, I blink heavily, then open my eyes wide, trying to get my shit together.

"Oh, Jesus. Fuck." Profanities and another unruly grunt comes from somewhere deep in my throat.

No one has ever paid so much attention to the area, and it's like she's tapped into some secret button to an instant fucking orgasm, because it's taking everything in me to hold back.

She begins moving both hands, synchronizing them in rhythm with her angelic voice, which are full blown words that I hear nothing of.

One hand massages my balls while the other strokes my cock, nothing short of some Jedi fucking mastery with the flawless amount of pressure and twisting.

"Mimi," I whisper, my tone dripping with desperation.

Her eyes connect with mine and the energy between us is like a wild force of nature. She appears collected as she expertly strokes my cock in front of a crowd full of people, hiding behind that professional mask of indifference, but I know she's just as affected as I am.

Her nipples harden behind the thin fabric of that stupidly small, transparent sports bra, and there's no hiding the blush covering the top of her chest and neckline that's fully exposed to me.

I turn my attention to the crowd again, avoiding eye contact with her because it will be my undoing. Seeing the need behind her eyes is too much for my body to handle.

My fingertips dig into my thighs as I hold on to any piece of myself to remain in control.

I can't lose control. I won't lose control.

Seeing the couples in the crowd, everyone is on edge. You can feel the hunger for sex in the air.

Some are kissing, some are naked, some are caressing each other. Another couple is face to face, looking deep into each other's eyes.

Hudson made his way back to Ember, his arms wrapped around her waist from behind as she observes the room, attempting to maintain her control and professionalism.

Dane disappeared and I have a feeling he found a couple to run off with.

Out of fucking nowhere, an indescribable pleasure radiates through my entire body as she presses underneath my balls at the base of my cock. A rope of milky cum shoots out of the tip, landing on my thigh, and my body jerks back in response.

It felt like the sensation right before a climax, except there was no build up or warning. My hips thrust upward as a reflex like it wants more before my brain catches up. I press into my elbows, my abs contracting as I sit up, attempting to pull myself away.

"What the fuck was that?"

Pressing her hand to my chest, she stops me from moving. Her eyes meet mine and I lose myself in her again. My control fades with every goddamn look she gives me with those cocoa-colored eyes drowning with lust.

"Let go, Seamus," she whispers to me. Pushing into my chest, she forces me back down on the mat.

Lifting my chin in the air, I push the back of my head back down onto the mat, and take a commanding breath. I allow my breath to release slowly, as my shoulders melt into the floor.

Let go.

I close my eyes, telling myself to focus on her touch and the sounds around me. Whimpers and moans play like an orchestra in the room, echoing off the walls and throughout the vast space.

Instead of thinking of everything I need to maintain control or avoid the feeling of Mimi touching me, I drown myself in her.

Her hand that wrapped around my arm that first day.

The feeling of how that felt before I even knew what she looked like.

The angelic sound of her voice as she first told me her name.

The gorgeous contours of her face, especially when she smiles and her eyes shine with a blinding light brighter than the sun.

The feeling the first time I pressed my lips to hers—the feeling that's never been replicated with anyone else.

The way her teeth pull in her bottom lip when she's turned on.

The way her eyes widened before rolling back behind her eyelids when I pressed my cock into her the first time. That exact moment when she gave herself to me fully.

My cock begins to harden, painfully. Mimi relentlessly continues, managing to touch every inch of my body even though her pure focus is just on my cock.

"That's it," she whispers, so only I can hear her.

"Let go, Seamus."

26

NAOMI

Seamus is finally starting to relax as I watch his cock continue to swell. It's so stiff and rigid, like him, but also ready to lose control. Just like him, in his current state.

Maintaining the pressure at the base of his balls, I slow my strokes and lighten my touch as I twist over the mushroom tip of his cock. His thunderous groan is like a megaphone announcement throughout the room.

A few heads turn our way, and I can't help my sly smile when I look at his delicious body and needy face.

I know I told him to let go, but edging him a little further—for educational purposes, of course—is the best thing to do for the students.

I release his cock and it remains ramrod straight up in the air, twitching like it's searching for more. I tease him for a moment while I remind the students a few techniques before looking back at him, and when I do, I'm struck with an overwhelming desire that I can no longer hide.

His lips are parted, his jaw slacked. He blinks heavily behind squinted eyes and furrowed brows, and I've never been so turned on by watching a man on the verge of coming.

Wrapping my hand back around his length, I give it one long stroke before massaging his balls again. Then I begin the systematic caressing, stroking and pressing of Tantric.

He bellows out a mournful cry that catches the attention of everyone.

"Fuck. Jesus. Goddammit," he whimpers out other profanities as his entire body tenses.

All eyes are on us, well, him, specifically. The students hold their breath as his cock grows harder and harder, his trembling body matching the unsteadiness in his voice, full of anguished moans.

A sharp groan permeates the air as his abs crunch up, forcing a jerk of his upper body as his cock spasms, erupting urgent and fast.

His cock pulses as it paints ropes of milky cum over his strained body and I continue to squeeze the shaft, caressing it carefully putting a tiny bit more pressure behind his balls.

"Oh God, Mimi. Fuck," he moans again, even louder this time as more cum jets out, dripping over his still hard cock.

Softening my touch, I begin to slow and allow him a moment to catch his breath. All the muscles are twitching as his body visibly melts into the mat.

When he opens his eyes, I can't help but smile, noticing the built up tension behind them has faded. Now, they are pliant. Relieved, almost. A light that wasn't there before shines through, softening his usually dark orbs. It's like seeing a physical burden lifted off someone and they can finally move without restraint.

I glance around the room, and he follows my gaze. All the couples are solely focused only on each other. An overwhelming calm washes over me as I see how beautiful everyone is, meeting each other in their current space, feeling comfortable and open.

Ember's eyebrows raise at me with a close, lipped smile, just as happy with the outcome. Our look is brief when Hudson pulls her away urgently and I have a feeling I won't be seeing her again today.

I have no idea where Dane went, but the couple that was sitting next him is gone, as well. And I don't see Christian Ford or the couple he was with.

A slight tinge of worry hits my stomach. I look around the room, but don't see them anywhere. I hope they enjoyed it as much as everyone else did.

Seamus must sense my worry as he sits up on his elbows.

"I guarantee you, they are in a room together," he says confidently.

I pick up the towel I stored nearby and wipe off his body. I can't help but smile at both his comment and the mess he made on himself.

"I think I won that round, Rambo." My playful tone makes his eyebrows rise over his forehead.

"If points equate to orgasms, I guarantee I'll win by a land-slide by the end of the night."

I bite my lip to hide my smile, because damn after the performance of what we just did, I could use a few. Just being around Seamus makes my body quiver with need, but seeing his restrained demeanor lose all control and inhibitions—it has me reeling for so much more.

"You sound so confident," I challenge.

Pressing into his hands, he pushes himself upright and I stand to meet him. We exchange looks for a passing moment, and it's full of a craving we both can no longer deny.

"You're in for it now, sunshine." Bending down, he picks me up, throwing my body over his shoulder, and I squeal as he saun-ters off the stage. I smack his naked ass playfully.

"Put me down, you animal!" But he and I both know I'm far from serious.

I never want him to put me down.

"Not a chance. We're going on our date, then I'm taking you home , and you'll be screaming my name all night long."

He smacks my ass back and I know he means every word.

27

NAOMI

It only took Seamus a few minutes to get dressed before he grabbed a bag from one of the rooms at Afterburn, and then walked me to his truck. He let me walk this time, which is a nice change, but I sort of hated it.

The twenty minute car ride was short, but full of banter between the two of us, just like our days by the lake. This time, reminiscing on the moments earlier in the night when I had him on stage and, what I referred to as, *desperate* and *begging*.

He used words like *necessary* and *essential*, stating it was for educational purposes as opposed to actually being lost in the moment.

"The penis doesn't lie, Seamus. You were so far gone and had no control over what I was doing to you," I tell him.

"Penis?" he questions. "Are we in the PG-13 version of the conversation now?"

"Penis is used during basic conversation. Cock and dick are reserved for the moments of madness, during actual sex," I reply, factually. "Using cock and dick too much is like swearing too much. Takes away its power."

"There will never be too much cock talk when you're talking

about mine." He passes me a sexy look before his gaze returns to the road.

He's still wearing his all black attire, but his button up shirt now has a couple loose buttons at the top and his sleeves are rolled up just under his elbows, exposing the tight lines of his mouthwatering forearms.

A light from the passing street light shines through the front windshield, and his strong form sits stoic on the console as he drives us to wherever he has planned for our date. He told me I didn't have to change, so I'm still currently wearing my all white leggings and sports bra with a light pink, oversized hoodie.

I'm a little disappointed I didn't get to wear the outfit I specifically bought for our date, but at the same time, it feels like the old us.

Seamus' truck veers onto a side road and we continue down the dirt path, going up a small, windy road that leads up a mountain.

We pull up to a wooded area, and I'm surprised when he pulls in and backs up in an open spot shaded by massive trees. There are no other buildings around, and I squint in confusion as I look around, seeing nothing.

"Stay here," Seamus says as he jumps out of the truck.

The dome light pops on as he opens the back passenger door, grabs a couple of bags, then shuts the door. The overhead light fades away immediately, leaving me in the dark as I look out over a stampede of silhouetted trees.

The only source of light is a sliver of the crescent moon, and I'm shocked when I shift my gaze to the sky, how clear it is tonight.

Seattle is known for its drab weather, and the thick, dense fog makes us forget we have a blue sky sometimes. Tonight's midnight sky has shed its layers, exposing itself to us fully.

A surge of anxiety runs through me as the minutes pass.

I have practiced some exposure therapy sessions, forcing

myself to hike through wooded areas and other things that my therapist had suggested to overcome some of the recurring panic attacks. This one I feel like I've mastered, but I've always been moving through it, not staying still.

I glance around again, and even though it's dark, it appears to be just woods and open air. I don't see a lake, thankfully, because I'm not sure I could stave off the panic attack if I had one.

The dome light slowly turns on, and my elbow falls to my thigh when my door pulls open.

Seamus stands with his phone in his hand, the flashlight shedding light on the ground so I can step out of the truck. I slide my hand in his extended one, giving myself something to hold on to.

"This way," he says, leading me to the back of the truck. He doesn't let go of my hand and he gently pulls us forward. I smile to myself when he rounds the back of the truck, popping open the tailgate. He's acting like we are going to climb a mountain and it's imperative that I hold his hand, but no. We literally just rounded his truck and walked to his truck bed.

With the truck gate open, he presses a button on the inner left side, and a string of twinkling lights glow soft white, trailing the sides of the truck.

A small gasp leaves my lips as I see a mound of fuzzy, warm blankets and a long, soft pillow laid across the back. A set of binoculars and a plate full of snacks sit on either side of bed.

I turn to look at Seamus as he appraises me with so much adoration. Between the gorgeous man in front of me and this entire set up, it's all so romantic.

It's also *so* triggering.

28

SEAMUS

"What's this?" she asks with more confusion than excitement.

I wasn't sure what I was expecting her reaction to be at the recreation of our nights at camp, but she's hesitant and totally on edge. I know the last time we saw each other was in this exact setting, minus the truck, but I want to explain everything. I want to share with her what happened and show her how much that short time meant to me.

"I wanted to relive my most cherished memories with you." My reply is instant, because those are the nights that are a constant loop in my mind, and she has no idea how much they helped me get through the last ten years.

I lived off the memory of her for too long, and now I intend to live off her presence.

A hint of a smile hits her lips before it falls again, as she takes a deep breath. She lifts her chin and rises to her full height as she turns around. Placing the palms of her hand on the back of the truck bed, she gracefully bends her knees as she jumps, sliding her butt onto a secure spot at the back of the tailgate.

"Well, now that you've got me here, what are you going to

do with me?" she asks the same exact question from years ago in the same playful tone.

Stepping between her legs, I meet her face to face and smile at the memory of everything that happened that night.

"Wanna play spin the bottle?" I playfully banter back.

Her neck cranes back as she pins me with a look of curiosity.

"Was that a joke, Rambo? Has my old Seamus finally returned or are you still the rigid Mr. Matthews?" Her lopsided smile melts my cold, dead, black heart.

Every encounter we've had since that night at Afterburn has been tense. She's on edge and uncertain, and I can't seem to say the right things. The years of holding myself back, not getting close to anyone, and years in the service have changed me. I'm not the same Seamus she knew those couple of weeks, but I've never felt closer to him than I do when I'm with her.

Her chocolate brownie eyes sparkle in the moonlight and a light sheen of gloss shines over her lickable lips. My eyes bounce between both, because I don't want to stop staring into the eyes that I've been craving for a decade, but I'm dying to kiss her.

There's no denying the sexual chemistry between us. The spark is like a gasoline fed fire that ignites into an uncontrollable inferno, and I feel her burn everywhere. But we need to talk before anything more happens between us that she can try and regret.

"Let's find Orion." Using my old friend as an icebreaker, I climb into the back of the truck and lay down with my arm splayed out to the side, inviting her in. She follows effortlessly like she always did and it feels like a lifelong puzzle is complete.

We lay in perfect silence, the scent of pine trees and sap heavy in the air. The breeze cascades through the brush, creating mother nature's soundtrack, and it's something I've been craving almost as much as I've craved her touch.

I stare up at the sky, breathing her in, feeling her mold against my body like a glove that was made just for me.

"That night was the best night of my entire life. Followed by the worst twenty-four hours after." I tell her, as she tips her chin up, resting it on my chest and I tilt mine down to meet her gaze.

"Tell me about it?"

29

SEAMUS

18 years old

"Did you see his face?" Mimi squeals. "He's always been such a jerk, I'm so glad I finally did that." She's on cloud nine after jabbing Nathan straight in his nose. I guess adrenaline will do that to you. Her giddiness is contagious as we laugh and tip toe run to our hidden area by the lake.

"That was the hottest thing I think I've ever seen," I say to her as we settle down by the water. I pull the rolled up blanket out of the bush where I've been hiding it and place it down on the ground. I always keep it here along with a spare sweater, in case she gets cold.

She plops down and runs her hands underneath her legs, making sure her dress isn't bunched up or showing anything, then criss-crosses her ankles in front of her as she leans back on her hands.

I kneel up beside her, but as I attempt to sit down, she tsks, holding up her finger.

"Aren't you supposed to be naked?"

I cock my head at her, confused at her assertiveness, but fuck, I can't say I don't love it.

"Like I said, I'll show you mine, if you show me yours." I banter back, reminding her of what I said earlier.

"You first." Her response is immediate, like she already decided hours ago this was going to happen.

"Are you sure you want to do this?" I ask. After our make out marathon the other night, she told me that she was a virgin. I didn't love hearing her go out of her way to say that, because I'd never want her to think that this is what that is all about. But I also can't say I haven't fantasized about this.

"I regretted not doing it the other night." I love hearing her confession.

I press into my hands, pushing up to my full height as I kick off my shoes and turn around to face her. I glance around the bushes, the trees, the lake, and everything that surrounds us. It's quiet, serene, and only the music from the dance hall can be heard in the far distance.

I attempt to wrap my hands around the bottom hem of my shirt, but I forgot it was a button up that Shane let me borrow, so I change direction and begin to undo the buttons.

I feel a tad awkward because nothing about me feels sexy, just the gorgeous girl in front of me whose lips part slightly as the shirt begins to flay open.

She bites her bottom lip which gives me a bit of confidence.

I continue taking off my clothes, until I'm standing in just my boxers, taking another glance around to make sure no one is around.

"Like what you see?" I ask with more confidence than I feel, and she nods quickly, still sucking on that bottom lip. "Your turn."

Bending her knees, she pushes herself up, standing only a few inches from me. Reaching over to her side, she unzips her dress, pushing the straps off her shoulders. The shiny fabric falls quickly, pooling at her wedge heels.

She's not wearing a bra, just pink, cotton underwear, and my mouth falls open.

"Holy shit."

Her breasts are fucking perfect. They look soft and full, and the silky strands of her long, onyx hair drape over the front of her, covering only portions of the peaks of her breasts, acting as the perfect tease.

A breeze blows between us. It's warm and light, but strong enough to blow some of the hair that was covering her chest behind her. Her arms instantly come up to cover herself.

Knowing she feels exposed and uncomfortable, I step forward, placing my hand on her waist and pull her close to me.

Leaning down, I kiss the shell of her ear, debating on so many things to say. I want to tell her how beautiful she is. How I've thought of nothing but her since we met. How I wish we could stay like this, here, forever, hiking during the day and looking at the stars at night. She makes me feel like my life has a purpose.

"Promise me this doesn't end after camp. Promise me we're more than this." I pull back to look into her eyes. I need her to see how serious I am.

The smile behind her eyes shines through, even in our dim surroundings. And when she nods, I can't help but crush my lips to hers. The kiss is frantic and messy, it's nothing like the other ones we've had.

It's like we've finally given ourselves permission and we've both been unleashed. I feel so goddamn desperate for her.

I wrap both my arms around her body as her arms circle around my shoulders.

Bending our knees, we both kneel down on the blanket, not allowing ourselves to break from our kiss.

The clock tower bell chimes, echoing through the camp-

grounds. She pulls away to glance over her shoulder to where all the cabins are.

"It's midnight," she says as my eyes bounce between her and the cabins, not caring at all what time it is. She's got me on edge, literally, but more so because I think she's worried about getting caught, that she's going to bail right here and now.

"Happy Birthday," she says softly, as she turns back to me.

Shit. I completely forgot it was my birthday.

"I don't have flowers for you, but I've been wanting to give you something else."

My breath hitches as she dips her hands inside the waistband of my boxers, then wraps her fingers around my cock, stroking the length. She leans forward, pulling down the fabric with one hand as she continues to stroke with the other.

She wastes no time as her lips enclose over the tip and she pushes forward, taking more than half of it in her mouth. Warmth radiates through my entire body as she bobs her head back and forth. I can't help but fist a handful of her hair to help me feel grounded.

Her tongue makes circles around the tip before she pushes me further into her mouth. She continues to repeat that movement, spreading fire through my veins each time she plunges forward.

An animalistic grunt comes out from the middle of my chest, and I throw my body back on the blanket as her head bobs up and down over my aching cock.

"Jesus, Mimi. Fuck."

My body movements are choppy and she's absolutely relentless. It's taking everything in me to hold back.

I look down at the same time her eyes lift to meet my gaze. I've never seen anything sexier than her on her knees, with her mouth full of my cock, eyes locked on mine as she moans like she's the one getting pleased.

My hips, having a mind of their own, pump forward. My cock hits the back of her throat, making her gag. She pulls back, slightly out of breath and coughing.

"Shit. I'm sorry," I say, as I sit back up.

"It's okay," she says, as a giggle escapes her.

I lift her chin to make sure she's really okay, and when that seductive smile hits me, I feel it to my bones.

"Fuck, you're perfect."

Crawling over her, I hover my body over hers, my painfully hard cock pressing between us.

Reaching down, I tuck my hand into her panties and my fingers graze over her already soaked pussy.

"You like sucking my cock." It's a statement, not a question, because it's obvious, but she nods anyway.

Running the tip of my finger over her slit, her mouth drops open and she moans louder than she should. I cover her mouth with my hand and continue to massage circles over her clit. Her eyes widen as she bucks up into my hand. I release the hand covering her mouth and bring a finger up to my mouth, doing the universal shhhh *sign.*

Pinching the bundle of nerves, she gasps and another begging moan echoes through the trees. I immediately reach down, wrapping my hand around her throat in an attempt to get her attention.

Instead, her eyes widen as her mouth falls open even further. Little groans vibrate from her chest as she pushes up into my grip on her neck. I grip a little harder and she fucking explodes. Her climax is sudden and so hard. She's bucking into my hand as she gasps for air.

She loved my hand on her throat.

Jesus, that was so goddamn sexy.

My cock aches from watching her fall apart like that.

"Fuck, Mimi. I need you." Releasing my hands, I tuck my fingers into the sides of her cotton panties, ripping them down

her legs. Lining my body flush on top of hers, I grip my cock, squeezing the base as I press the tip at her entrance.

"Tell me if it hurts." I press in slowly. The tip disappears and I press in further. I can't help but moan at how good she feels. The sensation of her tight, wet walls swallowing my cock, the desire in her eyes, all of it feels so fucking good.

I'm halfway in when I feel resistance and a bit of pressure. I pause, taking in her expression, but she just nods and pulls my hips closer.

I thrust in deeper, and it's as if I push past a wall. She whimpers and I remain motionless inside of her.

"You okay?"

Her eyes are closed as she nibbles on the inside of her lip, nodding, her eyes still slammed shut.

I stay still for another moment, then she rolls her hips up into mine.

"Please move. God, please move," she begs.

My cock twitches at her begging.

I pull back and slowly press back in, repeating that movement a few times before she begs again.

"Seamus, I'm okay. Please…give me more." My eyes roll to the back of my head as I hold my breath, attempting to reel myself in.

Her fucking begging gives every cell in my body its own personal orgasm, exploding like fireworks, making my entire body shutter.

I lean closer into her, using one hand to prop myself up and the other to move between, pinching her nipples and rubbing her clit. She wraps her legs around my waist and I plunge back into her.

Our breathing is labored, and uncontrollable moans echo through the trees around us, but right now I care about nothing else but her. Let them catch us. Let the world see what she does to me.

"Oh God, Seamus. I feel like I'm going to explode." Keeping my pace, I reach down and swipe at her clit again. I watch as my cock moves in and out of her. Her arousal and pinkish specks of blood streak my dick, and it hits me that I didn't even think about a condom.

"Fuck," I blurt out as her hips roll into me, her legs tightening around me, pulling me even deeper inside of her.

"I'm coming. Don't stop, please God, don't stop."

I tell myself to hold back as her walls contract around me. I have to pull out. Fuck, her pussy is like a vise around my cock, and I grunt out as I feel my orgasm coming.

I thrust twice more, my cock jerking, before her legs loosen their grip. My orgasm hits me as I push back and finally pull out, cum already dripping from the tip.

Wrapping my hands around my cock, I stroke myself through my orgasm, grunting as I watch the ropes of white cum paint her stomach, pussy, and the blanket we're laying on.

I didn't mean to do that, but I couldn't pull any further away so I just literally came all over her.

She looks down at herself, mouth dropped open, then peers back up at me.

"I'm...sorry. I remembered right before I came that we didn't use a condom. I fucked up." I sit back on my heels in defeat. My body high from my orgasm but freaked the fuck out about, one; not using a condom and two; I just used her body like a cum rag.

She laughs. She fucking laughs.

"I can't believe you did that." Still giggling, her arms are splayed out like she just got doused in slime. Which isn't entirely far off.

"Is this funny?" I ask, laughing too as I grab my boxers, using them to wipe her off. It's the only article of clothing that we can spare without missing clothes when we get back to our cabins.

"I should have said something, too, but I was so worked up.

Thank you for pulling out," she shyly admits as she starts to dress.

I still feel horrible. But she's right, At least I pulled out.

I grab my clothes and start to dress quickly. I have no idea how much time has passed—or, frankly, what planet I'm on— so I'm surprised when I glance around and the lights from the main hall are all off.

She bends forward slipping on her underwear, but pauses as she looks out into the distance.

"Oh my God. I see him." She's tilting her head slightly to the right.

"See who?" I ask, ducking behind the bush as I grab her arm to bring her with me, looking around for someone who might be headed our way.

"No. Silly. Orion." She whispers his name in amazement, then points to exactly where my old friend lives in the sky.

Standing to my full height, I smile as I pull her into me. Wrapping my arms around her body, I kiss the top of her head.

"We only have two more days," I say, as reality hits me again.

"Let's make the best of it," she replies as she turns to face me.

Her arms wrap around my shoulders as mine wrap around her waist. Dipping my forehead to hers, I wonder how she was able to work her way into my heart so quickly, branding herself there so easily.

"Is this what love feels like?" she whispers, unsure and vulnerable.

I crook my finger and lift her chin to look at me as I grow a smile I can't hold back. "I think so."

I kiss her like I'll never be able to do it again, because I'm terrified. Terrified to think after two days I won't have this same feeling. The one where my heart beats faster the moment I see her, the feeling of pure adrenaline whenever I just hear her voice. The sensation of complete happiness when I see her smiling.

Finally pulling apart, I finish buttoning up my shirt as she begins to step into her dress. She pauses, leans down, and squints as she looks past me.

I turn around and see two camp leaders with flashlights heading where the guys' cabins are.

"Shit." I duck behind my go-to bush and flail my arm out to barricade her behind me.

"Go, Seamus. You have to go." She tries to push me out on the side of the bush. "Go around the backside."

She's right.

"You're so beautiful," I say as I cup both my hands around her cheeks and kiss her hard before letting go. I race toward the bushes, giving her a quick glance back, still beaming a wide smile, then bolt over to the cabins.

Sneaking in the backdoor, I enter through the showers and crouch down through the doorway until I'm able to jump into my bunk.

I tuck myself in under the blanket, knowing the camp leaders are making rounds and I don't have time to change into anything else.

I'm still riding my Mimi high, wondering how the hell I got so lucky that she picked me. In two weeks, she's taken my sour outlook on life and given me a hope I never knew existed.

The cabin of our sleeping quarters' front door creaks open, and I see a camp leader and the camp counselor walk through it. One turns off their flashlight while the other covers it to give just enough light to look around the room.

Shit! *I duck further down under my blankets to hide. My thoughts wander in a million different directions. Did they find Mimi? Are they looking for me?*

My eyes are half covered, so I don't see anyone before they tap on the side of the bed. I peek over the blanket, pretending to have been sleeping, I blink heavily as I open my eyes.

"Seamus, you need to get up. Please come with us." Their tone isn't demanding or harsh, like I'm in trouble for something. It's…soft…concerning.

"Why?" I ask, pushing up onto my elbows. "What's going on?"

"Your mom's in the hospital. It's time to go home."

30

NAOMI

Present Day

"They urgently rushed me to the hospital" He pauses and swallows hard. "She died before I could make it there."

"Oh, Seamus. I'm so sorry." My voice cracks and my words feel broken. My hand is covering my chest like my heart physically hurts at the pain of his words.

"There was so much confusion and I felt so lost. I didn't know what to do. A couple days passed—I don't know, maybe it was three—when I finally was able to pick up the phone and call the camp to find you, to talk to you. And I live in so much fucking regret waiting that long."

He palms his face. The pads of his fingertips pinch into his eyelids as if he's clearing them of unwanted tears without me realizing.

"I called and everyone was already gone. Apparently, they had closed down the camp. I just called back at the right time and was able to talk someone into looking up your name, but they couldn't find anyone by the name of Mimi, and I didn't know what your last name was. Two weeks, everyday together, and I never asked you your fucking last name."

My heart is breaking for him, for the loss of his mother. And for us, for the time that was stolen from us because of a series of unfortunate events.

I want to tell him about how that was also the best night of my life, followed by the worst twenty-four hours, as well. But, the mood is somber enough. I don't need him to feel anything except the emotions he needs to work through right now. I don't know this version of Seamus well, but I have a feeling he's never talked this deeply about us or his mother with anyone.

"Does Hudson know?" I ask, curious if he's ever opened up. Because if he has, it would have been with him.

"He knows she died while I was away at camp. He was at the funeral with me. But I never told him about you. I never told anyone. For a while, I thought you were a made-up dream. Something I conjured up to get me through." He huffs out a heavy breath and runs his hand through his hair.

"Then I scolded myself for attaching myself to you. Questioning whether or not you were a figment of my imagination or a real life angel whose memories I clung to because I needed them to survive."

All these years, I've taught myself to hate him, to try and forget the time we shared because the memories were just too painful to push through some days. Yet, this entire time he's been clinging to them like they're his lifeline.

My heart hurts, it feels heavy in my chest as I breathe through the pain.

We both suffered in different ways because of our circumstances.

"I looked for you, I tried to search for any link I had to try and find you. I knew Shane's last name, *Smith*." He rolls his eyes. "Do you know there are fucking thousands of Shane Smiths in Texas?"

I laugh at the lightness that's finally coming through and nuzzle into him further.

"When I saw you at Afterburn that night, all dressed in halo white, I almost died. You went from being a spirit in my dreams to being an angel in reality, and I had no idea how to process it. That was until you kicked me in the nuts and then I really wanted to die." I toss my head back in a laugh and cover my face in embarrassment.

"I had ten years of built up anger to unleash." I smack his arm playfully.

"Oh I know, and you unleashed it in one swift kick, sunshine." I laugh again, the memories of our nights together flashing in the forefront of my mind.

God, I've missed him.

"I'm glad you did, because I knew at that moment it was real. You were real," he says as he tucks a stray hair behind my ear, tugging gently on my ear.

"So, you looked me up after that and bought my neighbor's house?" I ask, raising a questioning eyebrow at his tactics.

"I was determined. I *am* determined." He shifts on his side to face me fully.

"In my head, you've always been mine. But I won't stop until the entire fucking world knows it."

"Seamus…" I whisper.

"I won't stop, Mimi. I'll live next door, watching you, because I can't keep my eyes off you. I'll protect you even if you don't need it. I'll never give up on the idea of us."

I open my mouth to reply, but he holds a finger up to my lips.

"I know it will take time to trust me, I'll spend the rest of my life earning it."

I shake my head. I understand the circumstances as to why he left. And in my heart, I always knew he would have never left intentionally like he did. But that night changed…everything.

When he left, a fear of abandonment branded itself to me,

and the repercussions after left long term scars that I still have no idea how to process.

I've never been able to get close to any man. I've avoided opening up emotionally and physically, withholding my deepest sexual desires with any of the men I tried with.

Albeit, there weren't many. But those men also never tried to make me feel comfortable. I always used the excuse, that I liked giving pleasure and being in control as a reason to avoid them touching me or having to get physical with them in other ways, but I know I need to be honest with Seamus.

"I need to tell you something. But I'm afraid of what may happen if I do," I confess.

His brows furrow as his dark eyes fill with concern. He pushes himself up further on his elbow, giving me his full attention.

"You know you can always tell me anything, nothing will change how I feel about you."

I doubt it.

I roll over onto my back and close my eyes as I take a deep breath. I just hope what I am going to share with him doesn't change how he feels about me.

I open my mouth to finally share with him what's been weighing on me for a decade, but a large water droplet lands on my nose and splashes over my cheek. Then another on my forehead.

Suddenly, a flash of lightning pierces the sky, and heavy rain-drops begin pelting on everything. What feels like buckets of water come barreling down, it's instant and overwhelming.

"Oh my God!" I scream as we both urgently sit up at the same time, ducking our chins into our chest to avoid the flash flood from careening down on our faces.

"It wasn't supposed to rain tonight!" Seamus says loudly over the water that's beating against all the trees around us.

The slapping of the droplets overlap each other as the rain

gets heavier and heavier. It only takes seconds and we're completely drenched. Seamus pushes himself out of the back of the truck bed, his feet slapping down onto the already muddied ground before one foot slips from underneath him.

He uses one hand as a base on the back of the tailgate to balance himself and holds the other out to help me down.

A beat of thunder rolls through the air, slipping itself in between the pelting of the rain before another flash of lightning cuts through the sky.

"This is the Pacific Northwest. You should always anticipate rain." I have to yell over the sound of the rhythmic downpour and crackling thunder.

Sliding my hand into his, he pulls me down to a standing position at the back of his truck. It's a stark contrast how soft his touch is, how gentle he is, considering the mayhem of our current situation.

"This isn't rain, this is a goddamn monsoon." He steps around the back of the truck, still holding my hand, but as I go to follow, I lose my footing and begin to slip forward. He grips my hand to prevent my fall, but it's completely useless. It's like gravity is forcing me down. Instead of letting me go, he attempts to pull me forward, his own feet slipping from underneath him, and I fall face forward as he lands straight on his ass.

"You've got to be fucking kidding me." He's holding his hands out to his sides, looking at the muddy damage decorating his body, and I can't help but laugh.

It starts as a small giggle, then ascends into a full body, rolling onto my back, holding my stomach jerking as I laugh. Nothing about it is attractive, but neither is our current situation.

"Is this funny, sunshine?" His tone is deep and serious, yet as his eyes peer over to me, there is a touch of playfulness that I remember in my old Seamus.

But I know that modern day Seamus is dying inside. The heavy rain makes his face shine in the moonlight, the speckled with mud particles dress his cheeks and forehead while his hair is completely drenched and plastered to his head.

He sits up, swinging one mud-caked leg over my body, straddling me completely. His knees dig into the ground as he leans over the top of me, protecting me from the rain.

"You better stop laughing," he says with a tinge of a smile behind his serious tone.

Of course, I don't stop laughing.

So he leans further down, slamming his lips into mine. I greedily accept his kiss as my laughter instantly turns into a needy moan.

31

SEAMUS

What the hell good are weather apps and meteorologists if they can't manage to actually get the weather predictions correct? Seriously, they have one job.

I can't say I mind too much, considering it's landed me straddling Mimi with our tongues dancing together, drenched in the rain.

Something shifted tonight.

I don't know if it started with the Tantric massage, and if that really is some magical gateway to an open connection that we both needed, or if we're both just getting back to our roots of where we began together. But tonight, I feel it. We both do.

My tongue continues to explore her mouth and lips, and I can't get enough. I want more, but here in the woods, in the middle of an unplanned monsoon, is probably not the place to do it.

We're drenched, plastered with mud, and I couldn't be happier that I have a couple of dry blankets in the back of my truck for us.

"Come on." Pushing myself up, I take her hand as we both stand and trek through the mud to the passenger door of my truck. I grab the blanket from the back, quickly caping it around her, wrapping her like a burrito, then helping her into the front seat.

I run around the back, my feet slipping a bit in the mud as I close the tailgate, grab the extra dry blanket, and jump in the driver's side.

Starting the truck, I make our way back to our houses and she scooches over closer to my side, leaning her head on my shoulder.

I love her like this. It's like the old Mimi who was always so wild and free, who always wore her heart on her sleeve and a smile on her face. I feel my old self coming back, too. The one who had moments of happiness when my mother was around, because she made me feel like I meant something to someone.

Even with that, I can sense she's holding something back. I can only assume she's still reluctant to trust me due to our history of having ten years of feeling abandoned without any explanation. But I'm fine with spending a lifetime earning it back.

I lean down, kissing her wet hair, and I can physically feel her nuzzle deeper into me.

"They said your mom had an accident. Can I ask what happened?" she asks, quietly.

I think back on that moment. I remember my mind racing as to what kind of accident she had. I immediately thought she was in a car accident, and had no idea what to do or how to process.

I wasn't proud of the fact that I hoped, for a split moment, my dad was driving drunk and would finally get what was coming to him. But if that was the case, they would have told me something happened to my dad, not my mom.

When I realized what the actual accident was, I knew it wasn't a fucking accident.

"She *fell* down the stairs." I glance at Mimi as her eyes look up to mine, and she knows.

I retreated into myself that senior year. Holding in what I knew was the truth because no one would believe me. No one would believe that my father, Deputy Sheriff Matthews could be capable of violence.

My mother never reported any of her other *accidents*, so when I accused him of pushing her, everyone in the hospital just thought I was making something up to help with my grieving.

"My father was the Deputy Sheriff where we lived. No one believed me." I grip the steering wheel tighter, recalling all the moments of abuse and hidden violence my mother endured.

There is a distinct sound that leads to an indescribable fear when you hear the blunt force punch of a fist against a face. But when you know and love the person who is taking that hit, it jars your soul.

I had spent too many years doing nothing. Hiding like my mother had told me to and avoiding him when he was drinking. Remaining quiet for months after she died. The rage consumed me until I couldn't take it anymore.

"One night, a few months after she died, he came home drunk with a woman from the bar. I completely lost it. I called her a whore, tried to get her to leave, but he defended her. We were nearing Christmas break and I was close to graduating a semester early, pushing myself to complete my diploma so I could leave, but I couldn't stand the thought of him having another woman in our house—my mother's home—so I started a fight with him." I swallow thickly, recalling the moment I swung first and how shocked he was.

Mimi sits up and shifts her body to face me, giving me her full attention. I'm still hyper focused on the road, trying to see through the thick blanket of rain. It's heavy, but lighter than it was when we were in the woods. I know I probably shouldn't be having such an emotional conversation while driving through an intense rainstorm, but I've always strived under these conditions.

"I beat him so badly he was hospitalized for a week. He gave me a choice; enlist in the military or he would press charges against me. He was a well-respected town cop and I was his *disobedient, juvenile son with a bad temper*." I air quote. "You know the rest."

Pulling into my driveway, I shut off the truck and turn to face her. The rain has stopped completely now, so when I turn off the ignition, there is nothing but pure silence that rings through the car between us.

The flood light that I installed beams on and light shines through the windshield, bringing me a view of her gorgeous, gold speckled, dark chocolate eyes. There's a sorrowness behind them, but full of pride. Like she's proud of me, and I've never had someone look at me like that. Not since before my mother died.

"I don't know the rest. The rest is your life. It's what has made Seamus…Seamus. I'd like to hear the rest whenever you want to tell me." She leans in, kissing my shoulder she was just leaning on. "Now come on, let's get our muddy asses out of this truck and into my house. We need a shower."

She reaches for the door handle, letting herself out, and when she looks back at me, it's like I'm falling in love all over again. Giving me a playful wink, she dips her head at her front door with a smile, and I'm a total goner for her.

My God, this woman.

Something has shifted between us and she's opening herself up, allowing me in. Not only does it feel like the old us, but it feels like a more powerful us. And I won't take it for granted.

I have no idea what I did right in this world to have her come back into my life, but I'm never letting her go.

My phone buzzes in my pocket as I reach for my keys and wallet, but I ignore it as I exit my truck. I trail behind her as she unlocks her front door. My phone buzzes a second and third time. Now I'm curious. Pulling it out, I glance at the messages to see Rocco sending me a few images followed by a text message.

Rocco: I'm not sure what you're looking for, but if it has anything to do with the court case she and her parents had, those are completely sealed. But, because I'm me, I should have the details on that before tomorrow. In the meantime, her full medical background starting from when she was eighteen years old is here.

I don't really need to worry about digging into that too much right now, but as I go to shut off the screen, my finger grazes over the image and the screenshot enlarges.

The image of a medical record pops up and the first line reads: ***Termination of pregnancy.***

Dated only a couple months after she turned eighteen.

It's like I got dropped out of a tornado and everything around me is spiraling. I stumble, taking a long stride to catch myself. I've never felt so taken off guard before, so unprepared for something so shocking.

My breathing picks up and all my emotions are battling each other simultaneously.

Anger, sadness, frustration, rage.

"Seamus?" Mimi calls out as she looks at me concerned.

I look up to her, in shock, my breathing still labored.

"You had an abortion?"

32

NAOMI

*Y*ou had an abortion?

Four words totaling one question I've been dreading hearing from him. Something I knew he would say once I told him, but I didn't have to tell him. Somehow, whatever he's looking at already confirmed it.

"How do you know that?" I ask, my voice barely audible.

His face falls, like he wasn't ready for that confirmation.

I glance down at his phone in his hand. "What are you looking at?"

"It's true?"

Although his face is sheet white, his emotions are written all over his face for the first time ever. Morphing between confusion, sadness, and anger.

My door is wide open, but I'm turned facing him, his foot on the first step of my porch, rooted there in shock.

This is not how I envisioned telling him, and now I'm so mad at myself for not telling him sooner.

"Please come in, so we can talk," I tell him, holding out my hand, begging him with my eyes.

Please take my hand.

He looks at it, then back at me, tilting his head with a look like he doesn't know who I am anymore, and it's breaking my fucking heart.

"You knew my last name, you could have found me. You could have told me. Why didn't you fucking find me?" He takes a step up as I step forward, and we're now level like we were the first night I found out he moved in next door.

This is a side of Seamus I have never seen. Even when we were kids, he was never angry. He's always been so controlled, and even more so as a military trained adult. He's the most difficult man to read. But right now, anger drips off him in waves, and I feel it all the way to my bones.

I push my hand closer to him. "Please, come inside."

Instead of reaching out for me, he runs both his hands through his hair, taking another step back. His eyes are bouncing all over the place, like he's trying to piece everything together in his head with all the unanswered questions.

"I could have been there for you. Regardless if you kept it or not. I could have been there, Mimi. I could have…" I cut him off, because his words are like daggers to my heart.

"It might not have been yours."

His foot slips off the last step as his feet stumble to the ground. His brows are furrowed, his eyes are boring into mine, and he looks like he's in physical pain.

He's pacing, mumbling to himself. Probably going through the entire two weeks in his head, wondering if what we had was real.

"Seamus," I call out his name, because I'm losing him.

He's always seen me, watched me. And when I would look into his eyes, I could see so much desire and need. Now they are vacant. Dead.

I imagine they look exactly like how he's felt the last ten years, disassociating himself from everything he saw and felt during his time in the military. Protecting himself from feeling anything.

His back is now facing me as he stares at the ground. His head hangs heavy, like he's defeated and he has come to terms with what he just heard, and whatever reasoning he's settled on. He's getting lost in his head about what this is, and I *need* to explain.

"I need you to come inside, Seamus. I gave you the chance to tell your story, you need to let me tell mine," I say, my voice soft but stern. I need to pull him back to me.

He can step away and choose not to listen, or he can turn around and hear me out.

I can't hold back anymore. I never talk about it and never share what happened. Only my parents, Penny, and my therapist know, but he deserves to know and I *want* to tell him.

I was forced to tell my parents what happened, forced to tell the police, and my therapist, and Penny found out just by way of coming into my life shortly after that time.

This is the first time I've ever felt the desire to tell my story because I want to, and not out of obligation.

"Nathan raped me."

NOTE TO READER

A VERY IMPORTANT TRIGGER WARNING:

Your mental health is important to me.

The following chapter contains content that can be extremely triggering.

The following scene is violent and completely non-consensual. If that is triggering for you, please consider skipping the next chapter.

The book is written in such a way that allows you to have the full experience of the story without reading it.

SKIP TO CHAPTER 34

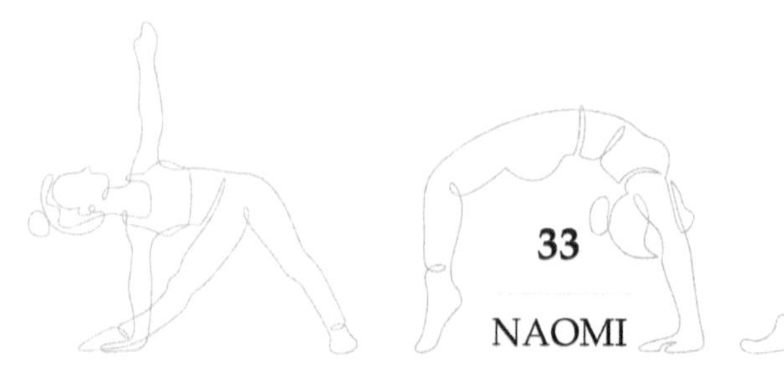

33

NAOMI

18 years old

I watch Seamus run toward the bush barrier that separates us from the view of the cabins. He takes a quick glance back at me, wearing a contagious smile before breaking out into a full sprint behind the hedge.

My emotions are leapfrogging everywhere. Excitement, giddiness, worry for Seamus not being able to make it back in time, and sadness that we only have another full day before camp ends.

Holding the sweater he left, I hug myself with an uncontrollable smile and sniff the fabric that still smells like him. It's a mix of the woods we spent so much time in, the scent that makes him distinctly him. Like fresh linen and cedar.

I glance down, attempting to find my dress and shoes, when I hear the snap of a twig behind me. I immediately duck down to hide myself, but before I can, I hear a man's voice sing-songing, "I see you."

Nathan.

I stop and turn around, hiding myself with the sweater. I only have my underwear on and minimal protection from the hoodie, so I crouch down to cover myself as much as possible.

"What are you doing here?" I grit through my teeth.

"We're just out for a late night walk." He slurs the last few words a bit as he walks toward me, and I notice he has a beer bottle in his hand.

"We?" I ask, looking behind him, but don't see anyone. He ignores my question as his hooded, bloodshot eyes rake over my body.

"I'm just leaving," I say as I pull the sweater over my head. Luckily, it's huge on me and falls just above my knees. I stand, grabbing my dress in one hand and shoes in the other.

"No, I think we should hang out for a bit. I mean, you owe it to me for almost breaking my nose," Nathan says, stepping directly in front of me, lifting his chin with a slight turn to show me the swelling and bruising.

"I'm sorry about that," I say, even though I'm not at all sorry about it. Moving around him, he sidesteps in front of me, stopping me. I step to the other side and he follows, blocking me again.

My heartbeat kicks up another notch and my breath is short. I'm trying to maintain my composure and not show him how terrified I am, but I'm failing.

"Nathan, let me through." He just stands in place, staring at me with evil laced in his eyes. I look down at the beer bottle he's holding, knowing that is contributing to his erratic behavior, unsure how many he's had tonight.

Looking over his shoulder, the pathway is there, lit up by just the moonlight, and I am desperate to just run for it. The lake is directly behind me, and there is no other way to get out.

"I'm going." I push past him, but as my shoulder brushes his, he grips the nape of my neck, pulling me back. My hands fly up to my head, attempting to pull him off, but he's too strong. The

sting of hair pulling and the yanking of my neck makes me squeal out in pain.

"That's not the only thing that's going to make you scream tonight, you fucking whore." He slams my body into the ground, pressing my face into the dirt as I cough and breath in the earthy particles. It's like chalk on my tongue, and only gets worse as his hand presses harder at the back of my skull.

"Nathan, please don't do this." My words are muffled as more dirt smears on my cheek and over my mouth.

My fingers claw into the dirt as I attempt to push myself up, but he slams his knee into my lower back, pressing me down. He leans forward, his hands find my wrists, putting all his weight onto them.

"You're hurting me," I manage to spit out, but it sounds like barely a whisper, even though I feel like I'm screaming inside.

I kick my legs and use all my strength to move my arms. I manage to get my right arm out from his grip, but he uses that free hand to grab a handful of my hair, pulling hard before slamming my face back down onto the ground.

A twig breaks underneath my cheek, and the sting that cuts through my skin feels like salt on an open wound.

For a brief moment, I'm in denial. That this isn't really happening. This can't be happening.

But I put myself in this position by sneaking out with Seamus, and it's my fault I'm here.

And it's my fault I hit Nathan, that I made him so angry that he's paying me back for embarrassing him.

Everything is my fault.

Tears stream down my cheeks and all I can do is beg and plead with him to stop. The volume of my words vary between a whisper and a scream, and I can't decipher or process any of the words I'm using.

"Nathan, please stop," I beg. "Stop!" I scream, as I throw my head back and forth.

"Shut up!" he screams as he turns me over.

Blinding pain explodes behind my right eye as he backhands me, and my body goes limp.

"I've done nothing but been nice to you, Mimi." Gripping the collar of the hoodie, he yanks it hard, pulling my neck off the ground as he tries to tear it off, but it's too thick and doesn't budge.

"Fuck!" he yells in frustration, and it's terrifying how angry he is.

A crash of broken glass echoes around me and he holds the bottle up to my neck. My eyes widen as I stare into his enlarged pupils, blown out and invading everything behind his evil eyes.

Pressing into the thick cloth, he saws mindlessly at the corner of the collar, and the fabric tears easily. My hair is a victim to his mindless cutting, and loose strands float around me, landing on my face and now exposed chest.

Tossing the bottle, he uses both his hands and rips the sweater down the middle. The sound rings through my ears. His unwanted touch gropes me aggressively as I plead for him to stop. But he just keeps going. I squint hard, hoping this is a nightmare, but when I reopen my eyes, he's still there, holding me down.

His fingernails pinch into the side of my hips gripping my underwear, then he yanks hard, using my own body to rip them off. He tosses them away, leaving me completely naked.

"No." I try to protect myself with my heavy arms, but it's no use when he smacks them away.

He kicks my legs open as he unzips his pants, and the weight of his body sits heavily on my hips. I scream when he pushes into me, and the excruciating pain travels from my core all the way to my throat. A thousand needles pierce my insides. My organs explode and my heart feels like it dies.

My heart, my mind, my soul. I can feel pieces of myself falling away.

This isn't happening. This isn't happening.

I squeeze my eyes shut and open them, trying to find clarity. Trying to understand.

Another hard thrust and I wail out again as he squeezes my breasts hard, the pain radiating through my entire body.

My arms fly up to protect myself, and I have one more burst of strength as I attempt to kick him off me, flailing my arms at his chest, swinging and hitting.

My weak pleas get louder as I push myself to fight.

Keep fighting, Mimi. Just keep fighting.

I have more in me. I have more fight left in me.

I manage to land one punch to the corner of his chin, making him slouch back briefly. Taking my chance, I crawl away from him, clawing at the dirt in the ground to help my get away. My bare feet grip enough of the earth to push myself away but his hand wraps around my ankle, pulling me back as he hits me again. This time, the back of his hand crushes the side of my face, and it feels like my eardrum detonates behind my jaw.

"That's it." His exasperated voice sounds muffled, like I'm hearing him underwater. My vision is blurred and nothing makes sense anymore. I open my eyes and the sky is spinning. He's dragging me. The rocks and twigs bite at my back, but I don't feel pain anymore. I don't feel anything anymore.

Droplets of water splash around me. The lapping of waves mix with footsteps, and suddenly liquid ripples over my bare feet, traveling up my legs until my entire body is drenched.

The lake.

It's cold and bitter, harsh against my scored skin.

He presses my face further into the ground and the waves crash over my eyes, matting my knotted hair to my cheeks. I try to breathe, but it's a mix of air, and liquid, and pure fear. I choke on water and gag as I gasp for breath.

He loosens his hold and I push myself up, heaving, begging for him to stop.

"Scream again and that's what you'll get." He holds my cheeks with one hand as he grabs my wrists with the other, holding them over my head as the water laps around us. "Are you going to scream, Mimi?"

It's like staring into the devil's eyes as I give in to him, to save my life. My fight is gone and I have nothing left. I just need to survive.

I shake my head, my eyes so fucking heavy, and everything just hurts. Everything hurts so much. I squeeze my eyes shut. Tears blend with the droplets that coat my face as he pushes into me again.

I don't scream. I don't fight. I just wince with every numb thrust as the silent tears continue to fall.

The pressure is so painful on my weak wrist joints as he bears all his weight onto me. I wiggle my wrists, but he only presses into me harder, heavier. I've never felt so trapped, so lost, so powerless.

The lake water is cold as it bites my skin. His jerking movements forcefully pushes more water over my body. It beats against my face as I attempt to dodge the tide, but wishing I could disappear into it so it could whisk me away. Far, far away from here.

I glance up to the sky that I've fallen in love with, the sky that's brought me happiness and peace. The same sky that Seamus observes every night, and I allow it to take me away.

The stars begin to blend with the black backdrop, so I squeeze my eyes closed and reopen them, because I need the light the stars offer.

Orion glows brighter than ever. He finally showed himself to me tonight, and now that I can see him so clearly, I wonder how I never saw him before. It's like a beacon, like he's calling me with his stars that shine brighter than all the others in the sky.

I focus on the corners that create the constellation and pray. I never pray. But if there is ever a time to do it, I guess it's now.

Minutes go by. Hours maybe. Probably seconds. I don't know.

Everything hurts. Even the cold lake water feels like lava on my skin.

My body jerks without resistance as Nathan shoves into me. Blinding pain radiates from my uterus up to my throat, and it physically makes me feel sick.

Mentally, I want to die. I don't want to live through the memory of this night.

The mud and rocks pierce my back with each forceful jolt. I can't feel my fingers, my wrists anchored against the ground with the entire weight of his body, and there is nothing left.

I have nothing left.

"Nathan, please stop." My defeated, tearful voice cracks as I beg for him to stop, even though I know nothing will help.

In fact, I realize I just made it so much worse for myself.

"Shut the fuck up, I'm almost done." His vile voice is stern, and nothing in it sounds remorseful.

He palms my chin. His fingers squeeze my cheeks with alarming force. He grunts, pulsing inside me as he loses himself in the pain he's inflicting while taking his pleasure.

Squeezing my eyes closed, I press my lips together as I endure the torture and push through the disgust. The water laps over my mouth, covering my face. I choke as he pushes me further into the muddy water.

I struggle to breathe, kicking my legs as I toss my head back and forth, but he's too strong. He's too fucking strong.

He's going to kill me.

I whimper out in pain, in agony, in fear. I'm so scared. So, fucking scared.

"Please," the watery words bubble from my lips. "Please."

He releases the pressure on my neck and I'm able to lift my head enough to take a gasping breath, but it's temporary as the back of his hand crashes against my cheek. Blinding pain explodes behind my eyes as my body falls limp and his hand returns to the tender, bruised flesh.

I try to lift my arms, but they're so heavy. So, so heavy.

My vision blurs as his grip tightens, stealing my air. I attempt to fight to keep my eyes open. All I can see is Orion's outline and Seamus' voice telling me it's going to be okay.

Somehow, it's going to be okay.

I guess this is what happens before you die. Accepting it and telling yourself, it's going to be okay.

Nathan pushes my face fully underwater, and I squeeze my eyes shut, losing track of the light. My Orion. Our Orion.

My body is on high alert. My legs kick as I attempt to flail my bonded arms. The watery scream is useless other than to just further choke myself on the murky water.

Suddenly, the weight that was holding me down is gone, and I'm able to hold my head above water.

My wrists scream in tender agony. My head throbs and chest heaves. The sound of splashing and muffled voices fill my ears as another deep male voice yells, and the fighting continues.

Catching my breath, I blink my heavy eyes open, but between the water and the swelling, I'm unable to see anything other than two silhouettes, their shadows mixing with each other.

My head throbs as I attempt to hold my neck up, but it weighs a hundred pounds and nothing in my frail body is working.

I need sleep, but I'm not tired. Or maybe I am. I don't know. I'm so confused.

Everything is out of focus and dark. I squeeze my eyes shut and open them to clear my vision.

A figure stands over my body, startling me, and I attempt to drive my legs into the ground to push myself away, but my body won't respond. I'm so weak.

"No," I manage to squeak out as I shake my head.

"Mimi," he shushes, comforting me. "It's going to be okay."

I try to open my eyes wider, but only my right eye barely opens with enough clarity to see.

"Wes?" My fractured voice is hoarse and dry.

His arms wrap around my naked, battered body. One behind my back, another under my legs, and I'm lifted out of the water. I attempt to buck out of the hold, but he shushes me again.

"Jesus, Mimi. Hold on, I've got you," is all I hear before everything goes dark.

34

SEAMUS

Present Day

I hold Mimi as she sobs in my arms. Tears stream down her face in waves as she stutters through telling me everything that Nathan did to her when he found her that night.

Not only did he violently rape her, but he almost fucking killed her. Nearly drowning her in the lake as she begged for her life.

My own guilt pulls at me, feeding my fury. I left her that night. I fucking left her because of a stupid fear of getting caught out of bed.

I could have saved her.

I could have helped her.

This could have been prevented.

Instead, Wes was the one who found Mimi in time to save her life. He beat Nathan off of her and got her help.

I haven't asked any questions. I haven't said anything, but I'm raging inside. I want to kill something, anything. My body trembles with so much anger, and I know I'm on the verge of completely fucking losing it.

The only thing keeping me grounded is her, so I squeeze her body tighter, pressing my lips into the crown of her head.

I force myself to breathe, calming myself, and focus back on her.

At some point, she collapsed as she was telling the story, and I slid over to her wrapping my entire body around her, like she needed protection. Protection from the words she's held back saying, reliving a story that no one should have even experienced.

She's rocking in my embrace as she apologizes profusely, and that only just feeds my fury. She has nothing to apologize for, nothing to feel bad about, and the fact that she feels like she has to, makes my vision blur with rage.

Pulling myself back, I cup her face and stare into her gorgeous eyes. The ones I fell in love with so easily. The ones I've seen only in my dreams for the past decade that are now drenched in tears and filled with shame.

"You did nothing wrong, Mimi. Nothing," I grit out as I kiss her forehead, pulling her back into me.

I want to take her pain away. I want to strip her of the memories from that night, even if it erased the memory of us. I'd rather her remember nothing than anything at all.

We are still outside, perched against her front door on the porch, and even though I'm grateful for the crisp air, it's too cold and I need to get her inside.

I press into my heels without loosening my hold and bring her to a standing position with me. Cupping my arm behind her legs, I lift her to my chest, carrying her bridal style as I step through into her entryway.

I kiss her temple and whisper in her ear, "One day I'll be carrying you through a doorway because you'll be my wife." A wrecked sob heaves out of her as she grips me tighter, pulling herself even closer to my body.

I've never been inside her house, but I've seen most of it

through my side window, so I don't need her to tell me where to go. I already have the layout visualized in my head.

Lavender and honey, a scent so distinctly her, fills my senses as I enter through the front door. I kick it closed behind me and pass the kitchen and living room, heading straight to her bedroom.

The herbal floral scent is stronger in this room, and it invites me in as my legs move easily inside the dim space.

Twinkle lights line the bookshelf, giving just enough light to see my surroundings. It's simple and clean, unlike usual Mimi nature. A yellow and blue velvet patterned chair sits in the corner stacked twenty items deep with articles of clothing. I can assume she tried on, before taking them off and tossing them there.

Placing her on her unmade bed, she curls up tighter on the bed, but doesn't release the fisted grasp of my shirt.

"Please don't leave me." Her soft voice cracks and it breaks my heart. She doesn't want to ask me for anything, but she knows she needs it.

"Never."

I'm never leaving her again.

I crawl into the side of her bed, pulling her body flush with mine, and wrap my arms around her.

We lay there motionless as the minutes tick by, and I mentally recap our time at camp, our nights together, and that final night that's always been known as the best night of my life.

To find out it's probably the worst of hers because of what happened, is a confliction of feelings I can't put into words.

My phone buzzes in my pocket. Once, twice, and on the third time I know it's Rocco. I shouldn't check it now. I shouldn't look at the details I know he's sending to me.

But I need to know more.

Mimi's breathing has evened out and her body lays heavy against mine.

Knowing she's finally asleep, I pull out my phone and read the messages.

Rocco: Got the files. I'll link them to you.

Rocco: I'm, uh…let's meet in the morning. I'll bring you the files.

Rocco: 0600. I'll come by your house.

Seamus: Send them to me now.

Rocco: I don't think that's a good idea, boss.

Seamus: Send them.

Rocco: It's not good.

Seamus: Send the fucking files!

Anxiety fills my bones as the link pops up. I know this is a complete invasion of her privacy and I shouldn't be digging further into what she has already told me, but I need to know everything.

Clicking on the link, a summary list of items appears.

- *Court Order*
- *Hearing*
- *Jury*
- *Witnesses*
- *Evidence*
- *Trial*
- *Sentence*

I IMMEDIATELY CLICK on *Sentence* to see what happened to Nathan.

Fifteen years with the possibility of parole after ten.

"You've got to be fucking kidding me." I didn't mean to say that out loud, but I couldn't help myself. That sentence is complete bullshit.

Clicking back to the main screen, my finger hovers a brief moment over *Evidence*, as I look down at Mimi's gorgeous face as she sleeps in my arms.

I don't want to see how the night ended for her. I don't know if I can handle seeing the photos of her like that, but she deserves for me to go through this with her.

I tap on the link, and the images that appear make my fucking heart stop.

I knew it was bad. I had no idea it was *that* bad.

Mimi's battered face and bruised body in sectioned images.

Her eyes swollen beyond recognition. Her lips and cheeks bruised with bite marks and cuts over her jawline and ears.

Her wrists have a distinct black and blue line where he put a majority of his weight, holding her down.

There are so many bruises, and every image of her face and body is so swollen, I hardly recognize her to be the same person.

Images of the lake, her dress from that night, and shoes lay haphazardly near the blanket we laid on every night, and it's too fucking much. I toss my phone aside and wrap my arms around her again, tucking my face into her neck.

"I'm sorry, I'm so fucking sorry." My cracked voice begs, pleads.

Why did I leave her there? Why did I fucking leave?

The intense rage is still licking at my veins and I can physically feel my blood pressure exploding from my pores. I have to force myself to calm my short breaths and just focus on the presence of Mimi comforting me, but the knowledge of what he did to her makes me feel a vengeance I've never felt in my life.

Even the anger I felt toward my father doesn't rival the sensations rolling through my body at this moment.

The uncontrollable wrath that led me to almost beating my father to death has haunted me my entire life.

It wasn't a mistake and I don't regret it. But it put me on a path that I didn't have control over, and even though I was built for the military and loved almost everything about it, I hated that I felt trapped because it wasn't my choice. I was forced to do it because of him.

I have never made another mistake out of a fit of fury again, and I won't start now. But Nathan will get what's coming to him.

Picking my phone back up, I text Rocco.

Seamus: Pull everything on Nathan Simmons.

35

NAOMI

My eyelids are well baked and stuck together as I attempt to open them. Rubbing the back of my hand over the crusted lines, blinking heavily, I bring myself back into reality.

My face is tight from the streams of tears I recall crying as I shared my story with Seamus, and he surprised me by holding me instead of responding with the rage I was expecting.

I suppose I should have expected him to refrain from showing any emotion, but I really wasn't sure what to expect.

I partially expected him to leave, probably needing space, but as my salted vision clears I not only see him lying close next to me in my bed, I feel the warmth radiating from his skin.

He stayed the night in my tiny, messy bed, even though he probably hated every minute of it.

His naked chest is exposed with my pink sheets covering the rest of his body, and it's a sight to be seen.

Never did I imagine Seamus Matthews lying comfortably in my bed, with one massive bicep over his head and the other covering his torso, blending with the light pastel tones.

I glance down at my floor. His clothes are scattered on the ground, jeans still muddy and darker in some spots from the rain.

I'm sure it absolutely killed him to throw his clothing on the ground like that, but it probably beat lying in bed with dirt-covered, damp jeans.

Although my body is wrecked from the emotional destruction I put it through yesterday, there is a sense of relief. A lightness I haven't felt in years—actually ever, I think. Like this was the therapy I always needed.

I always felt guilty choosing to have the abortion and deciding never attempting to get in contact with Seamus.

Well, that was a mix of feelings; because I never told my parents about Seamus, so they immediately thought the only chance I was pregnant was because of Nathan.

My rapist.

A statement that's taken me years to own and accept.

There was a chance that the baby was Nathan's. But, there was a chance it was Seamus', too. And that thought has always weighed heavily on me.

I knew I was too young to be a mother, but I've always known I wanted to have kids. So the fact that Nathan took that choice from me, forcing me to live with the *what ifs*, is something I know I'll never get over.

He stole that night from me. He stole years of peace from me, lacing me with trauma that's followed me longer than I'd like to admit. And because of it, I've never been able to give myself to another man.

I've dated, had some short term relationships with men, but the physical part of those relationships never went beyond hand jobs or blow jobs.

Sex created an anxiety that I couldn't get past. And for the first time, I don't feel that apprehension. Not with Seamus.

He now knows about that night, he knows about the abortion, but he doesn't know that Nathan also took my sexual desires and shoved them so deep that for the last ten years, I've never felt comfortable sharing them or myself. I've been too ashamed to want the things I desire in secret, and I wish I could muster the courage to share that with him, too.

I glance back over, appraising the cords of his muscles and the strong lines of his neck and shoulders and I feel…aroused. It's a foreign feeling to me. Especially because he's done nothing to get me there and I'm literally just looking at him. Okay, drooling over him.

God, he's a sight.

I want him to take me. I need it.

I dip my head under the sheets, covering myself as I move between his legs. One knee is bent to the side, while the other leg is stick straight and slightly splayed open.

I'm not surprised he's wearing black boxer briefs. I wonder if he owns anything other than black. The fabric hugs him perfectly, and I can see the outline of his cock through the thin material.

I bit my lip as I dip my fingers in the waistband, tugging them down slightly, exposing his half hard cock.

Jesus, he's big even when he's not fully erect. I thought the same when I performed my Tantric massage on him, but up close and personal, he's monstrous.

I lick my lips and wrap them around the tip of his cock. His breath catches in his throat and a slight moan leaves his lips as his hips buck up slightly. Pressing in closer to him, I take him all the way to the back of my throat.

His moan is loud as it echoes through the room, and fuck, it turns me on. I clench my thighs together as his cock hardens further in my mouth, and I let out a desperate moan of my own, needing more.

"Oh, fuck," he hisses and I bob up and down with more intensity. The tip of his cock pierces the back of my throat at each pass. "Fuuuck," he elongates before another, more urgent, "*Fuck*," vibrates through the room as he pulls himself from out of my grasp.

His legs disappear from under the covers and the telling sound of my nightstand drawer opens with a harsh scrape, followed by a resounding thud.

I circle my arm up over my head, exposing myself from under the covers, to find Seamus standing with his boxers pulled half down over his hips, his hard cock exposed as he looks dumbfounded down at the bright pink, rubber vibrator in one hand, while the other is splayed out toward the bed.

My jaw drops and I roll onto my back in a fit of laughter.

"What the fuck, Mimi?" He stands, dropping his tense shoulders as he tosses the sex toy back in my drawer before shutting it closed.

"What did you think was happening?" I ask, still laughing.

He throws his hands up to his sides and rolls his eyes before sitting back down on my bed.

"It took me two seconds too long to realize I wasn't in my house, and that dildo was not my gun." I laugh even harder as I wrap my arms around his shoulders and pull him back down on the bed.

He gives up a smile and covers his forehead.

"Hudson is right. I've completely lost my touch. One visit from you that night at Afterburn and I've never been the same." He glances down, as his arm splays open for me to lay in his nook.

I give him a tightlipped smile and squint my eyes as I study his gorgeous features. I remember laying just like this all those nights at camp, staring up at him. It's the same now, except his jawline is harder, more prominent. It's scattered with a small amount of stubble in the morning, and he's got a couple of wisdom lines on the corners of his eyes. The scar over his eyebrow is still there, but has grown larger with him. I remember the details of it as I flashback to all the memories that I've had of this exact moment.

"I haven't been with another man since you," I admit.

36

SEAMUS

My jaw clenches on its own at her confession and my eyes squint in confusion.

"I mean, I've done things with other guys." She shrugs, and I think my molar just cracked in half. "I dated a few guys here and there, but I could never get past just hand jobs and BJs. I think most of them thought I was some controlling dominatrix or something, because I would never let them touch me. I just never…I couldn't…I was never comfortable with it," she says out loud, like it's been haunting her all this time.

I can't imagine living with that. The desire to want more, but being so terrified of getting it because of what happened to her.

Although, I can't say I'm not happy about the fact another man hasn't touched her that way. But I still hate that she has gone through the past decade pushing down her sexual desires because of one man's actions that's now defined her life in ways that have been out of her control.

"I need you, Seamus." She nuzzles into me as her hand skirts over my chest. Her fingertips graze delicately over my skin and it sends shivers all over my body, igniting fireworks in my cock, instantly feeding my half-hard erection.

Fuck, what I wouldn't give to take her how I want her. But now is not the time for that.

I pull her hands up to my mouth, kissing her knuckles before holding them still over my body, preventing her from continuing to touch me. I want her more than anything, but finding out what happened to her stalled any thoughts I've had of taking her in all the ways I've wanted to.

I peer down at her, but she's turned away and her deep sigh is an instant realization that I just massively fucked up.

Yanking her hands out from mine, she pushes herself off the bed and violently grabs an over-sized pair of pants, stepping into them before ripping them up to her waist.

"You're going to treat me like everyone else, like I'm glass on the verge of shattering." Her arms flail out to her sides and drop down heavily. "*Oh, don't push Naomi too far, she'll break.*" She air quotes with her fingers in a sardonic, sarcastic voice.

"Mimi…hey, let's just take it—"

"Take it slow? Yeah, I've heard that, too. *Take it easy on yourself, give yourself time*," she continues with a mocking voice as she mumbles to herself, to me, saying things she's been told and heard over the years.

Words like, violent crime, victim, PTSD.

"No one ever cares what I want," she whispers to herself.

I should be shocked by her erratic behavior, but fuck, it makes total sense.

It's been ten years of living with the nightmare of what happened to her. Dealing with the loss of a pregnancy and taking away so many choices and freedoms. I can't even imagine the roller coaster of emotions it's put her through.

She finally shared she wanted more, wanted me, and I just rejected her.

I put her in the same category that everyone else has her whole life. Making her feel fragile and weak.

Goddammit, Seamus.

She forcefully pushes her feet into already tied running shoes, and I'm completely confused. She's never once worn sneakers out of all the times I've watched her, and I haven't missed a day, a moment, or an outfit.

"Are you going running?" I ask.

It's both literal and figurative being that she's running away, like the first night we reunited.

"I need to get out of here," she admits, still looking around the room for something.

Ripping the covers off, I stand and block the door.

She's not leaving, not like this.

"Fuck it. I don't need a hair thing." Turning, she sees me standing in front of the closed door. "Get out of my way, Seamus." Her voice is lighter now. She says it factually. Not angry, but more so defeated.

"No."

"What are you going to do, lock me in here? *Protect* me from what's out there? Tell me I can't do something because it's not safe? Newsflash, *Rambo*, everyone who knows already treats me like that, and I'm sick of it. I never wanted that from you. I should have never told you."

She reaches around me to grab the door handle, but I step directly in front of her, blocking her reach.

She looks up to the ceiling with a long exhausted breath. "Let me go."

"Never." Not in any capacity will I ever let her go again. "What do you want?"

Her eyes snap to meet mine.

"Tell me what you want." My voice is soft but demanding, making her breath hitch.

I step toward her, making her step back, our legs mirroring each other's movements until the back of her knees are flush with her bed. I hover over her, with the foot size difference between the two of us, as she gazes back at me with a fire in her eyes.

That's my girl.

"I am going to give you every fucking thing you want, but you need to tell me exactly what that is."

Her tongue darts out over her bottom lip, before taking in a deep breath.

"Go on," I encourage as I dip my head into the side of her neck, my lips kissing up the column of her throat. "Tell me everything."

Another choppy breath leaves her lips before she finally speaks.

"I want you to take me, just take me like a normal person."

I don't think I can do that because I'm too controlling and too rough, but I can take her in ways I think she can handle.

Shit. There it is. Exactly what she didn't want. Me, holding back. Not treating her *normal,* as she says.

"What if I like full control?" I ask. "What if I want to tie you up, tease you, and take full control of your body for as long as I want?"

A long moan leaves her lips as her hands cup my face, her fingertips dip into my hair gripping tightly, as I continue to explore her skin with my tongue.

"You want that, sunshine?"

"I trust you." And Christ, those words are like a dagger straight to my cock.

"You need a safe word. Something that will make me stop if it's too much," I tell her cautiously because I don't want her to feel like I'm underestimating her, but this is something we should have regardless.

"Rambo."

"It can't be a nickname," I reply, kissing along her shoulder.

"Sylvester."

What the hell.

I peer up at her, eyes closed and content as I caress her with my mouth.

"You're not saying another man's name while I'm touching you." She gasps as I nibble hard but playfully on her skin. "Try again."

She hums for a moment and her reply makes me smile.

"Orion."

I fist her hair, pulling her head back gently, exposing even more of her neckline. I graze my lips over her ear and trail over her jawline before slamming my mouth onto hers. I catch her moans with mine as our tongues dance together, moving and connecting like missing puzzle pieces.

Pushing her back, her knees bend as she sits on the bed. I crouch down with her, still kissing her as I pull each of the shoelaces loose, then grab the back of the heel and yank them off. Dipping my fingertips into the waistband of her pants, she naturally lifts her hips before I easily yank them off.

The excess material gets caught on everything and she laughs as I shake them off her legs with the grace of a baby giraffe.

"What the hell is this made of, a curtain?"

"They're harem pants, they have a drop crotch." My eyebrows raise to my forehead.

"Well, I'm going to drop in your crotch. Scoot back." She giggles, as I crawl over her forcing her to lie back.

My lips make their way up her legs and over her torso. I grip the hem of her shirt and tug it over her head, tossing it onto the floor, not caring about the mess I'm making around me because I'm solely focused on Mimi's gorgeous body splayed out in front of me.

One I've seen every morning since moving in next door, but nothing could prepare me for the feeling of hovering over her naked body as she gives herself to me again. It's like everything I've worked for in my life is finally gifting me something I've desired for so long.

"You're so beautiful." I kiss the channel between her breasts, my tongue trailing down the center of her body, shifting over to her hip bone. I kiss one before moving to the other and stall at the sight.

Placed between her hip bone and navel, right under where her underwear would normally hide, is a tattoo of Orion. It's small, petite, and utterly perfect.

Tiny black dots connect the larger stars at each end point, and those are colored. Dark pink, purple, and blue stars make up the corners of Orion's constellation with the most simple, yet intricate detail.

She lifts her head, sensing I've stopped, and sees what I've seen. A tight lipped smile reaches her lips and she shrugs.

"I suppose you've always had a claim on me."

Pushing myself up, I slam my lips to hers, wrapping one hand behind the nape of her neck while the other cups her face, taking her mouth in all the ways I've wanted to from the moment I saw her again. I've held back too long and I can't hold back any longer.

I lean over her and she lays back. I push her arms over her head, leaving them free and loose, but allowing her body to be fully exposed to me.

I flatten my tongue over her puckered nipple, sucking it into my mouth as she moans my name. She's so sensitive to my touch, but I'm just as responsive to her reaction.

My cock leaks precum onto the fabric of my boxers, and I realize my own PTSD when I came in my pants far too early from just hearing her moan my name.

I try to think of anything platonic and boring, but the sounds coming from her, her gorgeous, naked body and wet pussy that's rocking up into my hips completely takes over.

"Seamus, take me. Please," she begs, "I need it." Her eyes meet mine again and they're pleading just as much. She needs this. More than just for the relief of an orgasm, but for something more. Like she's been waiting years to give herself permission for sex to be good, to be pleasurable.

"Okay, sunshine, but I owe you another orgasm first." Technically, I already gave her the one I *owed* her but I think I like this never ending debt, and I'm not ready to be rid of it.

Pressing in my palms, I dip down, kissing Orion before I place myself between her legs.

I don't waste any time as my tongue swipes between her slit and she flinches, gasping.

So fucking sensitive. So fucking sweet.

Flattening out my tongue, I swipe again, but with more pressure. Her hands fly down, gripping my hair tightly as she curses. I wrap my lips around her clit and flick my tongue as I press one finger, and then another deep into her core.

"Fuck, oh my God. Seamus." Her words are mixed between a scream and a squeal, and I'm just as desperate for her.

Thrusting my fingers in and out as I lick and suck, I imagine all the years dreaming of having her this way. Timeless, limitless, in the comfort of a bed, exploring every inch of her body, and I can't help but groan with a satisfaction I never thought would be fulfilled.

Everything about her is perfect. Her body, her mind, her soul. The one inch Orion that brands her skin—and me—to her. All of it.

I hum again. The vibration hits her clit and her breath catches in her throat.

"Oh God, I'm so close." Her fingers tighten even harder into my scalp and her thighs close in against my face. I curve my fingers up and continue pressing in and out, fluttering my tongue faster over her clit.

"Fuck, I'm…coming." She clenches around my fingers. Her body tenses and arches as she moans through the most beautiful orgasm. Finally, she releases the kung-fu grip she had on my hair and the tender pain hits me instantly. My scalp burns with relief, but it was worth every fucking minute.

I sit back on my heels, pulling her languid body toward me.

Not bothering to remove my boxers, I pull my cock out between the front closure and stroke it, smothering the excessive amount of precum that's already leaked out.

Her mouth drops open as she watches me massage myself from base to tip.

Other than the first time with Mimi, I've always worn a condom. And it's been a while since I've been with anyone. I was required to get tested just to enter Afterburn, so I know I'm clean.

"I want you raw with nothing between us." It's a question and a statement. I smack the tip of my cock on her swollen clit and she gasps, biting her lip as she tosses her head back, nodding.

"I need your words, sunshine."

"Yes, please, yes. Take me any way you want. I need it."

"Fuck." More precum drips out of the tip. I swipe it through her slit and press into her entrance. Her tight warmth sucks me in and I squeeze my eyes shut at the sensation. "Jesus, Mimi. You feel so fucking good."

I press in deeper. She wraps around me so tight both our moans blend like a symphony of sounds that were meant for each other.

I hover there for a moment, taking in the sensation of feeling her, having her, then push all the way to the hilt. She gasps and moans, gripping my forearms as her nails dig into the skin. I still, giving her a moment to adjust, kissing her neck and chest, her lips and ears. Exploring every inch of her skin while my cock soaks in the heat of her wet pussy.

I could live here and my life would be complete.

"I could stay here the rest of my life," I say, sharing my thoughts with her.

"That's nice, Rambo, but right now, I need you to fuck me." She lifts her hips, circling them, forcing me even deeper, and I drop my mouth open as her pussy swallows even more of my cock.

This little minx.

Pressing my palm into her low belly, I stop her from circling, pushing her gently into the mattress before I pull all the way out and pump into her.

"Oh, fuck!" she screams. "So good," she whispers under her breath.

I continue to piston in and out, pulling out fully, leaving just the tip, then pushing back in, finding the perfect rhythm for us both. My cock hardens even more, how that's even possible at this point is a complete mystery to me. Her pussy clenches around me and I can't help but squeeze my eyes shut as I throw my head back.

"Please choke me. Choke me like you did the first time." I bring my gaze to meet her, my eyes wide at both shock and desire for her asking me to do that.

That was one of my favorite things about that first night, taking her as I wrapped my hand around her neck. It was rough, but still gentle enough that she pressed deeper in my palm. I realized then I needed that sort of control, that kind of rougher sex, and I hated that I liked it as much as I did.

Hearing her ask for it sends fire shooting through my veins.

"Please, do it."

"Fucking hell, Mimi."

I move my hand that's pressing into her low belly and wrap it around her throat, gentle at first as I lean in. I watch her carefully as I move in and out of her. Her mouth drops open as her breath shortens.

Just like the first night, she pushes her neck up into my palm, needing more.

I squint and clench my jaw, attempting to mask the desire burning through me, but also balance the pressure to make sure I'm not hurting her.

She looks at me with concern. Her brows pinch together, like she's worried of what I will think, and shame crosses her face before she eases back down.

"Don't you fucking do that, Mimi. Never be ashamed to ask for what you want. Not with me." I dip down, bring my chest closer to hers, then press my thumb harder onto one side of her neck, squeezing my fingers into the sides of her throat. Enough to give her what she needs, but not cut off her air completely.

My eyes flicker over to her hands to make sure they are free to move, and they do as they come up to grip my hair again, clearly comforting her.

"I'm close, Seamus." She chants my name like a prayer and I can't hold back any longer.

"Mimi, fuck, I'm coming." I groan long and loud. It's unlike my typical self when I orgasm. This time I can't hold back the desperate moans that are coming from my throat.

We come together, in synchronized motion and sound, and I've never felt an orgasm so deep and intense in all my life. Maybe it's her. Maybe it's the lack of latex between us. Maybe it's the missing link I've needed. I have no idea why this is all so powerful, but it's *everything*.

My words and moans are choppy and pleading as I spill into her.

I fall weak over her body, my forehead meets hers as I attempt to hold myself up so I don't bear all my weight on her, but she pulls me in, wrapping her arms and legs around me. I shift to the side and we lay together, breath heavy and labored, bodies damp with sweat and layered with so much satisfaction.

"Thank you," she says. "Thank you for not treating me like I'm broken."

37

SEAMUS

"Tomorrow?" My pissed off tone is clear even over speaker phone.

"You asked me for details *yesterday*, late last night, to be specific, and I'm telling you everything I know *today*," Rocco replies, annoyed but still concerned at my erratic behavior. Because, I never react to news, positive or negative.

Unless it has to do with Mimi.

I don't have a full plan set yet, but whatever I come up with he's got to be fully on board and fully in the know. So, I tell him everything. I tell him where Mimi and I met, how we reconnected, and what happened in the last few months since I decided to move in next door to her.

His silence says everything. He's probably cautious to reply with my unpredictable behavior because it's completely out of character for me. But now he knows and understands how serious this is, and what it means when he tells me that Nathan *fucking* Simmons has his parole hearing in Texas, *tomorrow*.

"I'll get the details of the parole hearing and call Miller. We'll be ready to go within the hour." He hangs up and my phone disconnects.

I glance over at the black screen, then out the window to Mimi's house. I know she's still sleeping because her bedroom lights are still off from when I left this morning.

I wrote her a note that I was going home to shower and change, even though my legs felt like cement bricks trying to leave this morning. The only thing that got me out of there was the fact that I have every intention of returning back to her bed before she wakes. I never want to leave her alone, but I know the more I cling to her, the more she'll feel like I'm coddling her, which is exactly what I know she doesn't want.

Before Rocco called, I was dressed and ready to head back over to Mimi's, but when he told me about Nathan, I robotically grabbed my overnight bag, knowing I was going to be on the next flight to Texas with my guys. Already conjuring up a plan to make sure he never becomes a free man, by either finding out my contacts with the courthouse judge or doing it the old fashioned way the moment he steps outside the prison.

I've thought of a hundred different ways to kill Nathan since seeing the evidence and photos Rocco sent me yesterday. The fact that his request for early parole is granted is like giving me a winning lottery ticket. He won't survive an hour outside those prison walls with what I have in mind for him.

I don't know who the judge is or what the details of his parole are, but I'm surprised that Mimi didn't mention anything about it after she told me, which leads me to believe she doesn't know. She should have been informed and given the choice to stand in the courtroom and tell her story to the parole board.

Studying my bag, I stop myself again. If Rocco, Miller, and I fly to Texas to take care of Nathan the way I want to, I'm taking away her choice yet again. Something that's happened far too much in her lifetime.

Fuck.

Thinking about the fear she's lived in for the last decade— the trauma, nightmares, and memories she's had to suppress to survive, the baby she lost, that was taken from her without choice. I pause, grieving for a moment for myself. Wondering if the baby she was pregnant with was mine, feeling just as powerless with the lack of choice.

I won't be the one to take that away from her. Not now, not ever, in anything in her life.

I glance back over at the window, seeing the room still dim, but bright art fills the walls with only the light and love that Mimi brings.

She's managed to become a strong, beautiful woman. Remaining to be the positive, giving person I knew when we were kids, never allowing that extreme trauma to define her, and she thrives regardless of all of it.

I pick up my phone, tapping on my photos app, bringing up the last picture I took.

Mimi is lying in her bed, one arm tucked under her head while the other is draped over the side of her body.

Her olive skin glows under the natural light, with her pink lips parted and a beauty mark that adorns the left corner of her chin. Her thick, dark hair splays over the pastel pink pillow cases, mixing with the ungodly sight of her ruffled, messy comforter. The contrast between the mess of the world around her and her ultimate perfection, defines who she is in every way.

I know exactly what I need to do.

Swiping out of the app, I click on my contacts and type in Christian, and click on the phone icon.

"Seamus." He answers in one ring. I can hear in his tone my name was equally a statement, as it was a question.

I run security for the club he owns, but doesn't manage. I should be calling Ember for anything related to Afterburn, so I know he's surprised by my call. But I need the resources of our local billionaire, and I'm never ashamed to owe any decent person a favor if it gets me what I need.

"Everything is fine at the club," I state immediately, so he isn't concerned about Afterburn or anyone in it, but I cut through the bullshit because I know he doesn't have time for it. "This is personal and I need a favor."

"Okay," his voice even and sure, "what do you need?"

"Can I borrow your plane?"

AN HOUR LATER, I'm packed and walking out my front door, locking it before walking down my front steps to Mimi's house.

In the span of the hour, we were able to secure Christian's plane, confirm the details and time of the hearing tomorrow afternoon, along with the name of the parole board members and the judge overseeing the proceeding that's making the final decision.

Judge Morrow is known for his unconventional methods and ridiculously mild punishment for criminals who deserve much more than the lenient sentencing he gives them. He's as corrupt as they come, and I've learned that Nathan has managed to make friends in all the right places.

Nathan's attorney, who happens to be his brother-in-law, runs in the same circles as Judge Morrow, and neither have anything guiding their moral compasses. Judge Morrow's influence on the Governor's parole board members was yet another shock to discover how deep their pockets go.

It reminds me of my father's connections, how the wrong people who knew the right ones could get away with practically anything.

I've come to the conclusion that the entire directory of government officials in their so-called justice system deserves a visit from me and my team after Nathan is dealt with.

But that's for another time.

Mimi woke up about half an hour ago, a little earlier than she normally does, but I wasn't ready to come back over without having everything in place.

I need to tell her about Nathan and give her the choice of what she would like to do, but want to assure her that I have every detail covered, and I wasn't coming back over here until that was done.

Flipping the latch on the door of her side yard fence, I push it open and walk down the opening between our houses. She's already made it to the backyard for her yoga session and it took all my willpower to continue to pack my bags instead of taking in my customary morning view.

Rounding the corner, the fountain that sits in the middle of her backyard is running, creating a river flow soundtrack behind the light curtain of mist that hangs heavily in the yard.

Mimi's mat is splayed out at the edge of her cement patio, right before it reaches the grass. Her toned arms hold her body in a perfectly aligned plank pose and the lines of her athletic body are on full display. Wet cotton balls form in my mouth as I follow the outline of her black lace underwear and pink sports bra.

Breath fog floats away from her lips as she lowers herself to her mat, shifting on the tops of her toes and arches upward, before pressing back onto the balls of her feet.

Watching her from my window is like a personal performance that only I got the pleasure of witnessing. Seeing her flow close up in finite detail is majestic and it's just for me, well…not that I've given her a choice. I've invaded her personal space since the day I moved in. But she knows about it, and I smirk at the knowledge that I know she likes it just as much as I do.

"That is new." She turns her head to see what I'm referring to and I tilt my chin up at the pink and black criss-cross sports bra she's currently teasing me with.

"You would know." She's breathless as her knees and forehead come to mat and she relaxes into a pose, hiding her smile.

Yes, I would.

"How did you sleep? I ask.

She takes in a deep breath, releasing it with a content sigh. "So good." She shifts her gaze to me, smiling. "Thanks to you."

I don't know that I've ever blushed in my life. But here I am, sitting in a plastic patio chair with my favorite girl while she stretches in her underwear, cheeks burning.

Fuck, I'm a goner.

I smile back, unable to avoid it. "Good."

Her gaze shifts to my overnight bag that I placed to the chair next to me and she urgently sits up. Her smile drops as her eyes bounce between me and the bag.

"What's going on?" Her brows pinch together as she stabs me with a look that could demolish a building.

Glancing down at my bag, I realize my mistake. I should have left it at the front so she didn't feel the need to put up her defenses. I know how deep her abandonment issues run, but she'll never have to worry about that. Ever.

Leaning forward, I look her dead in the eye.

"You never have to have that look on your face again because I'm not going anywhere, not unless you're the one to tell me to leave. And if you do, I'll tear my heart out and leave it here with you before I go. I want you, all of you, for as long as you'll have me."

She bites her lip to smother her grin, and that's exactly what I wanted to see.

I steal a moment to take her in again, because Nathan and everything surrounding him is going to consume the next twenty-four hours once I tell her. She might know, although I don't think she does, but her decision will affect us and what happens.

"So, what's going on?" Her tone is as soft as the smile that still graces her face, as she tilts her chin toward my bag.

I decide I need to just spit it out. There is no easy way around this conversation.

"Nathan's been granted a parole hearing…tomorrow." Her face instantly falls.

She definitely didn't know.

Her gaze drops to the ground and she's deep in thought. Palming her forehead, she runs her fingers back over her hair, pulling it to one side as her eyes bounce back and forth between random spots.

"They didn't call me. Shouldn't they have called me?" Her gaze returns to mine before dropping again. "That doesn't make any sense. My mother told me they denied his request for a hearing a few months ago. I don't understand."

She sits back on her butt and bends one knee, pulling the heel into her inner thigh, then extends the other leg and she leans forward. Her eyes are distant while she continues to talk to herself, as she robotically stretches.

"They denied him, but his attorney filed an appeal and the parole board accepted it." Thanks to his attorney, aka brother-in-law, more than likely paying them off in some way.

"So, he's been given a parole hearing. It's just a hearing so it could turn into nothing and he stays in prison, right?"

"It could," I reply. "But if he's granted parole, he'll be released in a few weeks, maybe sooner."

Her brows pinch together and she looks out over the fog and beyond the span of her backyard. I think this has always been a safe space for her. The petite yard, surrounded by lush, green trees and the mist that drifts between the fence line and the grass have probably provided her the serenity she needs to feel secure, safe.

But she has me now.

She bites the inside of her cheek as she wraps her arms around herself, and I know her mind is trailing off.

I slip off the patio chair and kneel next to her on her mat, mirroring my arms around hers.

"Christian's plane is waiting at the airport. If you want to face him we can fly there today and show up tomorrow. You have the right to share your story with the parole board, but if you don't want to say anything, you can still go and just show your face, or stay here. You are in full control of whatever you would like to do," I tell her as I hover my mouth over the back of her neck, wanting to be as close to her as possible.

Nathan's attorney clearly got this approved under the radar without informing anyone, so their plan is to get this hearing done, approved, and get him released without anyone being the wiser.

The prideful part of me wants to tell her that so she shows up and ruins that plan for him. Man, I'd love to see the look on his face when he sees her in the courtroom.

The protective part wants her to stay here so I can take care of him without her knowing any different.

"Maybe he's changed. He was young, he had been drinking. Maybe he deserves a chance?"

What the hell? He sure the fuck does not.

I saw the pictures of what he did to her. He does not deserve clemency. Not from her, not from anyone. If Wes had not stepped in and stopped him, I have no doubt he would have killed her in that lake.

She glances over her shoulder to look back at me, but she's not angry or upset. She wears a somber, yet hopeful look, like she's dying to hold onto it.

I've always been a fucking chameleon when it comes to facial expressions. A professional at showing zero emotion and giving away nothing. But the insanity of her comment might as well be written in permanent marker all over my face.

"Okay, I know he doesn't *deserve* it. But regardless, he's going to be let back out into society, either now or in the next five years. So, I suppose that's just my hope speaking for all the other women out there." She turns back to overlook the yard again.

I had Rocco dig deeper into Nathan while we were waiting for Christian to confirm the details for the plane. Rocco discovered multiple accounts during Nathan's time in high school of girls filing complaints with the principal. Even one of his female teachers brought his behavior to light, but all were swept under the rug.

Complaints of sexual assault and random acts of violence have followed him since he hit puberty. Those were silenced and went unpunished. So, no I don't think this is a man who knows how to control himself while sober, and especially not while under the influence.

Mimi wraps her pointer and thumb around her wrist and looks down, deep in thought. She squeezes a few times before moving her grip up and popping her knuckles.

"I need to go. I want to go. They need to hear my story."

That's my girl.

She presses into her palms and I reluctantly release her as she stands.

Standing with her, I try my best to not seem protective and overbearing. Turning, she cups my face and presses her soft lips to mine. I lean down as I wrap my arm around her waist, pulling her closer to me. I hate how close I need her to be to me to feel like I'm doing what I was born to do. Protect her, love her, revel in her forever.

I lean down and press my forehead to hers, breathing her in. The faint scent of lavender wraps around me like a warm blanket.

I knew she would want to go, and I want her to. She needs to tell her story, but this changes everything about what this mission is now.

What started out as a covert operation with Rocco and Miller to get rid of Nathan Simmons, is now a protective detail for Mimi, not just physically but mentally. And I've never been so uncertain about the outcome.

38

NAOMI

They are going to let Nathan go, I can feel it.

I don't know if that's my fear talking or my gut, but either way, the discomfort I've felt since Seamus told me about the parole hearing has been forefront and center.

I've been on a roller coaster of emotions in the short span of an hour. All the things I've learned about stress management, dealing with anxiety, and working through emotional distress have apparently left the planet.

Meditative mantras, breath control, cognitive thinking. Yup, all sucked into a black hole.

I want to believe Nathan has changed. I want to believe what happened to me was alcohol induced and not his normal behavior. But the nefarious look in his eyes, the pure evil that lurked behind them while he held me down, still haunts me daily.

"We're here." Seamus' voice rips me out of my daze and I blink quickly, fading out of the trance I was in before I recognize the view.

We're at the airport, but we are on the tarmac near where the planes take off and land. A row of smaller charter planes are all lined up outside of warehouse style storage units, large enough to fit said planes.

My brows pinch as I turn to look at Seamus. He has a concerned, but adorable smile on that handsome face of his and somehow he's able to pull a smile from me.

"This is Christian's plane." He tilts his head at the monstrosity of the so-called plane.

The sleek, silver and gold crested plane—that's twice as big as the other charter planes—sits like a princess at a royal tea party. The built-in airstairs are pulled out and placed outside the entry door with two of the classiest dressed crew members I've ever seen waiting at the top.

Even the stairs are lacquered and shine like no one has ever stepped on them.

"It's a mansion with wings," I whisper-yell as Seamus exits the vehicle. Christian's plane makes the other charter planes look like Pilot Barbie's playhouse.

I lean down to gather my purse as the passenger door opens. A gentleman dressed in a suit holds his hand out to help me out of the truck, but Seamus comes to his side, shoos him away, and replacing his extended hand.

I'm unable to hide my eye roll at his protective behavior, but smirk because the other half of me finds it adorable and endearing. I realize this is going to be a constant battle of either hating it or enjoying it. For now, I slide my hand, unable to hide the smile and revel in it.

He guides me to the plane and steps behind me as I climb up the stairs. Ducking through the entryway, it's exactly as I expected and yet still, I'm in shock. The interior of the plane is just as overwhelmingly gorgeous as the outside.

Coffee and grainy, leather notes hit my nostrils as I take in my surroundings. Plush, beige leather seating is lined throughout both sides of the plane. The neutral, earthy colors match the luxurious feel with touches of blue and brown accents throughout.

Everything looks expensive, including the two mastiff looking bodyguards sitting on each side of the aisle. Thankfully, they chose their seating properly, because if they were both on one side, the sheer weight of them would probably topple the plane over.

They both stand looking straight ahead, as if they are a mirror image of each other. I glance back at Seamus who is following my steps through the entry door.

"At ease, boys." The men deflate and their hands release from behind their back, again in sync.

Seamus places his hand on my low back and tips up his chin down the middle of the aisle, silently bossing me around, and I can tell by the look on his smug face that he likes it. It makes me want to rebel, but I'm completely out of my comfort zone here, so my feet carry me down the aisle, past the security team that doesn't seem to know how to make eye contact.

"Mimi, this is Rocco and Miller." He points to each one as he introduces them. They both glance my way at the same time as they tip their heads and jinx each other saying, "Ma'am."

Oh, this is way too awkward and formal.

"Great to meet you!" I say cheerfully as I step forward and airplane my arms around Miller's neck. It feels as if I am hugging a stone statue before I release and do the same to Rocco. He's just as stiff, but finally his hand grazes behind my back, giving me a soft embrace, and as I pull away I see a small smirk cross his lips.

I turn around to see Seamus granting me a patronizing look.

"What? I'm a hugger." I shrug.

"Come on, let me show you the back." He guides me toward the rear of the plane. "Wipe those smug looks off your faces," Seamus mutters to Rocco and Miller as we pass, and I can't help but smile.

Seamus was always very respectful and thoughtful. He still is, especially with me, but his age is now showing his experience, and his protective nature sending tingles down my spine. I've never had a man elicit these sensations from me so easily. I have no idea what I want, but I know Seamus could do anything to me in my current state and I would let him.

I push down those feelings and attempt to hide them away since that's the last thing I should be thinking about. Except that's impossible when Seamus opens a door to a full blown bedroom suite.

39

SEAMUS

Mimi's face is full of shock as she steps through the bedroom suite door. Her lips part as her eyes bounce around the room, taking in the built-in king size bed and mid-century modern decor. The bathroom ensuite door is slightly ajar, exposing the beige and brass tones of the tiling throughout. The shower is double the size of most showers in a standard apartment, and can fit three decently sized bodies.

I have a feeling Christian had that remodeled specifically for him, Jake, and Elena.

I've flown with Ember a couple of times when scoping out a few buildings in New York, but I've never spent time back here. I can't say the thought of taking Mimi in both this bed and the shower didn't cross my mind, because it did. Multiple times.

Mimi slowly crosses the room as she takes everything in. I can't help but stare at her as she wanders around. Her tight leggings hug every curve of her gorgeous legs and the over-sized hoodie does nothing to hide the fact that I know what's underneath it.

As if she could feel my gaze on her, she turns around and her eyes meet mine.

My breath is heavy as I take her in. It's like she can rip the air from my lungs with just a look in my direction. I've always known the effect she had on me. She's haunted me my entire life, and now that she's here with me, willingly, I have no idea how I'll hold myself back.

"Don't look at me like that." She bites the corner of her lip, contradicting her statement.

"How am I looking at you?" I ask, genuinely curious as to what she's feeling.

"Like an uncaged, wild animal."

I dip my chin to my chest, attempting to hide my smile, because that's exactly how I feel. And exactly how I've felt since the moment I saw her at Afterburn.

"You're right," I reply, stepping on the back of my heel with one foot removing my shoe, then I do the same to the other. I shrug off my jacket and drape it over a chair before throwing my hand behind my head, tugging my shirt off as I make my way toward her. She retreats backward before the back of her knees hit the side of the bed, and I stop in front of her, my body flush with hers.

"Everything in my controlled existence has completely gone up in flames since the moment you walked back into my life. And I wouldn't change a goddamn thing." I cup the back of her neck, pulling her lips to mine. She moans as she kisses me back, and I swallow the sound that makes its way straight to my swelling cock. Our tongues move together like they crave the touch and my hands begin to roam over her body.

She dips her fingers in the waistband of my pants, her knuckles caressing the sensitive skin below my navel, and I instantly feel out of control. I press my body closer to hers, but a knock at the door makes her flinch back, pulling herself away from me.

Goddammit.

"Don't go anywhere." I kiss her hard before stepping away, and I hate how empty it feels.

I crack the door open, blocking the view of the room behind me as Rocco stands on the other side.

"What?" He's completely unaffected by my abrasiveness.

"The pilot will only take his directive from you per Christian Ford's orders, and I have updated information about Mr. Simmons and his legal team."

Glancing over my shoulder Mimi's brows furrow and I know she heard Rocco, but I don't want her hearing any details of what we already know.

Did I plan on killing Nathan without anyone knowing the wiser? Yes.

Do I need to give her the chance to face him, tell her story, and get the closure she needs?

Also, yes. Unfortunately.

Which means I need to involve her, but right now I need to know what Rocco knows so I can figure out the next steps before sharing with Mimi.

I look back at her. "Give me a minute, okay?" She nods as I step out the door, shutting it behind me.

Rocco and I take a few steps toward the front of the plane where Miller is sitting, sorting through papers from the file Rocco pulled on Nathan.

The slapping of metal on metal snags my attention as the flight attendants retract the airstairs and close the cabin door. The cockpit door is still ajar and I can see the shoulder of the pilot and co-pilot as they flip switches and prepare for flight.

The pilot glances back at me and I give him a nod that we're good to go.

"What's going on?" I place my hands on my hips and roll my eyes, because I'm just now realizing I don't have a shirt on.

Miller glances up, snickers to himself, and looks back down.

"Wipe that smile off your face and tell me what's going on."

"It's not a smile, it's hardly a grin." Rocco smacks Miller's chest with the back of his hand. "What? He's got it bad. I've never seen him like this, just taking full advantage."

I glare at him, completely unamused by his amusement, fighting to block my own smirk because my boys see right through me, but I don't care about any of that when it comes to Mimi.

I'd happily tell the world how gone I am for her.

He clears his throat as my resolve beats out his. He begins to share the details of what he has found out about the parole hearing and the timeline of when they'll transfer him from the prison to the courthouse. He's even mapped out the route the bus will go and the guards that will escort the prisoner during the transfer.

I take in all the details that Miller and Rocco put together. Their plan is to take over the transport bus as it's on route to the courthouse, then take Nathan to a secure location.

My guys are good, really good, and I'm suddenly feeling very grateful they have my back, no questions asked.

Jesus, Mimi is rubbing off on me. I am getting soft in my old age. Who am I kidding? That's not age speaking. It's love. I'm desperately in love and happier than I've ever been, and it's making me ridiculously soft and weak.

And for some goddamn reason, I don't care.

Except when it comes to finishing Nathan and making the rest of his life—if we grant it to him—as miserable as possible.

"The plan is good, but I have a better idea. Remember when we had to break you out of that prison in Tijuana?" I glance over at Rocco and he spears me with the look of the devil.

"Yeah, it took you long enough, too." His reply is dry. Miller and I smirk as we look at each other, recalling that mission.

"Well, what if we get you in one this time?" I reply, looking back at Rocco as his face falls.

"That's a U.S. maximum security prison." He points at the paper, securitizing my comment.

"No, not there. We don't need to worry about the prison or the transport bus if we know his final destination. He'll be here until he's brought into the courthouse for the hearing." I point at the courthouse holding cells, which are minimally monitored compared to the prison.

Both Rocco and Miller stand a little straighter. Miller nods his head in a silent agreement as he looks over at Rocco. "He'll be a sitting duck, an easy target."

"You're going to kill him?" Mimi's voice rings through the air like a foghorn, and I turn to see her standing in the doorway, her arms crossed over her chest.

Shit.

I turn back to face the guys and whisper, "Set it up. But this is plan B. No one moves on this unless I give the green light, understood?"

The guys look confused, but nod. "What are we calling it, sir? The Op?" Miller asks.

A few things flash through my head, landing on only one option.

The hunter known for killing beasts.

"Orion." My voice is low as I respond to them before I step back and guide Mimi back into the room, shutting the door behind me.

"You're planning to kill him?" Mimi blurts out, her arms flailing out to her sides. She's pacing the room, unsure of how to feel. "I don't want him dead."

"I do." My response comes out as a cat-like reflex and I know I can't take it back.

I don't want to take it back, but I am worried about what she'll think of me. Will she hate how much I've killed? The things I've done simply because I was following orders? Some

I'm proud of, some not. Regardless, it's what I was trained to do. What I needed to do.

But I don't care. If I spent all those years training to do those things to bring me to this moment, to bring peace to her by ridding him from this world, it was all worth it.

"He raped you. Beat you until you were unrecognizable and almost drowned you in a lake. He ruined the memory of that night, *our night*, which has haunted you for ten years. Ten fucking years of your life was taken because of him!" I'm breathless as I step closer to her, aligning my body with hers. "So yes, I want to fucking kill him."

"I want to believe he's better than he used to be…" she replies almost inaudibly. Like it's hard for her to even say it out loud herself.

It should be.

He doesn't deserve that kind of forgiveness. Not from her or anyone else that he bullied and tortured in his years.

She needs to know everything before I let her make her decision. She's here so she has the chance to tell her story and keep him in jail. But, if he's granted parole and there is an ounce of terror that resides in her eyes, I need her to be okay with letting me do what I need to do. To keep her safe. To keep others safe, too.

I walk back toward the bedroom door, open it, and reach for the backpack placed on the chair right outside of it. Reaching in, I pull out thick manila folder with the photos from her attack and reports detailing all the other sexual harassment complaints filed against him.

Tossing it on the bed, the photos splay out in front of her, revealing flashbacks of that night. The very top photo is a picture of her beaten face, from the neck up after that night.

Surprisingly, her neck is untouched. Which is a relief considering what she enjoys sexually. If he would have held her down by her neck instead of her hands, her natural desire would be a fear she'd probably never be able to get over.

She'd react the same way she did when I grabbed her wrists and she'd battle even more demons within herself.

Using her fingers, she reaches down to spread out the pictures and she squints, as if in pain, when she sees them.

Her eyes are bloodshot and swollen. Her lips, puffy and bruised. A stitched cut aligns the top of her eyebrow and a bloody slit decorates her lip, matching the gash that crosses over her cheekbone.

The worst part of the bruising lies around the bridge of her nose, circling around her eyes. Different shades of black and blue, in depths I've never seen before.

Another one displaying her hands and forearms comes into view. You can see the outline of his fingers and palm print from where he held her down. One wrist is completely dislocated with striped bruising starting at her palm, all the way past her elbow from the abuse it took.

I've seen horror in my life. Lone body parts, broken bones, and more blood than someone should see in any lifetime, but I have to look away. To see Mimi like that, completely shatters me.

She stares down at the photo, stunned to silence. I don't know if she's seen these before, but I'm glad she's reminded of the pain and suffering he put her through so she can be okay with whatever decision that needs to be made.

Wrapping one hand around her wrist, she caresses the soft area and flinches. Her eyes are pained and I step toward her wanting to hold her, needing to do something.

"These are evidence pictures from the trial. Those were sealed."

"Not to me."

Her eyes snap over to mine, and I can't tell if she's upset or just confused and distraught.

My body has a mind of its own as it walks toward her, my legs taking me in the direction it knows my heart wants to go. I gently place my hands on her waist, pulling her close, and I swear it's like my body needs her to breathe.

"Some days I want to be able to forgive him, so I can feel like I can move on. Other days I fantasize about his death like it's the only way to get closure."

"You have the right to feel both ways at any given time," I reply reluctantly, because forgiving him is the last thing on my mind.

"I feel so confused and angry, and I want to scream and cry at the same time."

"What do you need right now?" I step toward her as she grips my shirt.

My hands roam under the fabric of her over-sized hoodie, caressing the soft skin of her stomach. Her hand wraps around mine, guiding it to her chest.

My fingertips graze over the satin hem of her bra and the sensation of touching her goes straight to my cock.

Her hips press deeper into mine and her breath hitches as she feels the length of my hard cock pushing against her.

"Tell me what you need, Mimi," I say again, my grip tightening over her hips.

"I've done nothing but try to accept it my whole life. Just accept what happened. *Forgive him*," she air quotes, "that's what everyone says I need to do to move on, but I'm so angry. I want to hit something, I want to be angry. I want to feel it. I want to hurt someone." Her hands grip the skin of my torso, as she shamefully dips her face into my chest.

Crooking my finger, I lift her chin and her teary eyes meet mine.

"Take it out on me."

Her brows pinch together as she begins to shake her head.

But she has no idea how serious I am.

"Take what you need. Give me your wrath. Let me feel it." I need for her to give it to me, so I can take it away and bury it so fucking deep she'll never feel this way again.

"Give me everything." I slam my lips into hers and she gasps, shocked by my aggression as I try to pull the rage from her. I grip her hair, tugging it behind her, hard enough to get a reaction but still gentle enough that I don't hurt her.

Her teeth are clenched tight as she peers through her long, waterlogged lashes, and I see it. The fury behind her eyes, the pain in her soul. "Give it to me. Don't hold back."

Spinning us around, she pushes me back until I'm standing next to the bed. She rips her sweater off over her head, throwing it to the ground, then tucks her thumbs into her leggings as she bends over, peeling them off her legs.

Fuck, she's always stunning, but she's out of this fucking world gorgeous when she's angry.

"These need to come off." I put my hands up in surrender as she tackles my belt, ripping it from the loops while simultaneously pulling the fly open with one hand.

She's incredibly talented when she's angry, too.

My jeans fall to the floor, pooling at my ankles, and I step out of them as I sit back on the bed. I have the perfect view of her body, standing over me as she reaches behind her back and unclips her bra. The dainty, lace strap tumbles down her arms and falls to the floor. My jaw slacks as her full breasts come into view, and I'm breathless.

She sets my entire body on fire.

I try to focus on anything else, thinking of the most unpleasant things, but it's completely useless when she pulls the sides of her thong down her gorgeous, toned legs and bares herself to me.

"Fuck. You're beautiful," I say, breathlessly.

I go to reach for her, but she grabs my hand and wraps it behind her waist as she kneels into the mattress. I scoot back until my back presses up against the headboard and I'm sitting upright as her body straddles mine. I've never seen a more beautiful sight than her naked body on top of mine.

The rage behind her eyes matches the passionate roll of her hips. She's fierce and confident, and I am so goddamn turned on I can hardly hold myself back.

Leaning forward, I wrap my lips around her taut nipple, flicking my tongue around the peak as I pinch the other. She gasps, tossing her head back, and her desperate moans are my kryptonite.

"Jesus, Mimi, you make me lose all control." All of the blood in my body is culminating between my legs, and my cock is rock hard, jutting between us.

She licks her lips as she glances down, seeing the precum laced tip throbbing and completely wretched. She presses her hips to mine, the underside of my cock aligning with her slit, and begins to move back and forth. Her wet pussy rubs against me, my cock dripping, mixing with her arousal, and I can't fucking get enough.

I pump my hips, matching her rhythm, and we moan in unison.

"Fuck, your pussy feels so good." I'm not even inside her and it's like my entire body is on fire.

She rubs her fingers through my hair, tugging my head back. I groan at the sting, but my cock pulses, liking the abuse.

"Give me your worst." I remind her that she can do whatever she wants to me. She can completely destroy me if it gives her the peace she needs.

"Fuck," she belts out as she clutches my hair harder and I bite back the pain.

My chest lifts as she yanks my head back, giving her easier access to press her body flush to mine. She wraps her hand around my cock, gives it a tug, then lifts her hips, placing it at her entrance before slamming down on top of me.

"Fucking Christ," I grunt out. Her pussy is tight and dripping, and she wastes no time as she begins riding my cock.

Her rage is swirling around us, like it's part of both of us—her story and mine. The perfect night that was tainted with pain, the years stolen from us because of the vulgar act of one man.

She's got a tight grip on my hair at the back of my neck and the other hand is pressing into my collarbone. Like she's holding me exactly where she wants me. Her moans are deep and guttural, and it's taking all my willpower to hold back.

"Fuck. Fuck." She squeezes her eyes shut as she grits between clenched teeth. "I hate him. I hate what he did to me."

"I know, baby." Her fingers tighten in my hair even more, the sting piercing my skull.

"I hated you, too. I hated you for all this time." Her hand moves to my throat and she squeezes her fingers against the sensitive flesh.

"And I've loved you every day since." I lift my chin, giving her full access to my throat. I push forward, giving her permission to take what she needs.

She presses her weight into me as her fingers tighten around the column of my throat, stealing my breath. My face flushes with heat, reddening with each second. I try to suck in air, but her fingers grasp harder around my neck.

"Harder, Mimi," I manage to gasp out, and the rage in her eyes explodes, pressing even more weight into me as my back pushes against the headboard.

My eyes widen as pressure builds and my balls tighten. My cock is throbbing and I realize it's too late to stop my orgasm.

Keeping my grip tight around her waist, I pull her down harder on my cock as I push my hips up. I thrust in and out, the friction is so goddamn unbelievably perfect.

"You were made for me," I manage to spit out. As inaudible as it sounded, I know she heard me.

She screws up her face and lets out a long moan. "Oh, God, I'm coming."

My orgasm hits me at the same time and I groan out muffled profanities as she rides my cock, robbing the air from my lungs.

"Fuck, fuck, fuck," I chant, unable to hold anything back. When she finally releases the kung-fu grip she has on my throat, I suck in a commanding breath.

Never would I have ever thought that would be something I would enjoy, but here I am, reeling after the most intense orgasm of my life. I have no idea if it was her anger, her passion, or the fact that she literally took my breath away, but I'm more than willing to try it at any point again.

She's still on top of me and I'm glad she's in no rush to move, because I could stay here forever.

"I'm sorry," she whispers into my neck, kissing the column where her fingers were tightest.

I sit up and force her to look at me. Her cheeks are flushed and there is a distinct look of satisfaction blanketing her. She covers her face with her palms and giggles.

"I don't think you're really sorry," I reply, smiling back at her contagious happiness.

"I think I just found my new version of therapy."

"I'll give you whatever you need, sunshine."

"Really?" she questions with both her tone and the look in her gorgeous, satiated eyes. "I don't want to hurt you."

"The only way you could hurt me is if you left me. That would probably kill me this time." I gaze deeper into her eyes, making sure she knows how serious I am. "Plus, you're like five foot nothing and a hundred pounds soaking wet. You couldn't physically hurt me if you tried," I playfully reply with a smile.

And then she slaps my chest. Hard.

"Ouch." I flinch.

"Oh, did that hurt?" Her snarky response has me smiling from ear to ear.

"You should do that more often." She tips her chin at mine, noting my lovesick grin.

I will, now that you're mine.

She glances down then around the room, pulling us back into the reality that we're living in. I'm dead set on revenge, but more than anything, I want her to get whatever closure she needs. If that means my Plan B doesn't happen, then it doesn't happen.

"I need to face him. I *want* to face him. I don't want to tell my story to fifty strangers who don't give a shit about what happened to me. I want to talk to him directly, before the hearing." She turns back to face me and her eyes are pleading.

I know the prison will allow for visitors, and I'm certain we can make that happen under the guise of another name to get him to come out and talk to her, but fuck, that makes me really uncomfortable.

Her in the same room with him, face to face. I don't know that I could handle her doing that by herself. I'd have to go, but I couldn't sit with them.

"Maybe we could get you in as a reporter or something. I wouldn't want him knowing in advance who he's meeting or have the upper hand. And, I would need to be there or else I can't let it happen."

"I want to go, as myself. I want him to know it's me who wants to talk to him."

"Mimi…"

"Please, Seamus. I need this."

I don't know what is going through her mind right now. Is she looking for a fucking apology? Does she really want to forgive him? Because that thought fucking kills me. But it doesn't matter. She needs this and I have the power to make it happen for her.

"Some people don't deserve second chances, sunshine."

40

NAOMI

Well, I slept like shit last night. I should have slept hard after that mile high orgasm, but the thought of facing Nathan and going to his parole hearing had my mind reeling a hundred miles an hour.

Seamus didn't sleep, either. I don't think he normally sleeps much, or if he does, he sleeps with one eye open like one of those psychotic drill sergeants.

He held me all night as we talked about random facts and things we liked or disliked. I think I fell asleep a few times, but woke up and wasn't sure how much time had passed.

We just ordered breakfast in the hotel, and I'm nibbling on some fruit and toast, trying to get my mind off the fact that I'll be face to face with Nathan in an hour.

Will he be remorseful? Will he take this opportunity to tell me that he's sorry? Will I care if he does?

I'm not sure why I feel this unrelenting need to face him, but I feel like it's the first step in the right direction in ten years. I've done nothing but talk out my resentment from that night. Wading through the shame, the guilt, the *what ifs* with my therapist, yet nothing has gotten me close to feeling like I'm on the right track for recovery until Seamus told me he got me a visitation scheduled.

The moment he shared that news with me, I felt instant relief. Simultaneously feeling a hurricane of nerves fluttering through me.

It's the first time I've been able to take control over what I have felt I've had no control over.

It's liberating.

The hotel door buzzes and clicks as it opens when Seamus returns from his meeting with Rocco and Miller. I have no idea what they have planned, but Seamus assures me it's clearly a backup plan based on however I want to proceed after my visit with Nathan.

He's a planner and has every scenario, moment, task, and detail planned out from the time we arrive at the prison to the moment we get to the courthouse.

In the last twenty-four hours, I've seen exactly why he was in charge of high profile missions during his time in the military and whatever "undisclosed special assignments" he said he was tasked to do.

He was built for it.

"Are you ready to go?" he asks, placing his keycard down on the table before putting his hands on his hips.

"I am." I lift my chin with more confidence than I feel.

"I still don't like this, Mimi," he blows out a long breath, "but I understand why you want to do it."

"Thank you for making this happen."

He nods curtly and pauses as his eyes rake over me.

Stepping forward, he wraps his arms around my waist and pulls me into him.

"The visitation room is large and there will be other people visiting inmates at the same time. They are allowing me to be in there, but I'll stand back and won't be visible. He won't know I'm there, but you will. If you feel threatened or need help for any reason, I want you to tap your right shoulder with your left hand. Do you understand?"

I nod and comply.

"Okay, let's go."

41

NAOMI

The lingering scent of pungent body odor and stale air hits my nostrils as we enter the check-in area of the prison. Seamus instructs me to sit, and points to one of the chairs in the corner as his eyes bounce around the room.

His body is tight and stern, as it usually is, but a touch more rigid than usual. He chose to wear a fitted, all black ensemble, feeding into the half-guard half-assassin look that I'm certain he was aiming for, and it does nothing except set my body on fire.

The long sleeve crew neck shirt that hugs his chest and shoulders with tailored perfection is tucked neatly into the black cargo pants, held snugly with a leather belt and combat boots.

Looking around, his outfit mirrors the security guards, save the badge and gun belts, and I wonder if that was his intention.

The guard who stands at the entrance of the prison doors glances up and eyes him as he approaches the check-in desk, standing a bit taller as they attempt to match his intimidating demeanor.

One finger knocking at the table, he grabs the attention of the security guard who is sorting through paperwork attached to a clipboard. His neck cranes up, the grove between his brows peaks as he stares at Seamus' hand before his eyes roam up his body, then instantly relaxes as he stands up quickly with a mile wide smile.

"Matthews, what the hell are you doing here, man?" The guard holds out his hand and Seamus slap shakes it as he pulls him in for a chest bump.

They share a few pleasantries before Seamus leans in and speaks to him in a hushed tone.

The security guard tilts his ear toward Seamus, but his eyes peer up toward me. He looks away then stands stick straight, giving Seamus a curt nod before sitting back down with his clipboard in hand.

Seamus pats him on the shoulder then retreats back my way, an unreadable look on his face—which is typical for everyday life, so I'm uncertain how to take that whole interaction.

"So, what was that all about?" I ask as Seamus sits down in the chair next to me.

He just shakes his head then says, "Nothing, he'll call us up shortly."

"But you know him?" I ask.

"Yes."

"From where?"

"We were stationed together."

"Hm, interesting," I reply. "Did you know he was going to be here?"

I ask because it's either a miraculous coincidence or planned exactly like Seamus needed it to be.

He takes in a deep breath and finally answers what I already knew.

"I had Rocco run all the names of the guards at this penitentiary. Whitlock," he nods at the guy at the desk, "got called in on his day off to be here today, because I need someone I know I can lean on if anything happens." He glances back over to me as his broad hand trails over the top of my thigh. "Nothing will happen, but it's always good to know people in the right places."

The concerned look on his face contradicts his statement.

What the hell am I thinking? Do I really need to do this? Confront Nathan? What for? What am I hoping to accomplish?

I know in my heart this is something I should do. Something I should have done a long time ago, but what if it makes everything worse and seeing him puts me in a tailspin I can't get out of?

I look up to Seamus who's studying me with concern. I see it in his eyes, too. I know he senses my doubt.

"Are you sure you want to do this?" he asks, his head dipping to look into my eyes.

I nod, urgently. "Yes."

"Naomi?" one of the guards asks, stepping in front of me. I look up and nod. "Come with me, please."

Standing, I follow him past the security desk Seamus checked in at and pass the two other guards. One holds a large metal door open with only a small square window that looks through it.

As I walk through the door, the quaint room has multi-sized lockers surrounding it with a few benches in the middle. The fluorescent lighting is piercing to my irises, and the stench in here is like taking a whiff of a carton of milk ten days past its shelf date.

I scrunch up my face in disgust. It's partially a relief that Nathan has had to live in a sewage smelling cell if this is anything like the jails.

"Put all your belongings in the locker, including all the jewelry you are wearing. Follow the instructions on the inside door jamb and pick a code of your choice, then I'll meet you over here for a pat down." He points at the corner of the room, a four walled cement cubby specifically for 'pat downs'.

I was prepared for this. Well, I expected it. I know this is standard, but it's all surreal that this is happening, and just behind that door I'll come face to face with Nathan. After all these years, I finally get to say what I need to say to the person I need to say it to.

I place my belongings in the locker and type in a code, 0722. It clicks in place as I close the small metal door and step into the corner of the room.

The guard glances at Seamus, then to me, giving me a once over before squatting down and cupping my ankle, patting all the way up my leg, then repeats the same on the other. He runs his hands over my waist and between my legs. There is nothing sexual about it, but when I turn to look at Seamus, his face is fire engine red. I can practically see the heat steaming off his head. He could probably fry an egg on top of it.

His fists clench at his sides while he tilts his neck from one side to the other, huffing out a long, drawn out breath. His eyes are dark as he pins the unknowing guard with a look that could kill an army.

Groping Guard makes me jump when his hand lands on my torso. He presses them underneath my boobs and into my ribcage, then moves his hands over my shoulders, down my arms, before grabbing my wrists. He flips them over, using a firm grip to inspect my fingernails.

I flinch and pull back on instinct.

My mouth drops open and I apologize, not wanting to seem suspicious. "You startled me."

"You're good to go in," he says as he gestures his arm toward the door.

I step through the archway and pause as Seamus steps into the space I was just in for this pat down, and the guard clears him.

Seamus places his hand on the small of my back, guiding me through the doorway as we enter the visitation room. The air is stale, the space is vast, and it's filled with metal, circular tables. It smells just as bad as the locker room.

Seamus' lips graze my ear. "Pick a table in the middle of the room. I'll have my eyes on you the entire time." Then he steps to the side, blending in with the wall at the back of the room.

I walk toward the middle of the room, as he instructed, and take a seat.

My hands begin to tremble at the realization that Nathan is just outside this room, waiting to come in. He must know by now that it's me, and that is both terrifying and liberating.

Breathe.

I remind myself as I close my eyes and draw in a deep inhale through my nose, expelling everything out of my lungs through my slightly parted lips.

Opening my eyes, I realize my back is facing Seamus and I'm not sure how he wants me to sit. Pressing into my feet I stand, glancing back at Seamus. His brows pinch together in confusion as his foot drags forward, before a loud clang catches both of our attention and the metal barrier separating us from the inmates opens.

My ass plops down on the seat, feeling as if I need to hide myself behind the table while Seamus steps back, pressing his back against the wall.

The men scatter in different directions, looking around for whoever it is that is visiting them. I keep my eye on the line of men as they disperse out before one of them stops next to me.

His arms are covered with tattoos that are barely visible under the thick layer of hair coating his forearms, and he's *huge*. His body is able to block the entire table next to mine as he looks down at me with a lopsided smile.

"You should come back to see me next week, darlin'."

I steel my spine and lift my chin. Before I can respond with a stern no, I'm interrupted by a far too familiar voice that makes my stomach burst and my throat constrict.

"Beat it, Charles. This one's mine, and she's here for me." I side-eye my view from *Charles* to the man who has consumed too many years of my life.

My rapist.

It took me years to call him that, to claim it. Not just the title for him, but the ownership of who he is to me. The word is vile, but what he did is worse. He deserves to wear the title as if it were tattooed permanently on his face.

I've thought about forgiveness and allowing myself the thought that he could change, he could become better. I would hang onto the advice of my therapist, telling myself to forgive so I could move on. But as he sits in front of me, forgiveness can never be given, because I can see in the dark orbs of his evil eyes, he'll never earn it.

My eyes quickly scan his body. His once boyish face is rough and hard. His body isn't excessively lean and fragile like I expected. He looks strong and healthy. Like he spends a majority of his days working out. He wears a smile like he enjoys the luxury and time he has.

"Mimi," he sits down across from me, intertwining his fingers as he places his hands on the table, "to what do I owe this pleasure?"

I swallow thickly at the distinct sound of his voice. It hasn't changed. It pierces me as it echoes through my eardrums, bringing forth the terror from that night.

For a moment, I feel like I'm falling. Dizzy from the adrenaline coursing through my body and torn between being fragile and weak, but still so mad and angry.

My eyes sink down into my lap and I feel like that eighteen-year-old girl again, sitting in the courtroom as everyone else spoke for her, about her, like I couldn't hear what they were saying.

I refuse to be that silent girl again.

Sitting to my full height, I confidently lift my chin as my eyes take in the weak, sorry excuse of a man.

"You don't deserve an appeal, and I'm going to do everything in my power to make sure it's not granted."

"Ahhh." As if he's possessed by Lucifer himself, he chuckles. Like I'm joking, or what I'm saying won't be taken seriously.

"How did you find out?" I remain silent, not answering his question as he shrugs. "Doesn't matter. By this time next week, I'll be outside of these walls, enjoying what I've been missing out on for the last ten years. Basking in the pleasures of what you took away from me. And nothing you do is going to stop me from that, sweetheart."

"The parole board will hear my story. They will see the pictures of what you did to me—"

He slams his hand down on the metal table, interrupting me.

"The parole board doesn't give two shits about your story. Texas has too many prisoners and not enough cells to hold them. My *crime*," he air quotes with his fingers, "is nothing compared to what some of these other guys in here have done."

"You raped me and almost beat me to death," I grit through clenched teeth.

"You wanted me for years, and when I finally gave it to you, you claim I took advantage of you because it was a little too rough for you. You women are all the fucking same."

I'm stunned for a moment as I try to understand what he's saying. But there is no use. It's impossible to understand someone who has made up an entire relationship in their head. Who justifies their actions because of their delusional interpretation of reality.

"Is there a remorseful bone in your body for what you did to me?"

He leans back, shaking his head as he chuckles to himself. "I didn't do anything to you. All those years you flirted with me, you were begging me for it."

I tilt my head, appraising him, realizing this isn't the first time he's given himself that excuse, nor will it be the last. Nathan Simmons is a natural born predator. Someone who will never take no for an answer and will always take what he wants. Right, wrong, or indifferent.

He leans forward over the table and aligns himself closer to me, whispering, "Do you know the things they did to me when I first got here? The things I had to do to get to where I am now? I dream of the day I can pay back my sweet Mimi with the same pain and suffering you've caused me, and it will come. It will come very, very soon, sweetheart. In fact," he pauses, lowering his voice even more, "I've always wanted to visit Seattle."

I gasp at his knowledge that he knows where I live.

"You think you're the only one keeping tabs on things?" he asks, smiling from ear to ear. "You've gotten to live your fun little life, free of restrictions on that cute little cul-de-sac. You even have a white picket fence and everything. It's adorable."

Dipping even closer to me, so he can lower his voice, he vows, "I will come for you, Mimi."

His rancid breath wafts through the air between us, and I screw up my face in disgust as his threats hit my chest like a ton of bricks. My lungs deflate and I gasp for air with the knowledge of what he knows about my life.

Turning to avoid his stare, I scooch back in my seat, attempting to create some distance between us. As I lift my hand to tap my shoulder, he slams his palms down over my wrists, pinning them to the table. Pressing into the joints he knows all too well.

"Where the fuck do you think you're going?"

42

SEAMUS

My eyes bounce back and forth between Mimi's hand and Nathan's mouth, as I read what he's saying to her.

He claims what he did wasn't a crime. Saying she begged him for it. Justifying his actions, acting like the complete narcissist that he is.

This is fucking bullshit.

Glancing around the room, I appraise the guards as they monitor the inmates. The same number of guards match the amount of cameras facing toward the visitation room. Footage that would miraculously disappear if they needed it to.

Which is why anything Nathan does or doesn't do during this visit with Mimi puts me on alert. The footage can be interpreted or used against her and it's putting me on edge.

I have no idea what Mimi was looking for, wanting to talk to him face to face like this. Acceptance, forgiveness, admission of guilt? None of which she'll receive from him. Some people are just born scum of the Earth, and there is nothing anyone can do to change that.

I watch as he continues to appraise her. His eyes swooping down to her chest and back up to her face as he continues to manipulate his words. He's been nothing but condescending and threatening from the moment he sat down, and I won't be able to hold out much longer.

As he leans closer to her, his face dips behind Mimi. Instinctively, I shift my stance so I can get a better angle at his face, but keep myself in the corner of the room, blending in with the guards.

Finding his lips, I read his words.

I have dreamt of the day that I can pay you back with the same pain and suffering you've caused me, and it will come. It will come very, very soon, sweetheart. In fact...I've always wanted to visit Seattle.

What. The. Fuck.

I keep my gaze locked on him as I take a step forward.

He mentions the cul-de-sac she lives on—that *we live on*—and coming for her.

I've had enough. My body jolts forward, rushing toward her. Mimi begins to lean back, but before she can stand, Nathan rises above her, slamming his hands over hers.

"Where the fuck do you think you're going?" he grits through clenched teeth, losing any control he was trying to maintain.

Mimi is shutting down. I can see it in the slouch of her shoulders as she looks down at her restrained hands.

"Get your fucking hands off of her!" I yell as I rush toward their table.

He's laser focused on her and ignores me, probably thinking I'm just a guard yelling out from the sidelines.

Just before I step up to the table, Mimi stands, ripping her wrists out from his tight grip, balls her fist, and jabs him straight in the nose.

De-ja-vu.

I stagger briefly from shock as I come up behind her.

He stands to his full height as he calmly lifts his hand to his nose, pressing into the nostrils, then peers at the red liquid laced over the tips of his fingers. Blood begins to drip, pouring over his lips and between the cracks of his teeth.

He's smiling, the blood adding to his devilish demeanor. His pupils are blown out as he stares at her like she's the only thing he can see.

"We're done here," I say, treading carefully because she's closer to him than I am. I wrap my hand softly around Mimi's elbow, attempting to pull her behind me.

"We're not done until I say we're done." His bloody hand lurches forward, shaping his fingers to cup her neck.

Grabbing his forearm with my free hand, I pull Mimi back and spin her away from him. With a flick of my wrist, I twist his arm behind his back, then push him forward over the table.

Leaning down, I drive all my weight over the top of him, squeezing the delicate joints in his wrists. I put as much pressure on them as possible, making him feel the pain Mimi felt when she was held against her will, then bring my mouth closer to his ear.

"You're going to regret everything you've ever done to any woman you've ever looked at. And Mimi, she's mine. She's always been mine. And the only thing she'll ever feel when she thinks of you is gratefulness, for how much you'll suffer when I fucking kill you."

In my peripheral vision, I see guards starting to approach. I let him go and airplane my arm out to push Mimi back. He turns as he stands, wiping his bloody nose with the sleeve, then looks down at the stained mess of his jumpsuit.

His nose is still leaking and I puff out my chest with pride that my girl did that.

As his gaze returns to us, he squints, brows pinched.

"I know you," he says as both a question and a statement.

"There's only one thing you need to know about me." I lean forward to speak directly to him. "I can make you silently disappear or make a spectacle of your death." I can't help but quirk my lips up with a smirk. "Either way, I promise you, it'll be the most fun I'll have in a long time."

He looks at the guards, as if to try and save him.

I push back and look over at Mimi. She stands strong with a fire burning in her eyes, like he fed her desire to finally feel the rage.

"Let's go, Seamus. *I'm* done here. I got what I needed," Mimi says, calling the shots.

I take advantage of her acceptance to leave and guide her out. I don't look back, but can feel his laser gaze directly on our backs.

As we exit the visitation room into the lobby, Whitlock is walking toward me from the entrance, his concerned eyes bouncing between me and the other guards.

"What the hell, Seamus?" he spits out. Calling me by my first name is a rarity, especially for a previous Petty Officer under my lead.

"You need to report his attack on Mimi to the warden," I demand.

"Are you out of your fucking mind? Nobody here is going to corroborate your story," he says, pulling me to the corner.

"He threatened her and he knows where she lives. What he did should prevent him from having an appeal hearing," I tell him, even though I know that's a fucking pipe dream.

"Every guard in this prison is on *his* payroll in some form or fashion. His family owns half the state of Texas, and his brother-in-law is running for assistant district attorney. I want to help you, but there is nothing we can do about that here."

He's right. I know he's right, and knew we would be power-less even if he physically harmed Mimi. Which is why I was so hesitant about bringing her here. He could have killed her in that room and they would have brushed it under the rug. It's their word against ours.

But as I peer past Whitlock, Mimi is looking down at her hands with a smile on her face that could rival a billboard advertisement. She's beaming with satisfaction, and her once heavy shoulders look lifted, weightless.

Her voluptuous, dark hair surrounds her face in waves. The light in her eyes, the one I saw the moment she wrapped her arm around mine that first day at camp, has returned with more intensity and strength than I ever thought possible. Even standing in this dingy locker room, she's never looked as beautiful as she does at this moment.

As if she can sense my gaze, she glances up, her smile grows even wider and with one brow hitched, she mouths, "Plan B?"

I can't help but smile back.

She finally sees what a threat he is, not only to her, but to other women. He's been keeping tabs on her, and clearly had every intention to find her and do god knows what when he was released. I'm glad he showed her his cards, because it justified her acceptance in what I've been wanting to do all along.

There's not an ounce of guilt on that gorgeous face of hers, and I fucking love it.

Pulling out my phone, I text Rocco and Miller.

Me: Orion is visible in three hours.

My eyes focus back on Whitlock as he studies me, waiting for my next move. He was only with my squad for a short time, but there's something special about the camaraderie of military brothers.

The loyalty never dies.

"I'm going to need your help at the courthouse."

Giving me a tight-lipped smile, he says, "Follow me."

43

NAOMI

Our pace as we exit the prison doors into the parking lot is walked with much more purpose than when we went in.

The feeling is completely different, too. There was always a sensation of dread, fear, and heaviness when it came to my thoughts about Nathan. Like that night would always be something I wore like a noose-fitted scarf around my neck for the rest of my life. And for years, everyone told me the only way to move on was to let go and forgive.

I was pushing myself to try to do that, but I realize now how much my heart fought me back on that. And for good reason. Because Nathan doesn't deserve that mercy.

That acceptance is providence.

For the first time ever, I feel like I'm floating. That night isn't sitting like a rock in my stomach or hovering like a dark cloud over my head anymore.

There is so much relief dying to express itself. I want to laugh and twirl like a twelve-year-old little girl through this parking lot.

But, due to the current situation, that would make me look like a psychotic Harley Quinn, so instead, I keep my stride with

Seamus, holding back a satisfied smile because I know what his Plan B is. Although I don't have any guilt or shame over that idea anymore, it's still concerning.

What the *actual* plan is, I have no idea. I just know it involves the well-earned death of Nathan Simmons. And where I had reservations about what was going to happen to Nathan, now I am concerned about what might happen to Seamus.

He rounds the front of the truck and opens my door, waiting for me to step in. He's focused on our surroundings, and as he glances around, I take a moment to really appraise him.

His dark hair falls with a slight wave, feathering just above his ear and rests in a perfectly straight line at the nape of his neck. His midnight orbs are the same shade as the deepest parts of the ocean, but where there has always been a lustful desire when he looked at me, now there is a vengeance intent.

I find it just as sexy knowing the story behind it.

A shiver runs through my spine as desire courses through my core. It's something that Seamus has always managed to bring out in me, like it's always been him and only him that my body has an uncontrollable sexual craving for. Something that went into hiding for all those years, but with him I feel safe, like I'm finally allowed to enjoy sex for what it is.

Passion, burning desire, and need.

Grabbing his shirt, I pull him into me and cup my hands around his face.

This is the first time since the day he moved in next door that his jawline hasn't been smooth. This impromptu trip didn't allow him to shave this morning, and he looks rugged and slightly out of control.

Wild, determined Seamus is a sight, and I fucking love it.

I've spent years trying to forget that night, not only because of what Nathan did to me, but because of how I felt when Seamus never came back.

There was so much resentment and hatred toward a man who had also experienced a loss I had no idea about.

We spent years lost from each other, and I saw the torture in his eyes when he told Nathan I was his. The same type of torture I live with when I think of what was taken from me.

I need him to know I'm his. Then and now.

"Fuck me." My confident words catch his attention as he peers down at me. His eyes ricochet between my lips, eyes, the truck, the parking lot, the prison, then back to me.

He looks at me questioningly, with both playfulness and concern, but I know he feels as feral as I do.

I can't help my lopsided grin as I bite my bottom lip and teeter my head back and forth, feeding into the playful side.

"Let's Roshambo for it." I lay my fist on my palm and peer up at him with a doe-eyed look.

Instead of matching my stance, he places his hands on his hips and he shakes his head. For a moment, I think he's going to reject me again, that he doesn't want to risk getting caught or taking me here.

His head falls forward to his chest as his lips form a thin tight line to avoid that rare smile I love.

When he lifts his head back up to face me, his eyes are dark and feral.

"You always choose paper."

And before I know it, he's grabbing me, hoisting my legs around his waist, slamming his lips to mine.

The handle of the truck door clicks open and gravity pulls me back as he sprawls me out on the backseat. He crawls in between my legs, never taking his eyes off mine, using only his foot to pull the door closed behind him.

I glance around the backseat and giggle, seeing his colossal form fill more than half of the air space in the truck, but he expertly maneuvers his hands, unbuckling his belt as he hovers over me.

His abs are on full display as his pants hang low on his waist. The zipper is splayed open at the center, his heavy cock weighted between his legs. The distinct outline of his swollen tip peeks through the thin fabric of his boxer briefs.

Jesus, it's like my very own, all-inclusive, live porno show.

His kiss is desperate as he trails his lips down my neck and over the peaks of my breasts. Tucking his hands into my leggings, he yanks them down, desperate to expose me, like my skin is the oxygen he needs.

I peer back into his darkened eyes, and the dark specks dance with a fire in them. Like he can't wait another minute to have me, and now there's no holding back.

It's the same way Seamus used to look at me, all those nights under the stars. There was more innocence back then, but still a burning desire that neither one of us could extinguish. And I see that hunger again, now with more power and urgency.

I've craved this. Craved him.

I've been desperate to feel the desire that he pulled from me, that I know now has always been his to control. I need him to take me, claim me like I'm his, because I always have been.

Reaching down between us, he pushes his boxers down and his cock springs free. It bounces between us, hard and erect. Wrapping his fingers around the base, he gives it a languid, long tug. His jaw slacks as precum drips from the tip, landing on the lace fabric of my already soaked panties.

Using his fingertip to swipe up his arousal, he presses it to my mouth, pulling down on my bottom lip as he caresses his finger over my tongue.

"Suck." His voice is demanding for only a moment until he loses his breath when I wrap my lips around his finger, lapping up the precum laced tip.

Hissing, he pulls back, using the same finger to pull my panties to the side as he swipes his thumb up my center, using it to coat himself.

"See how easily I lose control with you?" Stroking his cock with my arousal, another bead of precum falls. This time, the sticky liquid holds his crown as the other end lands between the crevice of my lips, connecting us. Like it was always meant to be.

Seamus leans forward, tapping his swollen tip at my clit, and I gasp at the sensation.

My pussy is already soaked and dripping. The wet slap of his cock echoes between us, mixing with the untamed moans coming from both of us, making our own personal soundtrack of sex, desire, and unrelenting need.

Pulling his hips back, he lines the tip at my entrance and pushes inside me, going at one controlled, agonizingly even pace. We groan in unison as my back arches at the invasion and it's like hot wax is poured over every inch of my body.

"Fuck, Mimi." He pumps into me, his movements exactly what my body was begging him for.

He's always had a hold on me, and as much as I've wanted to deny it, avoid it, and ignore what my heart was screaming for, it's useless. Loving Seamus is, and will always be, inevitable.

"I'm yours," I tell him, "I've always been yours."

His chest is flush with mine when he leans into one hand to hold himself up. Cupping the other around my throat, he pulls me close as our weighted breath mingles with each other. We're nose to nose as he forces my eyes to meet his. The pump of his hips slow to a painful pace, pulling all the way out before pushing back in just as slowly.

I can't help but whimper, rolling my hips as I try to wrap my legs around his waist. Needing more, craving more. But he's stronger than me, controlling every inch of his cock that pistons in and out, massaging my walls, teasing me, making me squirm and beg.

"This cock has always been yours, just like this pussy has always been mine." His words send a full shiver down my entire body, and I clench around him. My eyes squeeze shut, fighting the orgasm that my body so desperately needs.

"Look at me, Mimi." His voice is soft yet demanding. But I can't look at him. My body is on the verge of going over the edge, and my heart is ready to explode with it.

There's too much emotion swirling between us, and I can't trust myself. I want to tell him I'm sorry. I want to tell him I loved him…that I still love him.

"I…I…" It's there, on the tip of my tongue, but I can't. I'm too scared that once I open up to him, once I let go completely, I'll lose everything just like before.

He pushes himself up, and using only the fingers he has cupping my jaw, he tilts my face up, giving me a better angle to look directly into his eyes.

"I know you don't want to say it because you're scared, scared something will happen or I'll leave. But baby," he leans closer, pressing his forehead to mine, "the only time you'll see my back is when I'm shielding you from the pain of this world."

His eyes claim mine as my orgasm lingers between us. He is holding it back from me with his calculated control. Making me feel a high I've never felt.

This encounter with Nathan has brought him to another level. Me coming into his life derailed him, sent him off kilter. That confrontation with Nathan put him right back in the driver's seat.

"You don't have to say it, sunshine. I feel it." I moan, not just from his words, but his cock that swells inside me. I feel every ridge as he inches back into me. "Just like I've always felt you, no matter where I was—no matter what I was doing—you were the sun in my day and the stars in my night." He places his hand on my chest, feeling the pounding of my beating heart as tears pool at the corners of my eyes. "It's always been us," he whispers as he thrusts into me and he's no longer holding back.

My body writhes against him as I let go. Giving him both my tears and the orgasm that he's ripping from me, like he needs them both to survive. I call out his name, a few curses, and beg a little, too, I think. My body and my heart soaring together is a high I never thought I'd have.

"Fuck, Mimi." His eyes slam shut as his guttural moan echoes around us and his cock pulses inside me—filling me, claiming me. Every inch of my body is so sensitive and I can feel everything. Our pounding hearts, the sweat on our skin, his breath on my neck as he falls on top of me.

Our energy is cohesive now.

What initially tore us apart is bringing us back together.

It makes me feel alive...so fucking alive. And I know he does, too.

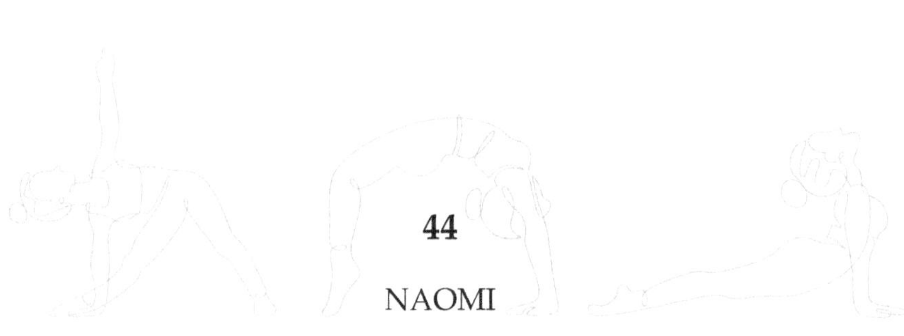

44

NAOMI

The high I felt leaving the prison has completely faded and is now replaced with nothing but fear and dread. Trying to control the emotional roller coaster I've been on in the last thirty-six hours would be like trying to herd a Tasmanian Devil.

I take a mental note to Google Tasmanian Devils and find out if they are actually anything like the Looney Tunes version, because something tells me that's not the case.

My mind wanders as I stare at the over-sized oak doors that lead into the courtroom.

It's the same goddamn courtroom.

The same courtroom I spent weeks in while they sorted through evidence of what happened to me.

Where they dissected every single moment of that night.

Where they showed everyone the photos of my beaten body.

Where Nathan sat, staring at me like he would kill me if I testified for myself.

Where his attorneys called me a slut, a tease, and vehemently claimed I wanted it.

Not only did they say I wanted it, but I asked for it rough, and egged him on. Like I was intentionally plotting this situation because of who Nathan is, because of his family name.

The anxiety I felt as an eighteen-year-old girl, who felt like she lost everything, cowered with their words.

I never testified for myself. I never stood up for myself. I never allowed my voice to be the defense I needed, or the therapy I clearly needed to speak out.

At the end, we still got something, but it was only because someone else I didn't know stood up for me when I couldn't stand up for myself.

Our attorney located a teacher at his high school who reported multiple situations where Nathan had sexually assaulted other girls. Apparently it was reported, but nothing was done and the teacher was eventually fired by the same principal she reported it to.

Turns out that the principal was somehow related to Nathan Simmons' father, and the teacher was related to Nathan Simmons' mother. So, when the teacher showed up in the court-room, there was a major outburst from his mother that caused a chain reaction, and Nathan jumped over the table in an attempt to attack her.

His attorney was able to pull him back before any physical harm was done and claimed he was just trying to stand up for his mother, but it still worked in our favor.

That teacher was brave for walking into the courtroom. She held her chin high and knew she was doing the right thing for a greater good.

If she hadn't testified against him—against her own family— my attorney said he may have just gotten charged as a minor, claiming it was alcohol induced on both our parts since that was another one of their claims. They brought out every lie possible and made me look horrible to the public to better his own image.

But because of that teacher, because of her bravery, Nathan was charged as an adult and my voice was heard, even though it wasn't my own. Nathan was sentenced, although it was shorter than it should have been, it was still something.

Fifteen years with the possibility of parole in ten.

It's funny how your view on time changes as you age.

At eighteen, fifteen years was colossal. *Fifteen years?* That was a lifetime through my naïve eyes at that time, and a part of me almost felt bad he was going to jail for that long.

Now, fifteen years is a blip. And my eyes are wide open to the fact that Nathan will never be right for this world.

Holding my chin high as I take a deep breath, I allow the air to expel out through my partially parted lips, feeling lighter than I've felt in my entire life.

"Are you ready?" Rocco asks. He stands calm beside me in jeans and a t-shirt, making him look like any other bystander. But his shoulders are tight, his stance is stiff, and his hands that are folded over each other in front of his body gives his identity away like it's written on a damn billboard.

Although it's not the same man who's brought me the comfort and security I need, I know Seamus is doing what he needs to do, not only for me, but for himself.

Plus, I've realized Rocco is even more fun to banter with because he's even more rigid than Seamus, if that's even possible.

"Yes, I'm ready, but are you, Tin Man?" I ask as my eyebrows lift to question his dense body language. "Relax."

He looks down, confused, then looks back up to me, still just as confused.

"This is relaxed." His shoulders loosen only a touch as he looks at his watch, then huffs an annoyed breath.

"I hate not being part of the mission, and I hate not having my earpiece." He gives the area we are standing in a once over before staring back at the door.

"You are part of protecting me, and Seamus said that was the most important part of the mission," I remind him of the words that Seamus said before we all split. "He said you were the only person he would trust with that."

"You're right," he hides a proud smirk that appears as quickly as it disappears, "I just hate not knowing what the hell is happening on that side."

Yeah, me too.

I know Seamus is good at what he does—what he's trained to do—but even with that knowledge I'm on edge, as well. Unsure if he'll get hurt, or caught, or the other twenty worst case scenarios that have run like a stampede through my head. But I also know I can't dwell on that right now.

I steel my spine, lifting my chin, pulling in all the brave bits that have helped me grow into who I am at this moment. The girl whose voice was stolen by fear and shame. The woman who now stands tall and ready.

Stepping forward, I grip the spiraled, metal handle and push the door open.

The scent of wood and leather surround me as I glance around the room.

There aren't many people here, the only ones I recognize are on the defendant's side sitting in the first row behind the attorney.

His parents. The ones who fed the courtroom lies about their son, about what a stand up human he has always been. The ones who practically own the small town they live in. The ones who called me a liar and a whore to protect their rapist son.

They are talking amongst each other, like this is the prelude at the cinema. Dressed like it's their first stop before Sunday brunch.

Rocco clears his throat, and not lightly. No, he made an intentional statement.

I hold back my smirk that feeds my confidence, and show it through my body language instead. Keeping my chin held high, the attorney peers up, looking over the heads of Nathan's parents.

The confident smile he was displaying falls the moment he sees me, and his parents shift in their seats, turning around to see what made him stiffen.

The disgust on his mother's face is as apparent as a blinding fluorescent light. His father's neck slowly swivels back up to their attorney who is looking back at his assistant, fumbling through papers.

In all my life, I have never felt so gratified.

I hold more power than I ever gave myself credit for. I always have. They just made me think I didn't. And now the roles are reversed.

The transfer of power is clear as I make my way through the middle aisle way, placing myself in the front row opposite them. His mother's loathing eyes follow me the entire way.

Sitting down, I scooch over, making enough room for Rocco. As he sits down, I lean forward, glancing her way. I'm unable to hide my smile as they move around frantically and whisper amongst each other.

His mother stays put, keeping her eyes on me. It's the exact same thing she did when I was eighteen and fragile, threatening me without words.

But it won't work. Not this time.

And, because I can't help myself, I wink as I give her my most proud smile.

45

SEAMUS

Courthouse security is a joke. Whitlock and I give each other the same knowing look as we enter the building, both dressed as guards with courthouse ID badges. We enter through the exit lane, bypassing the metal detectors like it's something we've done a million times before.

One guard glances up, tips his chin in a silent acknowledgement, then turns back to flirt with a tall blonde holding a jury tag in her hand.

In most cases, I'd be furious to see this. If he were one of my men, I'd punch him square in the nose then rip his arm off and beat him with it. But right now, being that I'm the one breaking in, I can't say I'm upset about their lack of *security*.

Our original plan was to have Rocco impersonate an inmate in the holding cell and Miller be one of the guards. Miller would move Rocco to share a cell with Nathan and take care of him with nothing but his bare hands.

An easy task for Rocco, probably would have taken him less than a minute. We'd erase any video footage of the event and he would sneak out with Miller as a guard.

Our plan was foolproof.

But after confronting Nathan at the prison, I knew it had to be me. I refuse to have him look at anyone else, other than me, while he gasps for his last breath.

Whitlock told us all the guards cycle rounds between all the correctional facilities in the county. From the courthouse to juvenile hall, the county jail and the prison. The agencies attempt to rotate them to avoid any hierarchy or favoritism with the inmates, but there is no avoiding that. Especially when most men, even the most dedicated guards, will do anything for power or money.

Needless to say, Whitlock having an in at the courthouse gave me the option to change the plan.

I side-eye Whitlock as we make our way down the tiled hallway. Our footsteps synchronize in rhythm as the sound bounces off the stale, empty walls. I'm unsure if he'll still have a job here after this, or even if he really wants one. Either way, I'll find another one for him with someone I know in Texas, but not before offering him a job in Seattle. I can use more guys at the club or expand the jobs I take.

I glance down the long hallways as we make our way toward the jails, taking in any possible exit routes and windows in case we need them. I rolodex the route, drawing a map in my head to make sure we have multiple options in case something goes awry.

We pass some guards who recognize Whitlock. They acknowledge each other and completely ignore me. They have no reason to question the other six foot something guy walking with him, especially since I fit the part so well.

And since he knows the courthouse floor plan, we ease through the halls at an even pace, then turn the corner to the holding cells. Whitlock scans his security clearance tag as he two-finger waves to the guard enclosed in the cement cube behind a small barred window.

A loud buzz rings through and the door clicks open, granting us entry. We walk through without hesitation, then the door slams behind us, locking us in.

Normally, going behind locked bars would make me feel trapped and suffocated.

Not this one.

This feels like providence. Like my destiny unfolding with each step I take closer to the cells.

I've done ops like this a thousand times. Countless missions, most of the time undercover covert operations that I'd get through without a hitch.

But this one is personal.

So. Fucking. Personal.

As we make our way toward the cells, her beaten, swollen face flashes in my mind. My fucking sweater ripped in half, torn from her body. The cuts and bruises that dressed her once flawless skin.

Because of that, I realize I should have left Rocco to handle this one. Too much can go wrong when emotions are involved, but I'll never be able to erase the images I saw of her in those photos. They are burned in my memory like a nightmare playing on repeat.

And by the way she broke down in my arms when she told me what Nathan did, the nightmare is branded to hers just the same, holding her hostage.

I will spend the rest of my life protecting her from them and freeing her of those restraints.

Starting with this.

Nathan's cell is in the far corner. Miller stands outside of it, listening to the incessant chatter Nathan spits out to him.

I pause, airplaning my arm in front of Whitlock as we wait in a dark corner, eavesdropping on their conversation.

"Nah, man. I never have. I bet it's fucking good, though," Miller answers a question neither one of us could hear.

"Man, virgin pussy is the best, and the younger the better.

Untouched and so goddamn tight. I'm telling you, blood is the best lubricant. Try it and you'll never be able to go back. Fuck, I can't wait to get the hell out of here." Nathan is practically salivating over his words.

Miller, who we strategically planned to be here, plays the part well and continues, "Damn, I'm jealous of you, man."

"I'll hook you up. Once I'm out, that's the first thing I'm doing. You can come with me while I hit up some of my old high school parties. Those girls can't handle their alcohol, it's a fucking slam dunk. Sometimes they have some fight in them, though. Like the bitch that put me in here. I can tell she wanted it, like she liked the fight, you know. Some girls are like that, just gotta put them in their place."

White hot rage burns through my veins, lighting my skin on fire. My fists clench and my jaw cracks as I envision what happened to Mimi that night.

He's a fucking predator, preying on young girls, taking advantage of anything in his path. I wonder how many girls experienced what Mimi did that he never paid the price for.

Whitlock's eyes widen as he stares over at me. He's preparing for…well anything. He turns his head from side to side, slowly, like a warning. Knowing I'm on the verge of losing it.

Taking a deep breath, I close my eyes and focus. Centering myself.

I smirk, wondering at what point Mimi's goddamn yoga techniques wore off on me while simultaneously realizing I'm minutes away from doing what I came to do.

An uncontrollable chuckle radiates from my chest.

Poor Whitlock probably has no idea what to do. Because I'm actually smiling. Smiling, ear-to-ear, while on the verge of a laughing fit in the middle of a kill mission.

His eyes say it all as they bounce questioningly around the room and over to Miller.

Miller squints to see our silhouettes hiding in the corner, and shakes his head with a tight lipped smile.

Kicking himself off the back wall, he walks past the cell in front of Nathan. "Well, shift change, *bro*. Can't say it was nice chatting with you."

"Wait, what? Where are you going?" Nathan stands, wrapping his fingers around the cell door as he presses his face between the bars. "Aren't you taking me to the courtroom soon?"

"Nope. Good luck," he singsongs to Nathan as he pats me on the shoulder passing by.

"I got the front," Miller whispers to Whitlock, rounding the corner to keep an eye out.

Walking out of the shadowed corner, I step into the light.

My eyes fixated on nothing but him.

"Hello, Nathan."

46

SEAMUS

He trips on his own foot as he backs away from the bars. Squinting, with a look of fear in his pale eyes, he quickly covers it up.

But, I already caught it.

He's terrified, as he should be.

"Well if it isn't my old friend, Semun," he says, faking confidence he doesn't have.

"I am far from a friend to you," I say as I lean up against the bars, peering into the small cell encasing him.

There's a three foot bench that lines the back of the cement wall, with a metal sink and toilet built into the far corner.

I can work with that.

"Everyone is a friend inside these walls, when you know the sort of people I know out there." He tips his chin to the exit door, like that's the only barrier between him and freedom.

I gesture to the keyhole as I glance at Whitlock. He tosses the keys to me and I slip the key in chasm and twist, unlocking it. The sound echoes off the cement walls and vibrates through the room.

He glances at the opening then to me, stepping back, as I step in.

"I have money. I have connections—"

"You have nothing I need," I calmly interrupt him, as I step toward the bench, pushing my weight into it to test its strength.

That'll do.

"Seamus, look…"

"Oh, now it's Seamus?" I huff out a chuckle.

He swallows audibly.

Maybe it was my laugh. Maybe it's my calm demeanor. Maybe it's sunk in that nothing he can say or do will get him out of this cell alive.

"I made a promise to you at the prison earlier today, and I always keep my promises," I remind him.

He bares his teeth at me, grunting in annoyance, but staying exactly where he is because he's trapped and he knows it. His fists clench at his sides, keeping in his angry outburst because he knows he's stuck.

"Silent or spectacle? I believe those were your options." I bend down and slide the skinning knife from my boot holster, crouch down on the floor, and use the cement to sharpen the blade. I lift my gaze to him as I slip the blade back in its holder, then look around the cell at the ceiling bars. "We could do a *Silence of the Lambs* tribute in here. That would be fun."

His eyes grow wide and I can see the rapid heaving of his chest as he tries to hide his fear.

"You'll never get away with this!" he screams as his voice cracks. Does he actually think the louder he is, the better chance he has?

I wince, as I rub my ear, annoyed.

"Desperation looks good on you," I say, as I pull my gun out of the sleeve, giving it a once over and checking the safety, then tuck it back into my belt.

He shifts his stance, and at first I think he's uncomfortable.

But as he stands to his full height, I see that his demeanor has completely morphed into something darker. His energy has changed, and when he dips his chin to his chest, I see the immoral darkness in his eyes.

"It looked better on her." His reply is an evil whisper in this dark cell, and his words penetrate me worse than any weapon could.

"The way she begged for my cock, telling me how much better I was than you. Whimpering when I slammed into her. Oh, she was desperate alright." His lips curve up into a smile. "She'll never forget me. Never. I will live in her mind forever, and there is nothing you can do about it."

"Seamus…" Whitlock's voice of warning is far away, but his words are nothing more than a name by the time it reaches me.

Fury licks at every corner of my body. My heart pounds behind my ribcage that rises and falls, as his words stab me like a knife to the chest.

It must be a minute that goes by as we stare at each other. My contained rage is still a wildfire burning under my skin. He just continues to stare me down with that sardonic smile, and he must think he's getting to me.

That's probably something he's gotten used to as an inmate in a prison that he practically runs with his family's money and connections.

But he has no idea what I've seen and the things I've done. Never did those jobs feel so goddamn personal.

Vengeance was never my motivation. But it is now and that centers me, keeping me focused and completely in control.

"Psstt…Seamus—" Whitlock whisper-yells through the side of the cell. I swivel my neck and look in his direction.

His eyebrows are pushed up to his forehead and his palm faces up as he gestures toward Nathan. "Are you done fucking with him yet?" He says, tapping the face of his watch.

"Yeah, I guess playtime is over, isn't it?" I ask, turning back to Nathan.

And now he can see the devil-in-hiding behind my eyes. The one I mask so well.

Nathan's brow pinches together as he steps back. I can see the realization that his taunting did nothing and how powerless he is when he's trapped in the cage with someone like me.

"Nothing you can say will stop me from what I came here to do, Nathan."

"Stop—"

"Stop?" I question, interrupting him. "Did you stop?" I tsk, shaking my head as I crouch down and grab the skinning knife from my boot.

"This will be what she remembers," I gesture to the knife, "because I'm going to whisper every single detail of how you begged for your life, while I fuck the memory of you out of her."

He takes a giant step back, cornering himself next to the sink and bench as he holds his arms out in front of him.

I jab forward, flicking my wrist once over his left arm then again over his right, slicing him between his forearm and his wrist.

He screams as he leans forward, holding his palms over his bleeding arms.

"That's the thing about this knife, it gets right under that last layer of skin and tears away from the flesh. Makes you bleed like…a lot." I shrug, kicking my knee into his face, cracking his nose.

Blood splatters on the ground as he falls to the floor. One hand covers his face, the other presses into the cement floor. Blood drips from the incisions on his forearms, and I can't help but think that he doesn't really need that wrist.

I step on his hand with one foot, kicking the base of his joint with the other, completely dislocating it.

It's a gut-wrenching, piercing scream that follows.

"Fuck you and that fucking whore," he manages to spit out before he pushes back on his haunches, leaning into himself.

Before he can hide, I grab his right hand and hold it in place on the edge of the bench, slamming my hand down over the top. There is the distinct cracking of tendons tearing and cartilage breaking as it bends backwards, that sounds a little bit like my new favorite harmony.

A mix of screams and begging cycle through the room and I bask in the soundtrack that I wish I could record for Mimi.

Blood drips from the cuts on his wrists, but the worst of it is misting from his mouth through the uncontrollable whining. I look down, inspecting my feet. He's making a fucking mess all over my shoes.

Grabbing the back of his neck, I yank him back on his feet and drag him in front of the toilet.

"You're making a mess and I don't appreciate it. Let's clean you up, shall we?"

Glancing in, it's not pleasant. It's stainless steel, with brown and white water marks, and I can't be sure the last time it was thoroughly cleaned. It even has some waterlogged toilet paper floating at the top, because whoever used it last didn't get it to flush all the way.

Darn.

"No, no…don't—" he words are drowned out by the sounds of bubbles as I press his face hard into the metal bowl.

"Oof, gross." Whitlock screws up his face and he looks away.

Pulling Nathan up, I lean down, whispering in his ear, "This is exactly how Mimi felt. Helpless. Disgusted. Violated." He opens his mouth to speak, but I slam his face back down, the metal bowl clanging as his forehead bangs against it. The water slushes around us, a mix of blood, watered down urine, and whatever else might still be residing in it splashes on the floor.

Holding his limp wrists behind his back, I step over him,

pushing more of my weight into the back of his skull. His feet slip from underneath me, and a gasp then gurgles follow when I act like I'm going to give him a chance to breathe, but slam his face back down instead.

A loud wail and muffled howl echo in the bowl as his body jerks, once-twice, then goes completely limp.

Releasing my grip, I stand, rolling my neck from side-to-side. Lifting my leg, I step over Nathan's contorted body and make my way toward Whitlock.

Miller stands next to him sucking on the traditional, celebratory lollipop. He tilts his head to peek behind me, the white stick hanging out the side of his mouth, and he's completely unamused by the lifeless body that halfway hangs out of the dirty toilet.

"Did you bring me a lollipop?" I ask.

"I had it ready before you even started," he replies as he hands me a red one. I quickly tear off the plastic and pop it in my mouth.

"Did you bring me a lollipop, too?" Whitlock asks, as he turns to him.

"Do you think I have an endless supply?" He arches a brow as he peers over at him.

"Seriously?" Whitlock looks between us both as we thoroughly enjoy our traditional post-op treat.

Miller sensually hums as he licks the lollipop, glancing over at him. Whitlock rolls his eyes, frowning.

"Jesus, do you always whine this much?" Miller grabs a handful of multi-colored lollipops out of his front vest pocket, handing him a green one.

He snatches the lollipop out of Miller's grasp, pulls the plastic covering off, then shoves the candy stick in his mouth, mumbling, "I just wanted a fucking lollipop."

Shaking my head with a smirk, I turn and take one last look at the first man I killed by choice. The one I actively sought after, for revenge, for my own personal justice…for Mimi. I can't justify this being an order or a job, but it feels the same. Like it had to be done. Because some people can't be trusted to live in this world.

"Alright, let's get the hell out of—" I'm interrupted as a man's thundering voice barrels through the room, matching the sounds of his urgent footsteps.

"What *the fuck* is going on back here?"

47

NAOMI

I've always thought of myself as a patient individual. One who allows nature to take its course. Who trusts divine intervention when it comes to karma.

Well, I was wrong.

The wait in this courtroom is excruciatingly long, testing every ounce of patience I have. Which clearly is none. And, I've completely justified my boyfriend—I guess that's what I'm calling him now—to take matters into his own hands, condoning it. In fact, I encouraged it.

But that acceptance is easy when I witness first-hand what the justice system is like.

It's the assistant district attorney and defendant being directly related to each other. Seeing that attorney shake hands with every member of law enforcement that passes by, knowing all their names and everyone in their family.

The same attorney who plays golf with the sheriff on Saturdays and drinks with the judge on Fridays.

The justice system that allows a rapist who attempted murder an undeserved appeal, attempting to go under the radar and let him free without telling the families he's affected.

So, at this moment, I don't believe in the justice of divine intervention. But, I do believe in protecting myself, and other innocent women, and that's exactly what Seamus is doing for me.

The minutes tick by and I find myself glancing down at my watch, checking my phone while my knee bounces uncontrollably.

"Stop fidgeting," Rocco whispers without moving his mouth.

He's right, but I'm losing my mind.

"How are you not worried right now?" I whisper back.

"I am," he says calmly, although his body is a lot more tense than when we walked in and the tip of his finger is tapping on his thigh.

I look down at my watch again, forgetting what time we even walked in. I can't even tell you how long they've been gone, because I don't even know when they really started. I just know we went our separate ways, at some point an hour ago, maybe two.

Suddenly, the sound of heels on the ground and a synchronized whoosh fills the air as the entire room stands up.

"All rise. Judge Morrow presiding," the bailiff's deep voice announces throughout the room.

Everyone stays standing until the judge sits and says, "You may be seated," as he puts his glasses over the bridge of his nose.

He skims the room and pauses abruptly when he sees me. There is a squint in his eye as he peers over to Nathan's attorney, back to me, then down at the file on his desk.

He's still and quiet for what feels like a lifetime. Lifting his eyes above the top of his glasses, looking at the courtroom, me, then back down. Repeating that numerous times.

"We're here today, in the presence of the parole board on behalf of the State of Texas, to discuss the provisional release of Nathan Simmons. Before we bring in the prisoner, does anyone have anything they would like to say?" He looks up and around the room.

Pressing into my feet, I stand. The wooden bench creaks behind me and everyone's neck swivels toward me in matched movement.

"I would like a moment to address the parole board, your honor," I announce, my voice strong, confident.

Rocco, still looking forward, gives away a proud, lopsided smirk, but it drops quickly when the judge replies.

"And you are?" His condescending voice echoes through the room.

I stand to my full height, lifting my chin even higher.

"I am Naomi Masumi, rape victim of Nathan Simmons." The words I've never been able to admit, say, or claim verbally, come out as a proud statement. Because I'm a survivor and I will no longer live in fear of hiding my voice or being ashamed of that title.

Whispered voices rise in the courtroom as the parole board members glance at each other.

Nathan's mother sits forward, tapping the attorney on the shoulder. She whispers something to him as she glares at me.

"All quiet down!" the judge booms through the courtroom.

Taking his glasses off and giving me a once over, he places the spectacles back on his face and nods at the bailiff.

"You'll have your time later to speak, young lady," he says, dismissing me. "Now, sit."

My eyes bounce around the room, as my cheeks flush in embarrassment. I glance over at Rocco whose brows are furrowed, and he looks…pissed.

The bailiff makes his way toward the back entrance of the courtroom when suddenly, and very urgently, another officer comes through it in a panic. His breathing is labored and there's a sheen of sweat on his forehead.

He pulls the bailiff through the doorway and it closes behind them, leaving the courtroom in only whispered silence.

There's commotion amongst the attorney and Nathan's family. The judge, just as confused as everyone else, pounds his gavel. "Order in my courtroom! This may not be a trial, but it's my courtroom all the same, quiet down."

The voices fade immediately and almost everyone straightens in their seats. Nathan's attorney stands and approaches the bench with preferential treatment. The judge leans forward, talking to him in hushed voices, and I can see the judge's eyes as they side-shift my direction.

The judge's lips move in response, replying back to the attorney, but there's no way to hear anything they are saying.

Rocco's body stiffens next to me, although his expression remains the same. When I look over, he's clenching his fingers around his pant leg. "He's agreeing with the attorney to postpone the parole hearing."

Just as Rocco goes to stand—to do God knows what—the bailiff returns into the courtroom and stands behind the judge as he whispers something in his ear.

My entire body is trembling and I'm unsure where to look or what to do. I glance down at my phone, still nothing from Seamus, then over to Rocco.

I can see the concern in his eyes, as they bounce between the bailiff, the attorney, and the judge. Then another proud, lopsided, very hidden smirk, appears and disappears just as quickly.

"What?" Nathan's attorney shouts out, his voice cracking as it practically squeals through the courtroom.

His head whiplashes our way before he makes his way back to his table where the rest of his staff is.

The judge rises from his chair as he tosses his glasses on the table, making his way to the doorway where there are multiple officers congregating, just as frantic as the first.

As I attempt to stand, Rocco stops me. "Stay seated, we'll be leaving shortly."

The judge returns to his chair, but doesn't sit. Instead, he places his hands on his hips and gazes down at it, before skimming the courtroom. His eyes deadpan to mine and the groove between his eyebrows is judgmental and glaring. Like he's trying to figure out a piece to a puzzle but he's not even sure where to start.

My stature remains strong, even though I have no idea what to expect. I don't know all the details of what their plan was. Seamus said it was better that way.

All I know is they were planning to break into the county jail. What sort of stupid ass plan is that? So who the hell knows.

Is Nathan alive? Did he let him escape so they could do something outside of the courthouse? What did Seamus do? Is Seamus okay? Were they even able to get into the courthouse? I can ask a million questions and probably get zero answers, but nothing could prepare me for what the judge says next.

"Nathan Simmons appears to have committed suicide in his cell," the judge grits out like it's painful to say. "He had some sort of shank, cutting his wrists, but when that failed, it looks like he drowned himself in the toilet or maybe the other way around. We don't know. There will be a full investigation." His eyes barrel into mine, like a threat, but I'm too shocked to register anything except the fact that Nathan is dead.

He's dead.

He's actually dead.

Relief blankets me, but it only lingers for a moment because I'm stunned to silence. I open my mouth to say something, but close it when nothing comes out.

"Who the fuck drowns themself?" Nathan's attorney shouts, as he runs his hands through his hair before snapping his neck my way.

There's no way they suspect I could have anything to do with this, even though their eyes accuse me just the same. Not only have I been sitting in the courtroom, in plain sight the entire time, the dumbfounded look on my face says it all.

How Seamus pulled this off and made it look like suicide is beyond me, but I can't say I'm upset about it. Since the moment I walked in this courtroom, it's like everyone else is the victim, and not me. His entire family and their narcissistic personalities, manipulating everyone around them to make everyone else feel sorry for them. And God forbid, this hearing take time out of the judge and attorneys' busy golf schedule.

Nope. I don't feel bad one bit.

I feel vindicated as I watch his family act like they've been personally attacked. They aren't grieving. In fact, they don't even look upset at the news of Nathan's *suicide*. Instead, they're pissed, talking amongst each other, pointing blame at whoever they can.

Rocco reaches into the inside pocket of his jacket, pulling out a yellow lollipop, rips off the see-through wrapper, and tosses it into his mouth.

"Come on, yoga girl. It's time to go." He stands and holds out his hand, gesturing *ladies first*, with a very satisfied smile behind the white lollipop stick.

What the hell is with the lollipop?

Making our way out of the row and into the middle aisle, I turn and head toward to the exit. His mother pushes her way in front of me and screams in my face.

"You did this! You put him there!"

"He did it to himself!" I bite back immediately. "He raped me. Beat me. He almost killed me!" I yell through the court-room. She flinches as she steps back in dismay. I can't say I blame her, the tenure and strength behind my voice surprises even me.

"He made his decision and—" I look back at the judge and his attorney, criminals just the same, then look back at his mother, meeting her eye-to-eye, "he clearly felt remorse for his sins. He couldn't even live with himself, and thank God for that, because the world is a better place for it." My tone is more calm and matter-a-fact now.

I lift my chin and step around her, not giving them a glance back as I walk through the large oak doors with so much more strength, power, and justification than the first time.

And as the doors shut behind me, it's like that part of my life is over. I'm finally free to move on, and this darkness isn't clouding over me. The doors bind together as my closure and I accept it freely.

I close my eyes as I suck in a deep breath and exhale. I'm unable to hold back my smile when my eyes open and Seamus stands directly in my line of sight. His back leans up against the side of the wall, one foot kicked back against the wall, his head tilted to one side, studying me with a lopsided smile of his own.

When I last saw him, and frankly almost every single time I see him, he's wearing a black shirt, black pants, black boots, and even his damn belt is black.

Not now. Now, he's changed into something mouthwatering and completely irresistible, looking lighter than ever with a glint behind his eyes.

Light stonewashed jeans work their way up his legs, a white button up shirt fits snugly around his torso with the top buttons undone, giving me a teasing view of his broad chest. The gray wool jacket lays over the top, the collar splayed, with his hair just clean enough to pull off his look, but messy enough to make him look like he just stepped off a runway.

He looks fucking edible.

Pressing into his foot, he kicks himself off the wall and starts to walk toward me. I pull my bottom lip into my teeth when I see that damn white stick peeking out the side of his mouth.

"Okay," I glance up at Rocco, who's sucking on the same stick, "what's with the lollipop?"

He just shrugs, a bit of a sad look crosses over him. "Not all missions end successfully, but when they do, this is how we celebrate."

When I turn, Seamus is walking with more purpose, and now the only black on him is his eyes that gaze into me so deeply, I feel it to my bones.

He wraps his arm around my waist and pulls me flush against his.

Pulling the lollipop out of his mouth, he presses his lips to mine and our tongues collide. The sugary sweetness blends over my taste buds, and I can't help but moan at both the taste and sensation.

I pull back, unable to hide my smile. "Did you miss me?" he asks, his eyebrows raised, unsure what answer to anticipate.

Before I can say anything, Rocco answers, even though he knows damn well Seamus wasn't talking to him. "Hell yes, what the fuck took you so long?"

Miller and Whitlock—I frown, realizing I don't know their first names, and I think that's weird—walk up to our small huddle, standing on opposite sides of Rocco.

"We were almost toast," Whitlock replies, as he bites into his green lollipop. "Right as we were leaving, another guard came up—he just started working at the jail, so I had no idea who he was—and busted us. He had his gun out yelling, *put your hands where I can see them*." He lowered the tenor of his voice to sound even manlier. "Then he takes one look at Seamus, puts his gun back in his holster, and they do some sort of fist bump secret handshake. Next thing we know, the dude is leading us out the backway and we were like ninjas in the night, never to be seen again."

A first-time, timid smile crosses Seamus' lips and he peers over at his guys and a sense of pride washes over me. I can see how much these guys mean to him and the loyalty they have. But it seems like everyone who's crossed paths with him feels that way.

"Alright, enough of all this." His arm falls from my waist, but finds my hand. He laces his fingers in between mine and gives me a reassuring squeeze. "You ready to go home, sunshine?"

I nod and smile back as Whitlock takes a couple steps backward with a skip in his stride. "We're going on the private jet, right?"

I laugh at the guys bantering back and forth as we walk out the courtroom doors and into the Texas sun.

When my parents moved me away from here after everything happened, it was to start a new life that I didn't want. It ripped me away from my friends and everyone I loved, everything that was familiar to me.

This time, I'm leaving Texas proud and happy, feeling more loved than I ever have, and it feels like going home.

<h1 style="text-align:center">48</h1>

<h2 style="text-align:center">NAOMI</h2>

One Month Later

"Yes, Mom, I will." I roll my eyes as I finish putting on my mascara. "I'm going over to his house in a few minutes and I will make sure to tell him about it."

I finished my morning backyard yoga session half an hour ago—half an hour later than I wanted to—because, well, my time management skills suck. I really do try to manage that better, especially because I know it drives Seamus absolutely crazy when I'm rushing to and from my classes or whatever else I planned, but didn't schedule properly in my day.

But I know he doesn't mind the extra time I spent in the backyard, as he watched my every move through his second story window.

Although I practically live at his house now, I still come over to mine for yoga and to toss my clothes around the room while I get ready. I don't think his daily structured routine is ready to live with my wild, untamed one twenty-four seven.

Although, with the surprise I have for him today, he might not have a choice.

"Are you sure you'll remember? You're a bit flighty, you know." My mouth drops open at my reflection in the mirror.

"Did you just call me flighty?" My tone verges on shrill since I'm completely offended.

"Oh, honey, you know you are. I'll just call him myself." She hangs up. She actually hangs up on me and my jaw drops even further as I let out a small gasp.

Ever since I brought him over and introduced him to my parents, they've been *obsessed* with him. I don't even think they like me, their own freaking daughter, as much as they like him.

After the event at the courthouse, we decided—I decided—to tell my parents about Seamus. To share with them the entire story at camp and everything that happened up till that night.

We did leave out two important details.

One, the fact that we reconnected at Afterburn, because my parents don't need to know about my shenanigans at a sex club.

And two, the parole hearing.

They heard what the public heard. Nathan Simmons committed suicide in his jail cell at the county courthouse.

Obviously, they covered that up to protect themselves because Seamus told me everything that happened in the cell.

I can't imagine a man with a broken nose, two broken wrists, slits over his forearms with his head shoved into a toilet, was in any way an actual suicide.

Either way, justice was served.

I still have passing moments of guilt, but now my therapy consists more of acceptance than it does forgiveness, and I'm grateful for that shift.

My parents didn't bat an eye, and when we shared more details about our experience at camp together, it just furthered their hatred for Nathan and adoration for Seamus.

It was an extremely emotional conversation between all of us, but one that was long overdue. And before the night ended, my parents were absolutely in love with Seamus.

Seamus admitted my mother reminds him of his mother, and there was some type of connection those two instantly had with each other.

And now, she won't stop asking us over for dinner or calling my boyfriend directly.

A clink at the glass of my side window takes the attention away from my blacked out phone I was still staring at in shock. I duck my head down to look through my window.

Seamus stands, shirtless, his hands pressing into the window sill as he just barely leans out his second story window with a beaming smile I rarely get to see. His corded arms branch up the window like tree stumps, and I somehow salivate uncontrollably in my mouth.

I click the lock on the side panel and crack open the glass.

"What the hell is taking you so long?" he asks in all his topless glory.

"You know, between you and my mother, I swear." I shake my head, biting my lip to hide my smile, because I still flush seeing him even partially naked.

"Get your ass over here, sunshine, I have something to show you." His dark eyes meet mine and there's a little something deeper in them today, an admiration that's always been there, but something slightly unsure behind them.

He has an expression that I can't read, and it makes me feel anxious.

"Okay, I'm coming right now." His phone rings in the distance and he glances down.

"It's your mother," he says, as he answers with a smug ass smile.

"Hi, Mrs. Masumi." He says all cute and adorable, then pauses. "No, she didn't tell me about dinner. She probably just forgot, she's a little flighty like that, you know." He shrugs his shoulders at me with raised eyebrows and a knowing look, mouthing, *get your ass over here.*

Fine, I mouth back, then shut my window.

They are going to be the death of me.

Seamus might want to show me something, but I bet my surprise is even better.

49

SEAMUS

I say goodbye to Mimi's mother, then press the *end call* button, tossing my phone onto the counter where my brushes and palettes are.

I've just finished the painting I've been working on for months, the one I started the day after I moved next door to Mimi.

It was the first time I looked out the back window and saw her in barely there underwear. She moved fearlessly through each pose, and I watched the lines of her body twitch and stretch as she paused, holding each position with a grace only she has.

At the end of that session, she removed her bra and sat in what I now know to be lotus pose, an overly-pretzeled way to sit with your legs crisscrossed. She pressed her hands to the center of her chest, as if she were praying, with her eyes closed and her lips parting between breaths.

Her forearms pressed gently against her breasts, covering her nipples, but showing the roundness of her full breasts that peeks underneath.

The way her hair fell over her shoulders as she tipped her

chin down, how her skin glowed against the sunlight that hit perfectly with the sunrise.

It was majestic, and I couldn't stop my hands from moving over my canvas, attempting to capture every single detail possible. I stayed up all night finishing the base of the image, but have worked endless hours perfecting every detail. And now, I'm ready to share it with her.

In fact, I can't wait, but she forces me to because she's late to *everything*.

I only spoke to her mother on the phone for a few minutes, so I suppose she is still making her way over here. However, I've learned when she says, *I'm on my way,* I know I have about twenty minutes to burn.

So, my shock doesn't hide itself when seconds later, she appears at the top of the stairs of my loft for the first time, her eyes wide with wonder.

She's my inspiration. My muse. She's been the driving factor since the moment I met her, even when we were apart she was there.

This room proves that.

Because now that she's back in my life, I haven't been able to stop painting.

Her eyes bounce between the portraits that surround the room and all of them are her, us, or a moment that we experienced together.

I watch her eyes as they explore the room, her lips parted in awe. Her feet gravitate toward one of the paintings on the opposite end of the room, the abstract image is of a man and a woman, us of course, kissing in the rain.

The canvas next to it is nothing but the night sky over a glistening lake, surrounded by trees with Orion shining brightly in the center. The two of us lay on a blanket near the shore of the lake, gazing into the stars.

"Seamus…" Her fingers are cupped softly over her mouth,

her words are barely a whisper.

"That one was the first canvas I ever painted," I admit, a shy undertone even I don't recognize.

I've never shown anyone my paintings, except Hudson and Dane the day they came over and gave me so much shit—I haven't invited them over since.

Who I am kidding, I never invited them over in the first place. But Dane has literally no limits or boundaries, and there was no stopping either one of them once they started inspecting every single thing in my loft.

This uneasy feeling is foreign to me. I hate feeling so vulnerable, but with Mimi, it's different.

I want to share everything with her. Give her everything.

Which is why the ring I bought a month ago feels like a fucking anvil in my pocket.

She steps to the side and I match her movement, stepping around the table that holds my latest painting. The one I need her to come see.

She moves around the room effortlessly as she observes all the images on the canvas.

It's all the colors and different ways I see her.

"Seamus, these are beautiful." She's glancing around the room as she passes by me, completely absorbed before she turns, stops, and stares at the one sitting on the easel, still drying.

I should have waited, but I couldn't.

Stepping behind her, I watch as she takes in the figures on the canvas.

A man, kneeling on one knee behind a woman, surrounded by paintings. And it's exactly as I planned.

She gasps, realizing what it represents. She turns around, seeing me with one knee planted and my fingers wrapped around a little, black velvet box.

I swallow thickly, the foreign feeling of vulnerability races up my spine because I want nothing more than for her to be mine for the rest of my life. I bought the ring the first chance I got after coming back home from Texas, because the thought of losing her again is my biggest fear.

I know it's only been a few months since the night at Afterburn, but it's been over a decade that I've known she's the one.

"There's only one thing I'm scared of in this world. It's living a life without you in it. It's the nightmare of the last ten years, knowing you were out there, but completely unattainable. You give me so much purpose and meaning that I probably don't deserve, but I'll spend a lifetime proving it, because I'll never stop loving you."

My throat bobs as I swallow down my nerves, opening the little black box. "Will you marry me?"

Her breath hitches as the tear that was threatening to fall drops down her cheek, hiding behind her hands that now cover her mouth.

The pink diamond is bright, rare, and represents everything she is perfectly. The tip of the pear shaped diamond shines with the slight tremble of my fingers, and it feels like an hour has gone by without an answer.

"Yes." A muffled squeal echoes behind her hands. Her head nods up and down and her eyes are beaming with happiness.

I stand, relieved, and so goddamn happy. I pick her up and twirl her around with an unrelenting smile. Her hands cup my face and she presses her lips to mine. Fuck, she tastes like sugar and vanilla with the scent of lavender that whips around us as I place her down on the table covered with my paints, not giving a shit about the mess.

Her mouth drops open as she leans into one ass cheek, inspecting her jeans.

She reaches behind her, worry laces her expression and she pats her back pockets and sighs in relief.

"What is it?" I ask, as I roam my hands behind her, running my hand over the spots where I know she's ticklish.

"Don't!" She giggles, attempting to pull my hands away, and I realize she is actually hiding something.

"Wait…you *are* hiding something." My face squints with concern, as I try to look around the back of her.

"Don't." She jumps off the table and shimmies around me, not turning back to me.

"Roshambo for it?" I hold my hand out in my palm. A close lipped smile dresses my face because I know she can't turn this down.

She turns on her heel, her head held high, palm in hand.

"But, I always choose paper," she says, her snarky tone on full blast.

"You won't this time," I reply, still smiling.

But, she will.

One. Two. Three, beating our fists into our palms.

Annnnnnnd, my scissors cut her paper.

She drops her hands in annoyed defeat as I reach around, dipping my hand into her pocket, expecting to grab out a piece of paper or something small. But it's a hard, plastic stick of some sort.

My eyes bore into hers and there's nothing but silence crackling in the air between us.

Pinching my eyebrows together, as her chest rises and falls slowly, as if she's trying to control her breath, and she looks worried.

A look I haven't seen from her since we came home from Texas.

Uncertainty, concern, panic.

I wrap my hands around the small plastic tube. It weighs nothing, but the tension of the unknown is heavy.

Keeping my eyes on hers, I move my hand around her body and hold it between us.

Her heart beats rapidly behind her pulse point, raising mine.

Without moving my neck, my eyes dip down and roam over

the pregnancy test, displaying two distinct, blaring pink lines. A relieved huff expels from my lungs and another fucking smile I can't hide beams over my face.

"You're pregnant?" I ask. She rakes her two front teeth over her bottom lip and nods.

I grip the pregnancy test like I need to superglue it to my hand. Cupping my hands around her face, I pull her into me, kissing her lips, jaw, nose, and forehead before wrapping my arms around her and picking her up again.

Her legs wrap around me and I walk downstairs with her, still kissing her anywhere I can.

"Where are we going?" she giggles.

"To *our* bed, where you'll be on bed rest until you give birth. The only time you'll leave is when we go get married, which will be tomorrow after I make a few phone calls."

"Seamus!" she belts out, hitting my shoulder, like that's actually going to do anything.

"I don't need bed rest and we can't get married tomorrow."

The hell we can't.

Turning the corner into the room, I place her down on the bed. Her gorgeous body sprawls out over the top of the covers. Paint streaks the fabric, as she presses into her hands and feet pushing herself toward the headboard. The stained covers bunch, and it's the first time that I don't care that we're making a mess of it.

In fact, I don't care if this entire house is drenched with Barbie dolls and Legos, I just want her and however many children she wants to have.

"How long have you known?" I ask, tapping the pregnancy test in the air.

There's a look of defiance in her hooded eyes. "Not long."

"How long?" I ask, more demanding this time. She knows I hate being left in the dark. She should have told me the moment she had to take a test.

She rolls her eyes. "Three days."

My eyebrows breach my forehead. "Three days? You've been holding this back for *three* days?"

I walk around the bed. Her eyes follow my movement as I place the positive test on the nightstand next to the bed, and open up the drawer.

"That's an orgasm for every day, sunshine." I pull out one of her vibrators.

"How did those get in here?" she asks, knowing all her toys are in her nightstand at her house.

"I bought duplicates of everything you had in your drawer," I state as I inspect the pink rubber toy, turning it on and off to test the charge, "and a few other items." I pull out a blindfold, rope handcuffs, and a leather chain and choker.

Her eyes widen and her breath becomes heavy. She might be anxious, but she's exhilarated, as well.

After we had sex the first time…again…I didn't need to say how much control I like to have, that much was obvious. But, I did mention to her that I wanted to tie her up, which I knew wouldn't be something in the cards for us considering what she went through.

She surprised me when she said she wanted to explore those kinks, that she trusted me and wanted to give up control. I immediately researched restraints that wouldn't hurt or intimidate her if we did try, and found these silk made rope cuffs. They look like an infinity loop and feel like butter. There are plastic clips at the end of the loop that you can easily press to make tighter or looser.

The leather choker looks like a necklace with a chain that dips all the way down the channel of your chest, but when you pull on it, the leather choker becomes tighter.

It might be too early for her to explore this, but she shared with me how badly she wanted it and I'll be ready whenever she is.

Her eyes flicker between the cuffs and my eyes, and when they land on mine, they are as feral as I feel. Her pupils are blown out and they don't stray from mine as she crosses her arms, gripping the hem of her shirt, lifting it over her head as she tosses it to the ground.

She leans back onto the bed, lifts her hips, and pulls the denim down her strong, luscious legs. It looks like every inch of her is flushed, or maybe she's just glowing.

She's always looked like a goddess with a golden hue to her skin tone, but now knowing my baby is growing inside her... fuck, she's absolutely stunning.

My lips part, attempting to get more oxygen as my eyes trail over her slow, deliberate movements. She uses her feet to push her jeans onto the floor, then reaches back, unhooking her bra. The straps fall forward over her arms and she slowly removes the fabric and throws it at me.

It bounces off my shirtless torso, landing at my feet, but nothing takes my attention away from her.

Her eyes are dripping with lust and need, and her expression is desperate.

The fact that she is ready and can't hide it sets me on edge.

All the blood rushes to my cock and my pulse goes into overdrive.

All my life, I have had the ability to control my breath, my pulse, my blood pressure, the expression in my face, and even my body language. I give away nothing.

Except when it comes to her.

She lays flat, raising her arms over her head and crosses them at her wrists. Her chin lifts in confidence, silently showing me how badly she wants this.

My grasp tightens around the soft fabric as it moves between my fingers. Pressing my knee into the top of the mattress, her body dips toward me as I lean over her. I can feel the heat of her body radiate against mine.

I pull the rope through the strap I placed at the top of the bed, then pull the loops over her hands, tightening them around her wrists.

I tug on the middle, testing the movement. They are tight enough to keep them in place, but loose enough to give her space to move.

As I back away, I trail my mouth down the crease of her jaw, the column of her neck, and over the lines of her collarbone.

My tongue caresses down her breastbone and over the skin of her breasts, before my lips wrap around her taut nipple and suck before nibbling on the peak.

She gasps, moaning, her chest arching into my touch.

"You're so sensitive." I continue to kiss my way down her torso and belly button until I'm hovering over her pussy. My hot breath is probably cool against the warmth I feel radiating from it. I squeeze my lips together, blowing on the sensitive bud.

"Oh, Jesus," she mewls, begging for more.

I stay hovering over her naked body, trailing my fingertips over the sensitive parts of her inner thighs, avoiding touching her in any place that I know she needs.

"More, please," she says, arching her body off the bed.

I stick out my tongue, staring up at her. If she wants it, she can take it.

Her eyes saucer when she looks down. Her lips part when she lifts her hips, pressing her clit on the tip of my tongue as she bucks her hips back and forth.

"Oh, God." She tosses her head back, but keeps the rhythm of her hips, aligning her clit in perfect symmetry with my tongue.

Her moans grow louder and I continue watching my gorgeous muse, move her body desperately, then grow frustrated, knowing she'll never get what she needs unless I allow it.

"Seamus..." Her voice is needy in my ears and goes straight to my cock as I pump my hips into the side of the bed.

I reluctantly push myself off the bed and grab her favorite pink vibrator.

"What's your safe word?"

"Orion," she says urgently.

Flipping on the switch, the buzzing sound rips through the room like a thousand bees are swarming around it.

I press lightly over her swollen clit. Her arousal beads off the rubber tip, the sound of the vibrating wetness now fills the room, mixed with the throaty groans coming from her chest.

I press the tip closer, then pull back. Soft, then hard. Repeating that movement until she's begging, pleading for me.

And fuck, my cock feels the same. I unbutton my fly and allow the denim to splay open, exposing the base of my hard cock that's pressing down between my legs.

"Mmm, fuck." I growl. Mimi stares between my legs as I pull out my cock and stroke it from base to tip. Using the precum to circle over the crown, I cover the tip and round over the top, then stroke down to the base.

She knows how often I watch her doing yoga in the morning —every fucking day—but she's never witnessed me take my pleasure. And by the way she's bucking and moaning, she likes it.

I continue to give myself long, languid tugs. My mouth drops open as pressure builds at the base of my spine, and I breathe through, holding myself back.

Jesus fuck, the things she does to me, stealing my control without even trying.

I push the tip into her clit hard, needing her orgasm like I need my next breath.

She screams as her hips buck and hands pull at the restraints. Her head is pressing into the mattress as she tosses it back and forth, her breath heavy and labored.

Pulling the vibrator away from her body, I toss it on the bed and push my jeans down my legs. Stepping out of them, I press my hips in between hers, the back of my cock rubbing between the arousal that coats her lips, and I piston my hips over her center, rubbing the crown against her clit.

"That's one, sunshine." I continue to buck my hips, running the tip over her sensitive bud. "Give me another," I demand.

My cock is throbbing, but I don't hold back and keep my pace. Her body trembles before another whimper and she comes again, groaning through another climax.

I pull back and lean over the bed, grabbing the blindfold and quickly placing it over her head. Her eyes were squeezed shut coming down from her orgasm, so she gasped with surprise.

Thank God it was only three days, because I can't hold myself back anymore.

Grabbing a small bullet vibrator, I hold it between my fingertips and graze it over the tops of her feet, over her calves, and up her inner thighs. She's begging, but this time it's for a break or to stop. She's mumbling, but there's a hint of smile behind that blindfold.

"Do you need to use your safe word?" I ask, placing myself between her legs and pressing my palms on the inside of her knees, spreading her wide.

"No…" she says questionably

I pinch her clit and ask again. "Do you need to use your safe word?"

"Ah, fuck. No."

"Good." I thrust into her. My cock is so fucking hard and already throbbing.

I reach up, cupping my hands around the base of her throat. Her lips part from the unexpected sensation, and I wondered how much she'd like this being tied up and blindfolded. I ease my grip, tightening slowly and her pussy contracts around me.

Fuck, she likes it.

I grab the leather choker and tuck it behind her neck. I

connect the chain and tug lightly at first as she takes in some air, then pull tighter as I thrust into her.

I watch her face closely. I want so badly to bring her the ultimate pleasure, but I'm not even sure she knows her limits and I refuse to push them too far, especially now that she's pregnant.

Then the thought of my baby growing in her hits me like a freight train. A sense of pride, ownership, and possessive rips through me.

My balls tighten and my cock jerks, and I need her to come with me.

"Tell me your mine." I rub my thumb through her arousal and circle it around her back hole.

"Oh fuck, I'm yours."

"Who's going to claim every inch of this gorgeous fucking body?" I ask, putting more pressure as I press into the tight ring.

"You, Seamus. You." I press the tip in and her pussy clenches against my cock, pulling out my orgasm with hers.

"Fuuuucccccck," I hiss out, my body falling over hers. We're both covered in a sheen of sweat, and only the sound of our labored breath fills the room.

I reach up and push the blindfold back, then snap the plastic clasps loose from the rope cuffs.

She pulls her hands down, and runs her hands through my hair, pulling my lips up to meet hers.

"I love you," she whispers into my mouth with a kiss that says everything.

She's always been the one to believe in karma and fate. I've never believed in signs, divine intervention, or some higher power creating our destiny. But the way we came back to each other will never cease to amaze me, and it will be the only time that I admit it was nothing short of a miracle.

I rub the pad of my finger over her Orion tattoo.

"It's always been you, sunshine."

EPILOGUE

SEAMUS

Three Months Later

"Dane…" I glare at my so-called friend as he taunts me while walking toward the stage. "Don't you dare," I threaten.

"What? It's just a little karaoke!" He shrugs with a shit-eating grin.

"Oh, Jesus, what is he going to do?" Hudson asks as he palms his face.

A normal gesture when we're out with Dane, I suppose.

Afterburn introduced karaoke nights due to Elena's love for karaoke, and while it's normal to see her and Jake take on a song or two, Dane isn't normally here to provoke us.

He's visiting before his backpacking trip to Europe, and God only knows what is going to happen with Dane and a mic.

As he steps up on stage, he introduces himself to the crowd before he walks over to the machine and chooses his song.

"I just want to let everyone know right now that I will not stop singing until those two," he points at me and Hudson, "join me."

Hudson's face drops and he slouches in his chair, as if he'd be more comfortable if the seat swallowed him whole.

I, on the other hand, just raise my eyebrows with a death stare, because I might actually kill Dane tonight.

He can sing out of tune all fucking night, nothing will get me on the stage.

"Nothing you're not familiar with, right, Hud?" I pat him on the shoulder, giving him shit because he did dance on a stripper stage in Vegas.

"Vegas was different," he mutters under his breath.

"You'd rather do *that*, than this?" I point at Dane as he picks his song on the machine.

"Neither, actually, so no matter what, we're going to hold out." He holds his fist out. "We're in this together…we are staying right here," he says as a statement.

I knuckle his fist. "Agreed," I respond just as *My Girl* starts playing through the speakers and Dane seductively walks over to Ember, who is getting a drink at the bar with Mimi.

Hudson stands immediately.

"Dane…" he threatens. Dane walks up behind Ember as he begins to serenade her. His hands softly press against the side of her arm and down to her hand as he raises it and kisses her knuckles.

He's singing quite good, actually, and Ember is blushing, her cheeks almost matching the color of her vibrant red hair.

Hudson backhands me, pointing to Dane, and I can't help but laugh as Hudson freaks out. But still stays put because we fist bumped on it.

Dane picks Ember up and spins her around, and she squeals with excitement.

"That's it." Hudson takes a step in their direction, but I grab his arm.

"It's fine. He's just—"

I glance over as he places Ember down then takes Mimi's

hand and walks her to the stage, sitting her on the edge. He steps in front of her and begins to roll his hips over her leg, Magic Mike style.

What the fuck.

I stand abruptly, now side by side with Hudson. He crosses his arms with a tight-lipped smug ass smile. *"It's fine, Shay,"* he says, mocking me.

Bastard.

My face must be beet red by now. I clench my fists as Mimi looks over at me, and she fucking smiles with a glint in her eye. She runs her hands over Dane's shoulders and through his hair, egging me on because she's a brat, then tosses her head back with a laugh when he nuzzles into her neck.

"That's it." I step around Hudson and now he's the one to grab my arm, but we both pause when he grabs Ember, sitting her down next to Mimi. Now he's tag teaming them as he dances and sings for both of them.

We would have won a gold medal in synchronized motion if this were a competition by the way we both rushed the stage.

We're steps away from the girls when Dane spreads his arms out, separating us from them and announces, "Ah, my backup singers have finally arrived!" He tosses each of us a mic and begins to sing the chorus of *My Girl.*

I roll my eyes and peer over to Hudson as he shrugs, and thankfully, we have consumed some alcohol tonight.

Hudson raises the mic and sings along, providing a balanced background to Dane, then I join in, singing the words to the Temptations classic, my timbre just a little deeper than the two of them, as we all sing the chorus in harmonious tone.

Dane still doesn't let us through to the girls as he wraps his arms around our shoulders. I belt out the song smiling, hating myself for actually enjoying this.

Thankfully, the song was almost over and we finished quickly, but admittedly—that was pretty fun.

Even though you'd have to torture me for an extended period of time before I'd confess that out loud.

I turn and pull Mimi into me as the song is over, and place one hand over her petite belly. She's finally starting to show, and she's never looked more gorgeous.

I don't know what I did right in this world to have her come back to me and choose this life with me. I find myself anxious for the first time, wanting to meet our child and be the father I never had.

"So," Dane comes up between us. "Have you found out if it's a boy or a girl yet?" he asks.

"We're going to have it be a surprise," Mimi says excitedly.

Dane flinches, like her words physically hurt him. "And you're good with that, mister must-be-prepared-for-everything?"

"Absolutely," I lie.

I haven't been able to prepare for anything specific, so instead, I'm just preparing fully for either.

"Well, I'm glad I'll be living here to see Seamus freak out when it happens."

I turn to face him, surprised.

He's planning a backpacking trip over the summer through Europe, which I knew about. But, we never know what he's doing or where he's going to end up most of the time. Frankly, I don't think he does, either.

Not that it matters for him. He's got a genius level IQ and has been independently wealthy since he sold off the platforms he created in college. He has only consulted for companies when he feels like it because he's never *had* to work.

Also, a permanent home somewhere where he's grounded for an extended amount of time? I don't think he's had that since college.

"Yeah…" He nods, a bit shyly, which is very unlike him. "I accepted a job here in Seattle."

"Really?" Mimi and I jinx each other in our response.

He laughs. "Yeah, Polytech University offered me a position teaching a course for their MBA program."

I'm shocked, but ecstatic for him.

He'll either be one of the best teachers those students will ever have or the next generation is completely screwed.

I half chuckle at my thoughts as I absorb his excited energy.

Patting him on the shoulder, "Well then, Professor Campbell. Welcome to Seattle."

THANK YOU FOR READING

I hope you enjoyed Seamus and Mimi's story as much as I enjoyed writing it!

I am a self-published author. If you loved this book, please consider taking the time to leave a review as it helps me tremendously!

www.berlinwick.com
Please sign up for my newsletter to keep up to date on my upcoming releases and receive exclusive content!

The Secrets We Hide
Elena, Jake and Christian's Story
A voyeur husband, a fiercely loyal wife and her billionaire boss... what could possibly go wrong?

Also by Berlin Wick

The Promises We Break
Hudson and Ember's Story
A drunken Vegas wedding turned marriage of convenience

ACKNOWLEDGMENTS

My husband… he's one of the good ones you guys. This book was written during a challenging time for us. Without his support, it would have completely halted the publishing of this book. My sexy, supportive loving husband - I don't know what I would do without you because, not only do you love my unconditionally, there is also a tad bit of you in every MC that I write - thank you for inspiring me. Oh, and thank you for buying me the Smut Hut.

Prior the the release of this book I kept my writing a secret. So only a couple of my close friends knew that I started authoring. I have recently, "come out of the closet", so to say and it's been liberating. SO, thank you to all my friends that have shown your support and cheered for me more than I can ever cheer for myself! I love the hell out of you guys so, so much!

During the writing of this book, my family and I went to our vacation home in South Lake Tahoe (we only get to visit there a couple times a year) and during our stay I thought the couch smelled kind of funny. I decided it was just me and my overly sensitive nose. Two days later, as I go to curl up in my favorite writing spot to take a nap, I nuzzle into my couch pillow and tuck my hands underneath it, getting all cozy comfy and I felt something weird. I blindly pull it out from under the pillow and … well, it was a dead rat. You can imagine what happened next. So, little rat. Thank you for keeping me company during the chapters of this book where I sat on your dead body and smelled your rotting corpse.

My Beta team — Ashley, Kelly, Susan and Amanda. I can't tell you how much I appreciate your feedback, your love, and all your constant support! Thank you!!

Hannah G. Sheffer-Wentz (English Proper Editing), for editing out all my grammar issues and providing all the hilarious commentary throughout. OPE!

My ARC readers and Street Team. Man, you guys f*cking rock. It's funny that I will drop the F-bomb nonstop in my book, and I probably said cock around 312 times in this one, but my first instinct was to censor that here. So, with that being said... You guys FUCKING rock. Seriously, without you I wouldn't be here.

Lastly, you the reader, the Goodreads reviewer, the social media poster, the romance lover. By sharing your thoughts, ideas, reviews, and love for the book, you help spread the word and grow us indie authors in so many ways. We would not be able to share our stories without you.

ABOUT THE AUTHOR

Berlin was raised in a tiny town in North Idaho who moved to the Bay Area, California, at the age of eighteen. She now resides in San Diego with her husband, two boys and her massive Cane Corso named Blu! Her bucket list items include skydiving, attending the Oscars, becoming a New York Time best-selling author, and cruising the world for retirement. She loves writing and reading, ANY and ALL kinds of romance novels, and loves engaging in the booksta community. You can find her most active on Instagram!

For the latest updates on upcoming releases please follow me on your preferred social outlet - Instagram, Facebook, or TikTok!

I would love if you would follow me on Amazon as it bumps us little indie authors up a notch or two in those silly algorithms.